JOURNAL OF THE LIVING

LIFE AFTER THE ZOMBIE APOCALYPSE

JOHN MORALEE

ISBN-13:
978-1517325077

ISBN-10:
1517325072

Copyright © John Moralee 2015

The moral right of John Moralee to be identified as the author of this work has been asserted in accordance with the Copyright, Design and Patents Act, 1988. All rights reserved. No part of this publication may be reproduced or transmitted in any form or by any means, electronic or mechanical, including photocopy, recording, or any information storage and retrieval system, without the permission of the author. Any person who does any unauthorised act in relation to this publication may be liable to criminal prosecution and civil claims for damages.

This book is a work of fiction. All names, characters, businesses, organisations, places and events are either the product of the author's imagination or are used fictitiously. Any resemblance to actual persons, living or dead, events or locations is entirely coincidental.

Visit www.**mybookspage.wordpress.com** to find out more about the author.

Genuine Placebo Publishing © 2015

EDITORIAL NOTE

Shortly after the zombie apocalypse, a survivor called Ben Smith posted a series of blogs on the internet, recording his life in Britain. The following is his complete journal. Only minor changes have been made to the original text, which can be found in the Ben Smith archive in the British Apocalypse Museum and on the Journal of the Living website.

The Editor, 2084

BEN SMITH'S JOURNAL ENTRY ONE

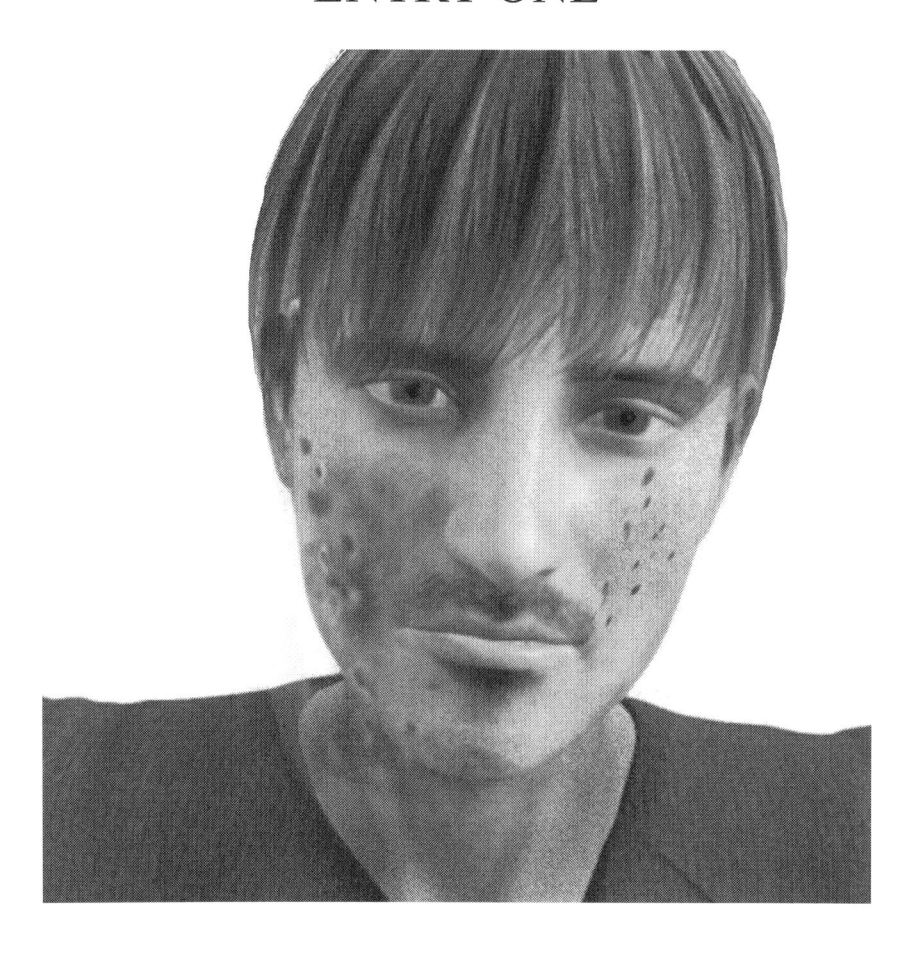

Ignore the blood on my face. It's not infected. It's mine. I cut my forehead a couple of days back raiding an Asda superstore in the territory of The Pure Bloods. On a whim, I grabbed this laptop from the electrical aisle. I thought I'd like to write a journal about my life when I had some free time between hunts and raids. This blog might be the only record of what happened to me. I'm going to fill these blogs with things I consider important, so other people, like you, can know what it was really like living in Britain after the zombie apocalypse.

It's no picnic, believe me.

Dear Reader, my name's Ben Smith. I'm a survivor of the zombie plague, living in England ten months after civilisation collapsed. I'm alive for now, but I'll probably be undead by the time you read these words.

At the time of writing this first entry, I'm hiding out in an old farmhouse a few miles north of Watford, watching a gang of Pure Bloods hunting for me and my friends. They want back the food supplies we grabbed in the Asda raid. They're coming my way now – so I'd better stop writing. I'll write some more when it's safe.

ENTRY TWO

The Pure Bloods have gone now. It's safe for me to write some more – telling you some things that you should know.

I'm a member of a small group of survivors. There are currently six of us – me, Sadie, Neal, Angela, Jason and Hayley. We don't have a permanent base because it's risky to stay in one place too long – but we do live together in a camp. It's currently hidden in a clearing deep in the woods miles from anywhere important. Our base consists of a camper van, some tents and lots of razor wire fencing. Sadie and Neal guard the camp while the rest of us scout out sources of food and essential supplies.

I'm the leader of the hunting party just because I'm the oldest. I wasn't anything special before Day One of the zombie apocalypse like a ninja or SAS captain. I was just an ordinary guy with a boring job in the City. I sat at a desk all day staring at figures while writing witty emails and tweets. Nothing I ever did meant anything. I made a load of money for myself and spent it on expensive toys like fast cars and fast women – but I didn't want to have real responsibilities, like getting married and having kids. Those were things you did *after* you were too old for clubbing and drinking all night. I didn't want to settle down. Not me. I was Mr Party. You wouldn't have liked me if you had met me a year ago. I was a thirty-five-year-old jerk acting like a hormonal teenager. I was forced into growing up by necessity. All the things I did back then were selfish and stupid – but now I have responsibilities.

I have to keep my family *alive*.

Robbing the Pure Bloods of their supplies was a pretty dumb move. They don't exactly forgive and forget – but since we're already on their hit list for just being untested I had to do it. We needed food and medicines from that Asda superstore because we were running out. Now we have enough food to last another month in the back of our van. We'll feast tonight – providing we get back to the camp.

I hid our van behind a disgustingly filthy cow shed that I knew the Pure Bloods wouldn't go near because of the smell of the dead animals, which must have been ripped apart by zombies a few months ago. The rotten carcasses are covered with flies. I would have been sick smelling the decomposing flesh if I had not become used to smelling bad things – but it barely registers now.

"Are we leaving now?" Hayley asked me a few minutes ago. She looked desperate to go back to the camp. Her big blue eyes stared at me from behind a fringe of long blonde hair that had blown in her face as the wind changed direction, making a whistling noise through the broken windows of the house.

"Not yet," I told her. "The Pure Bloods might still be nearby. We'd better wait a bit longer."

"How long?"

"They'll want to go home before it's dark," I said. "So we will have to wait another hour."

"I hate this place," she said. "It's creepy."

The farmhouse was creepy – but it was also deserted. The elderly residents had died upstairs by committing suicide in a bedroom with a shotgun. I'd found their skeletons lying on the bed next to the weapon. It had been empty – but I'd found some shells in a cupboard under the stairs. It had been a good day because of that. A shotgun was a great weapon against the living and the dead. It was better than the crossbow that I carried, except for its limited ammo supply.

After I had told Hayley she would have to wait here for a bit longer, she pouted and stomped off, acting exactly like a normal ten-year-old girl. She left the house through the kitchen and joined her teenage brother

Jason, who was crouched low behind a stone wall watching the road through his binoculars. He was wearing a camouflage jacket and dark jeans, practically invisible. Hayley sat down beside him and tore open a Snickers bar, stuffing it into her mouth hungrily. It was the first chocolate bar she had eaten in several weeks. I couldn't blame her for wanting to gorge on it.

"She's right about this place," Angela said, coming up behind me as I cleaned the dusty shotgun on the kitchen table. "It is creepy. I can feel the ghosts of those people disapproving of the way we've treated their house."

We had ransacked the house for anything useful. "We had to do it, Angela. It's better if we have their stuff than the Pure Bloods."

Angela sighed. I had not known her long – but I could see she was nervous. It wasn't the fear of ghosts, though. "I don't think we should wait, Ben. They didn't find us because they didn't look very hard. But another group could come back. We need to get back before it's dark. You know what happened the last time we tried to drive at night."

Zombies were not like vampires. They didn't come out at night. But they did get drawn to movement and sound. A whole herd of zombies had been drawn to the headlights of our van the last time we had been driving after dark. We'd had to smash into them to break through. It had been terrifying. I'd never turn on the headlights again – but driving in the dark without them would be just as dangerous.

I honestly don't know what to do. It's not like there's a manual for this situation.

Should we leave now or later?

If there's anyone out there, I'd love to know what you think we should do. Just send a message to my blog.

COMMENT FROM 'ANONYMOUS SOURCE': *Ben, you must not stay where you are. The Pure Bloods will come back soon. I've been listening to their radio signals. They are intending to sweep the area around you. They will bring more troops. GET OUT NOW!*

ENTRY THREE

Okay. I did what you suggested, Anonymous Source. We left the farmhouse straight away.

This is what happened after that.

We headed south-east towards London, which was the last direction the Pure Bloods would think we'd go. You had to be a little bit crazy to drive into zombie-infested areas, ignoring the warning signs left behind by the government, but we could not get back across the M25 border near Watford with the Pure Bloods hunting us.

After a couple of miles, a yellow sign appeared that caused me to shiver:

Danger Radiation

There was a radioactive zone ahead. At the moment the Geiger counter stuck on the dash was registering an almost normal background level – but we were heading into a radiation hot spot. Great. Zombies and radiation. What a combo.

Anyone sensible would have done an immediate U-turn because Greater London was by far the most dangerous place in Britain – but if we wanted to slip past the Pure Blood patrols we would have to continue.

That radiation sign reminded me of what had happened at the beginning of the crisis when nobody had even heard of the necrovitalis virus. Nobody mentioned the z-word at the beginning. The outbreak was treated as a mysterious disease that started in America.

DAY ONE

I was at my trading desk when I first heard about something happening. A New York trader – a buddy of mine – phoned me.

"Yo, Benny-boy," he said. "It's Chuck. Get this. I've just seen some weird things on the subway. It all started with this homeless guy biting an old lady's fingers off."

"What?" I said. "He bit her fingers off?

"Yeah. He chomped her fingers off like he was snacking on hot dogs – then he wouldn't even let go of the stump. She was screaming her head off – but nobody wanted to get near the guy. There was something seriously wrong with him, man. It was like he was totally nuts. He kept chewing on her hand until her blood sprayed all over. Some cops tackled the guy at the next station – but he bit them too. I got out of the train and saw the lady he'd attacked collapse from a heart attack. Next thing I know, a paramedic arrived and started pumping her chest. He saved her life – but then she starts going mental, attacking the man trying to help her. She grabbed his head and bit off his nose, tearing it to shreds. It was the most disgusting thing I've ever seen, man."

"Chuck," I said, not believing a word of his story. "You sure this wasn't a dream?"

"It was real, Ben. I'm deadly serious. I got out of that station fast, man. I saw dozens of people going crazy. They were biting other people and eating chunks of flesh. Then the ones bitten started biting other people. It was like instant rabies, man. I've never seen anything like it. Half the people on the platform were infected with whatever it was, attacking the rest of us. I was real lucky to get out of there. It's all over the news if you don't believe me. They're calling the Subway Madness. Look – I got to go."

"Thanks for telling me," I said, thinking that I would have to do some trades in pharmaceutical companies. A new disease meant big bucks for the industry. The cold, hard, cynical trader in me didn't care about what was going on in New York as long as it didn't harm my trades. I put CNN and Fox News on my screen to check out what was happening over there. The American networks were reporting an outbreak of a rabies-like disease, origin unknown. The weird thing was it wasn't only happening in New York. There were outbreaks in Los Angeles, Chicago, Miami, San Francisco and Washington, D.C. All big cities, all suffering outbreaks of a new disease simultaneously? Only one thing could explain that. A biological or chemical attack. I turned to my colleague Harvey, sitting at the next desk on the trading floor.

"Looks like we got a major terrorist incident in America, Harv. A biological or chemical attack in several big cities. Get your money out of the US now."

Watching the news showed the chaos in America.

Even then I was only thinking about the damage to the international markets. Terrorism meant new opportunities for investing – with the governments of the world increasing taxes to spend buckets of cash for military contracts to get those responsible. I needed to shift some money around before the markets reacted. For a few minutes, I had an advantage. My hands danced over my keyboard, making money for my company. In an hour I had made a killing thanks to my buddy in America. I called him back to thank him – but I only got through to his voice mail.

"Ben!" someone called out. It was Harvey. He was looking down the hall towards the elevators, where someone had just got out covered in blood. It was a dark-haired girl from the legal department called Mandy Something. She was staggering as blood poured down her right arm. She was begging for help. A group of concerned people rushed over, asking her if she was all right.

"No," she said. "I've just been attacked. I was about to leave for my lunch when this businessman ran into the building. He was snarling and biting people. It bit me as I tried to get away. It was mental. There were other crazy people outside, banging on the windows, trying to get in. I ran to the elevator to escape. I saw one of the security guards get his throat ripped open as the doors were closing." She sobbed and showed everyone the nastiness of her wound. "Ow! It really hurts. My arm feels like it's on fire."

There was a ring of teeth marks in her flesh. The skin around it was pale and slightly bluish. Blood was running down her arm, dripping on the carpet. Some people helped her to a seat. A woman with first-aid training opened a medical kit and applied some antiseptic and a bandage. Mandy's condition was deteriorating rapidly – too rapidly for it to be blood loss. Her skin was turning grey and mottled as her breathing became shallow and raspy.

Everyone had turned their attention on Mandy – forgetting about the elevator, which opened again. There was a security guard inside covered with blood. He staggered out and fell. His uniform looked like it had been caught in a shredder. His face, neck, arms and legs were savagely wounded. He was holding onto his stomach, keeping his entrails inside his chest. "They're attacking like maniacs. Don't let them come up here. Stop the elevator."

The elevator doors were shutting. I jammed my foot in the way. The doors stayed open. Harvey saw what I was trying to do. He brought a desk across to the block the doors from closing when I removed my foot. I turned around to ask the guard some questions – but he had stopped breathing. His eyes were open and he was definitely dead because his entrails had tumbled out onto the floor in a steaming mass. Remembering what my buddy Chuck had said about the paramedic, I didn't rush forward to do some heroic CPR, like stuffing the man's insides back in. It was just as well that I hesitated. Within seconds of dying, the security guard suddenly sat up, opening his mouth very wide, emitting a moan that I felt in my bones. He glared at me and crawled towards me, gnashing his teeth, leaving his entrails behind. There was no humanity in his eyes any longer. They were dead. I knew what he was – but the word "zombie" seemed so ludicrous, so B-movie that my mind rejected it. I would have stood there until he reached me if Harvey had not smashed down a swivel chair on his head. Harvey hit the security guard over and over until his head resembled a large squashed tomato.

"That guy was a zombie," he said.

I nodded. "Yeah. He was."

We both looked at Mandy, knowing she would be next to turn. We had no choice but to lock her into an office, quarantined from the rest of us. She lasted forty minutes before passing away. A minute later her pale dead face pressed against the glass wall. Then she began to moan.

There were twenty-two living people on the trading floor that day. We all knew it was safer to stay on the thirty-fourth floor than risk leaving. We barricaded the exits and waited there, expecting a rescue that never came. We were fortunate to have full water coolers and vending machines to use while we waited. We watched what was going on in London through the windows and on our computers until the power failed two days later. Then we used our phones to keep track of what was happening on the outside. Though it was obvious to us that the infected were zombies, the z-word wasn't mentioned by the authorities until three days later. By then the capital was overrun with millions of the undead.

For a while the PM stayed in Downing Street, protected by the police and the army, giving reassuring interviews to the BBC and Sky

News about dealing with the problem soon. He convinced a lot of people to stay in their homes, barricaded in, waiting for the army to rescue them from the zombies taking over the streets. He promised effective action in a few days – but he was lying. On the eighth day, the PM fled Downing Street in a black helicopter, leaving behind thousands of Whitehall staff to fend for themselves.

In a last desperate attempt at stopping the zombie plague from spreading, the prime minister decided his government would drop a nuke on London. Being a gentleman from Eton, he issued a warning, telling everyone in London to get out before the detonation in twelve hours.

Our safe haven was about to turn into a radioactive wasteland – so we all had to leave the building. We armed ourselves as well as we could with weapons made of the office furniture – then we descended the emergency stairs floor by floor. I grabbed a fire axe on the way. We encountered no zombies until we were on the eleventh floor – but then they appeared below us. Hundreds of undead employees. We had to fight our way down to the underground parking structure floor by floor. Of the twenty-two people in my office, only a handful made it alive and uninjured to the underground parking. My red Porsche was still in my private parking space when I got in it with a couple of other weary survivors. We drove it out onto the streets of London, which were eerily quiet. Harvey was in his blue Jaguar right behind me. Another two vehicles were behind us. There were zombies everywhere. We ploughed through crowds of them until we were out of the city heading north. We didn't slow down until we reached an army checkpoint. The soldiers detained two people with bite wounds. I heard gunshots and knew they had been summarily executed. Harvey was one of them. The rest of us were released and told to keep driving north, joining a mass exodus up the M1.

Exactly twelve hours after the PM made his announcement, a nuclear bomb exploded over the Square Mile. It turned the city into a radioactive wasteland, contaminating most of the south of England with the fallout. The bomb destroyed millions of zombies and thousands of innocent people trapped in the capital – but it proved ineffective against the plague. The zombies were like cockroaches. The ones that didn't die in the nuclear furnace survived and moved out of the city in search of new food sources. Instead of slowing the plague, the government made the zombies *hungrier* and *more dangerous*, scattering them into a wider zone.

I had been lucky enough to get out of London before the nuke exploded – but I was stuck in a traffic jam on the M1 when the mushroom cloud rose into the sky.

A few days later the prime minister was shot by one of his bodyguards. Then the country descended into total anarchy.

Now - Again

I ignored the warning sign and drove on. The Geiger counter stuck on the dash started to click faster after a couple of miles, making everyone nervous because the radiation around London was just as lethal as the zombies, probably more so because you could not see it. The radiation was still not at a dangerous level when I saw a crowd of zombies on the road ahead – several hundred of them walking and crawling over abandoned vehicles. They looked like an army of homeless people.

Our grey van was almost impervious to the undead because we had modified it, turning it into an armoured killing machine, but I was reluctant to drive on. You didn't look for trouble.

"What do you think?" I asked the others. "Drive through them or turn around?"

I knew all of the windows were protected by wire mesh. There were slits for shooting out. The doors had been reinforced. An escape hatch was in the roof that could be opened so somebody could shoot out as we were driving. There was also another under the passenger seat for emergency escape. We could confidently drive through a group of a dozen zombies or even fifty without a problem – but the number ahead looked like it was exceeding our capabilities.

Angela, Jason and Hayley answered me at the same time.

"TURN AROUND!"

I could see the zombies were reacting to our appearance, becoming more lively, no pun intended.

"We'd better turn around now," Angela advised. "I can't even count how many are coming, Ben."

"Yeah," I agreed. There were thousands of zombies coming towards us. All hungry for fresh meat. They had seen our vehicle and increased their speed. Some were very slow – but the freshest ones could run at the speed of a normal person without slowing down for miles and miles. Dozens were sprinting down the road, leaping over the fallen, racing each other. My heart thudding, I turned the van around and got the hell out of there. I didn't slow down until I lost sight of them in my side mirrors.

We drove parallel to the M25 for about ten miles before turning north, avoiding the major roads because they were controlled by the Pure Bloods. They had roadblocks on the M1 and every intersection of the M25 – but I knew it was possible to slip by them on the B roads and across fields if you don't mind getting out to push your vehicle if it got stuck in mud or a pothole.

I won't tell you our exact destination or exact route because the Pure Bloods might find out about this blog and use it to track us.

Now in the area around London you not only have radioactive

zombies – but you have thousands of very sick survivors living like wild animals. On the edge of the radiation zone you have the Pure Bloods. They are fighting a war to keep the zombies from spreading beyond the M25. They have a noble cause to eradicate all of the undead – but they kill anyone trying to leave the zone that doesn't surrender at their roadblocks.

They kill first and ask questions later.

To avoid them, we sneaked through small villages and along narrow country lanes until we were past the perimeter of the M25. Even then we remained cautious. There was still the chance of encountering some Pure Bloods – or some other gang – or some zombies. I watched the road ahead as I drove with Angela sitting next to me looking through binoculars. Hayley and her brother Jason were in the back with the supplies stolen from the Asda superstore. Hayley was drinking a Pepsi Max and burping as the fizzy liquid refreshed her. Jason was looking out of the back window, making sure nobody was following us. The van jolted over every pothole in the road – so I was only going forty.

To my right, I noticed a couple of zombies in a field feasting on the corpse of a crow. The sound of our vehicle had made them turn to look our way. One had only half a face. The other had lost its arms. They shambled in our direction, but they were soon tiny figures in my rear-view mirror. No threat at all. Just sad, pathetic creatures. I didn't see many more zombies on our journey through the countryside – but I stayed constantly alert because a relaxed person was a dead one. I opened my window and let some fresh air into the van. It would have been a pleasant journey if there had been no threat of attack.

It was getting dark so I looked for a place to stay the night. I picked an industrial estate where I parked inside a lock-up garage.

That's where I am right now, writing this journal.

I'll continue writing this after I get some sleep.

ENTRY FOUR

I'm wide awake and unable to sleep because I'm wired – so I'm back online, letting the others get some well-earned rest in the van. This internet connection is kind of dodgy – but it is pretty amazing I can a signal at all. After the national grid broke down you'd think nothing electrical would work – but this laptop uses a satellite link. I don't know how it works to be honest – but somewhere there must be a load of computers still working on solar power, keeping the internet functional even though most of the people who designed it are now long dead. Anyway, enough about boring technical issues.

I should tell you something about myself and my new family while I have the time.

You already know I was a banker before Day One – so no need to go over the embarrassing confession again.

Right now the 'me' from then wouldn't even recognise the 'me' from now. He wore designer suits and a big gold wristwatch that made his wrist ache because it was so heavy. He only wore it to show off his wealth. His bling was worth more than a family car.

These days I don't wear a suit. I wear a dark waterproof jacket with lots of pockets, all stuffed with life-saving items, including two machetes, a torch, a walkie-talkie radio, bandages, sterile dressings, alcohol, a claw hammer, and some fireworks that I could set off as a distraction in an emergency. I also wear black jeans and steel-toed boots. I look like I should be on the poster for a Robert Rodriguez movie: *Machete 3: Zombie Takedown*.

As well as keeping weapons on me, I always keep a hold-all of other weapons and tools in the van. My bag contains long-range weapons like a crossbow and a modified air rifle that is silent and lethal over a short distance. It also contains more fireworks, some knives, bolt cutters ... It's useful to keep it all close as a backup to my more portable weapons. I couldn't lug those things around all of the time – but it is good to know they are available if I encounter a tough situation.

That's enough about me for now.

Let me tell you some important things about the others.

Hayley and Jason

I wouldn't be alive if Jason and Hayley had not saved my life six months ago. I'd been living on my own, surviving day to day by looking for food in empty houses on a zombie-infested housing estate when some teenagers robbed and beat me. They'd left me to die in the street where the zombies were bound to get me – but I'd been rescued by a little girl. She had fought off the zombies with a nail gun while her older brother got me into the back of a van. Jason had driven the van back to their camp while I lay semi-conscious.

At the time the kids had been on their own because their parents had died. They looked after me for about a week while I was recovering from my injuries. Had the kids left me behind that day like most adults would have done, I would have died without a doubt. I would have been bitten and turned – but they risked their own lives to save mine.

I owed them more than my life.

I owed them my soul, which they had changed that day, by making me a better person.

Until then, I had been surviving on my own – Ben Smith versus the rest of the world – but they showed me it didn't have to be that way.

I became a new man, a man willing to do anything to help those kids survive.

Angela

Angela is the newest member of the family. I don't know anything about her past because she had never talked about it, though I know it must have been very, very bad.

One day we found her locked inside a garden shed. She was naked and half-crazy because she had not eaten anything in days. Someone had locked her in and left her there, trapped with just a bag of potatoes and a source of fresh water from a rain barrel. She would probably have died in a week if I had not busted the lock off the door to see what was inside.

I remember it had been dark in the shed, the smell foul, like death. I had shone my torch in and caught a movement in a corner. A flash of dirty red hair. Pale skin. Naked breasts. Then a wild thing launched itself at me, screaming. (Zombies don't scream. They moan and groan and snarl - but they don't scream.) But for a second I didn't realise the thing attacking me was a living breathing woman. It wasn't easy to stay cool when a screaming naked thing was clawing at my eyes with sharp fingernails. I pushed her back and raised one of my twin machetes, my favourite close-combat weapons. With her dirty red hair covering her face, her green eyes wide and angry, I had thought Angela was a recently turned zombie that I would have to decapitate before she bit or scratched me – but then suddenly all the fight went out of her when she noticed I was with the Hayley and Jason.

"Not them?" she mumbled. Tears of relief ran down her cheeks. The only sound out of her lips after that was a sob as she collapsed into my arms.

It had taken Angela a week to get strong enough to train with me – but now she was a hardened member of our little group. She was good with a crossbow and a crack shot with a rifle. She carried an axe in her backpack for close combat and a knife taped to her ankle. She was fearless – but not foolhardy. More than once, she had saved my skin and surprised me with her bravery. She was no longer the scared naked thing from the shed. She was a strong, beautiful woman, a valuable addition to our family.

Angela wears a black T-shirt and jeans with a green jacket over the T-shirt, her red hair hidden under a backwards baseball cap. She looks very sexy in a tough girl way, like Angelina Jolie playing Lara Croft in the *Tomb Raider* films. She is in her mid-to-late twenties, but I had not asked her exact age. She doesn't talk *personal*. Maybe one day she will open up and say something about her life before I met her – but she isn't ready for it yet.

I don't even know her surname.

Sometimes at night, I hear her moaning in her sleep, reliving in her nightmares the bad events in her past that were none of my business. She's doing it now. I'm tempted to wake her before she wakes the kids – but she would panic and slash at me with her knife. It is better to let her sleep on.

*

We all have things in our past we don't want to share. For me, it is my life as a rich and over-privileged banker, leeching off society. I want to forget about that arrogant jerk. He is dead as far as I am concerned.

It's a few hours until dawn. I'm yawning now. Must be tired. I'm going to shut my eyes for a bit.

ENTRY FIVE

The day was warm and sunny when we left the lock-up garage on our way back to the camp. It was almost possible to forget we were living after the zombie apocalypse. The countryside was beautiful. Spring daffodils lined the roads as we rode homeward, avoiding major towns and Pure Blood patrols. We were all in a good mood because we were so close to making it home.

Unfortunately, our good luck didn't last long. We were in the Thames Valley in sight of the Chiltern Hills when I saw something ahead that alarmed me.

There was a quaint village coming up – the sort of place you'd see in an episode of Midsomer Murders. There was a little church and some thatched houses and a small streets of shops that had once sold touristy things like genuine fake antiques. I'd been through it a dozen times – only something was different. Something was wrong. I slowed down on the narrow country lane approaching it.

"You see that bus?" I asked Angela. She had been half-dozing, but she snapped awake.

"Yeah," she said. "What about it?"

"It wasn't there last time. It's almost blocking the road – forcing us into a narrow opening between it and those houses. I think it's an ambush site."

Her eyes widened. "You think it's the Pure Bloods?"

"Maybe – but I doubt it. This isn't like them. They'd just do an obvious roadblock. This is more subtle. More sneaky."

"You want to go another route?" she said.

"Yeah," I said. "We'd better go back to the last intersection."

I braked and reversed down the lane because there was no way to turn around.

"Uh-oh," Jason said. "Ben, there's a big black car behind us!"

The car had pulled into the lane from behind a stone wall leading into a farmer's field. It was an SUV.

"Check it out," I said to Angela.

She scrambled into the back and looked out through our pair of binoculars. "There are four guys in it. They don't look like Pure Bloods – but they look like trouble. They've got guns. The driver's talking into a radio."

"Contacting the ones in front of us," I said. "Great. Hold on to something. We're in for a bumpy ride."

I accelerated and drove off the road through a closed wooden gate that broke apart on impact. Beyond the fence was a fallow field of black soil. The van had never been designed for off-road driving – but the field was flat and didn't slow us down much. After thirty yards something hit the van. It sounded like a coin tossed on a metal tray.

I knew what it was instantly.

A bullet.

They were shooting at us.

Ping. Another bullet struck the van. Hayley screamed because the bullet had shot through a crate of drinks near her head, spraying frothy foam all over. I was glad it hadn't been her head that it hit. Another bullet struck just missing Hayley by inches. Jason covered his sister with his body, protecting her, as another bullet hit our vehicle, making a dent in my door. I pressed the accelerator to the floor and yanked the wheel left, then right, trying to make whoever was shooting lose their aim. It worked – for a second. The next bullet didn't hit us. It raked up some dirt.

There were some oak trees and bushes on the far side of the field. We had to get to them. Ping, ping, ping. Holes appeared in the van. Pieces of metal ricocheted around like angry wasps. I felt something cut my neck. Angela yelped as she was hit somewhere. So did Jason. I veered between two trees over a bramble bush that sprayed the window with twigs and leaves as we hurtled down a steep embankment towards a fast-flowing stream. I couldn't afford to crash our van filled with vital supplies – so I braked and stopped us from falling into the water.

Everyone was yelling for me to keep driving – making it hard to think about what to do next.

I saw the stream was shallower about a hundred metres to my left. The pebble stones on the bottom were visible there. We could drive across there. I backed up, the tyres kicking up dirt. "Anyone seriously hurt?"

"No," Angela said.

"Jason?"

"No," Jason added. "Just a flesh wound."

"Hayley?"

"Nothing hit me," she said.

I drove along the edge of the stream towards the shallow section. The van struggled over the uneven muddy ground.

"Angela, keep looking out for them!"

"I am! I am!"

I was almost there.

"They're here now!" Angela yelled.

Looking back up the bramble-covered slope, I could see the black car had stopped at the top of the embankment. Its occupants were jumping out with handguns and rifles. They looked like thugs from a prison movie. They had shaved heads and hard faces. The shotgun was no match for them at a distance – so there was no point in using it. I had to just get us out of there. Quickly.

"Keep your heads down!" I ordered, moments before a bullet zinged through the rear window and blasted the flame-retardant stuffing out of the passenger seat where Angela had been sitting two minutes earlier. She was lucky to be in the back with the kids.

One of the men was running down the slope firing at us. He was a skinny rat-like man in a leather jacket. He was grinning and aiming a gun.

Angela poked the shotgun out of the side door and fired at him, catching him in the left leg. He fell with blood pouring from his knee – looking more surprised than hurt. He fired his gun again – but his aim was off. The bullet went straight into the blue sky. His injury made the other men stay back, dodging behind the trees, firing off shots that missed. Angela fired back, taking chunks out of the trunk of an innocent oak tree. She was wasting shells – but she was keeping them back. The sound of the shotgun made my ears ring.

I drove into the shallow river and up the embankment on the other side, hearing our van's engine groaning and straining. The van had never been designed for this abuse. I begged it to keep moving. It crawled up the bank. We got to the top with everything not tied down sliding on top of Angela, Jason and Hayley so they were buried in tins and packets and bottles and toilet rolls. The men fired a couple of wild shots before we were out of their range – then appeared to give up.

I drove about a mile through woodland until we reached another road – a dirt road through a forest. I increased speed then, eager to just get out away from our ambushers. I thought we had escaped fairly unscathed – but a red light was on the dash telling me we were running out of fuel. I couldn't understand it. I'd filled the petrol tank that morning from the cans we kept in reserve. We should have had enough to get back to the camp with no problems – but we were registering nearly empty.

I looked back and noticed the van was leaving a dark line of petrol on the road behind us.

"We're going to have to stop," I told the others. "We've got a petrol leak."

"We can't stop here," Angela said. "Those men will be hunting us."

"We can't drive on leaking fuel. We won't get another mile at the rate we're losing it. I've got no choice, Angela. We're stopping." I pulled off the road and stopped. "Okay – I'm getting out to check the damage. Angela – cover me. Hayley and Jason – keep watch for the ambushers. Jason – get in the driver's seat. Honk if you see trouble."

I took off my jacket before jumping out to crawl under the van, looking for the source of the leak. It was much worse than I feared. A bullet had ripped a fist-sized hole through it too big for a quick repair. The petrol was pouring out. It had already covered my T-shirt so I stripped it off and stuffed it into the hole until the petrol wasn't leaking out too fast – then I rolled out from underneath. I went back to the van to get a clean shirt on. I pretended I didn't notice Angela checking out my muscles – but a shallow part of me liked her interest in my body. When she realised she was staring, she looked away, embarrassed.

"So ..." she said. "How bad is it under there?"

"It's bad. We can't make it back to the camp – but I've patched it temporarily so it won't leak if we add some more petrol just to get us a few extra miles. Ideally, we need to hide the van somewhere until we get it repaired. Somewhere with fuel."

"I'll look at the map," Angela said, opening the glove compartment. "Maybe I can find somewhere nearby."

I grabbed our last can of petrol from the rear and topped up the tank with a couple of litres. That left the can empty. It'd get us a little bit further – but one bump in the road would dislodge the rag. I hurried back to the driver's seat. Jason hopped back into the back. I drove on. My patch job had stopped the petrol leaking onto the ground – but I doubted it would last long. We desperately had to find somewhere before it leaked again.

Angela was studying an Ordnance Survey map unfolded on her lap. "There's a small town coming up. Turn left ahead at the next fork, then right at the next one. It's about three miles. Can we make that?"

"Yeah," I said confidently, though I wasn't feeling it. The van was making disturbing noises. There must have been more damage done to it than just what I had been able to see. We were probably lucky the petrol tank hadn't exploded. Somehow my T-shirt stayed stuffed in the hole until we reached the town.

It was always potentially dangerous driving into a strange place without scouting the area from a good distance – but I didn't see anything worrying as we approached on a road winding down into a green valley. We checked it out with binoculars. There were several rows of houses built around a High Street. No zombies were visible on the main street. The town looked deserted. There were many places like it. Ghost towns. The living had just abandoned their homes to head north to the refugee camps in the highlands of Scotland. They had fled north hoping to find safety and civilisation, but I had heard the Scottish refugee camps had been turned into hellish prisons by the new regime up there.

I cruised into the town slowly, looking around nervously. The noise of our vehicle would disturb any zombies in the buildings. They would be coming out of their hibernation state, listening, moving, feeling hungry. The hairs on the back of my hands were standing up. I always hated the crawly feeling inside my chest when I was venturing into unknown territory. So far we were good – but I didn't like the quiet streets. I couldn't even hear a bird. There was a boarded-up house on my right with the words GONE NORTH written on the front door. There were also some empty shops with broken windows and abandoned cars. A dead dog was rotting on the pavement – but since nothing was snacking on it that was actually a good sign. It made it less likely there were any zombies around. They would have picked that corpse clean if they had smelled it. I passed a pub called The Red Queen. I idly wondered if there was any beer left inside.

Ah! There was a petrol station ahead with a large auto-repair garage. Just what I needed to find. I pulled into the empty forecourt, noticing weeds growing on the petrol pumps. The little shop looked like it had been looted because all of the windows were broken. The petrol station had been closed for several months once it ran out of petrol. The garage was around the side, where I could hopefully find the tools for making the repairs. The grey metal doors were closed. Somebody had sprayed a message on them in huge letters:

WARNING! ZOMBIES!!!

The three exclamation marks seemed a little excessive – but I appreciated the warning.

I looked at the fuel gauge. Empty. I couldn't drive the van much further on the fumes in the tank. I swore. The garage would probably have everything inside needed to fix the leak, including a pit for getting under it. It could even have some full fuel cans. What if the message was just a bluff to make people afraid of breaking in? I'd seen that before. Writing 'zombies' on anything kept people away better than a BEWARE OF THE DOG sign.

It was worth checking out. I got out and approached the garage doors. They were secured with a strong lock – but I could break it with my bolt cutters. I banged on the door just to see if there were zombies inside.

I heard moans and groans.

It was no bluff.

It sounded like about a dozen flesh-eaters were locked in, maybe more. They started pounding their hands and feet against the doors, shaking and rattling them, attempting to break out.

"Grrrrrr!"

"Grrrr!"

"Grrrrrrrrhhh!"

They sounded angry. I was lucky the door was made of solid metal. There were not going anywhere – unless I unlocked the garage. No way was I doing that.

I walked back to the van, sighing. "Okay – we got a problem. There are zombies inside – so we either have to take them on or leave the van here and look for alternative transport. We might find a car and some fuel somewhere in this freakishly quiet town – but it might not be as good as the van. Either way, we're stuck here for some time unless we get some petrol."

Jason was looking back up the road. "Uh – we have a bigger problem, Ben. The black car. It's on its way."

We all looked. The car was on the road leading down into the town. It was about half of a mile away – but it was moving fast. My heart did some dancing in my chest that hurt. "Okay – grab what you can. We've got to hide somewhere."

"We can't leave the supplies," Hayley whined. "We can't!"

"Hayley, we have to," I said. "Come on! Let's go!"

I grabbed my bag of weapons and the shotgun. Angela and the kids grabbed their backpacks filled with their essentials. That left a lot of food and other things left in the back that I was very reluctant to leave – but we didn't have the time to move everything. The ambushers were getting closer.

We dashed across the road into a side street of small shops. We turned a corner into a back street filled with green and blue recycling bins that had been left full of uncollected rubbish. It smelled like an open sewer. I could hear the car coming. We hid behind a disgusting pile of black bags and bins just as the black car drove past on the high street. It was moving more cautiously – at about twenty miles an hour. We peered around the corner, watching it. It moved on. I hoped it would keep going without spotting our van. But then I heard the car stop. I could see two armed men jumping out. They fanned out, looking around. One looked inside the van, seeing we'd abandoned it. "They're not here!"

"They must be nearby!" another shouted from the car. "Find them! They shot me!"

The man injured by Angela stayed in the car, pointing a gun out of a window. The driver also had a gun.

Our weapons were not a match.

We were better off hiding among the rubbish. The smell was likely to keep the men from exploring the back streets.

Just then something black moved between two bin bags. I feared it was a zombie – until it ran across my feet, revealing itself to be a black rat the size of a cat. The rat frightened Hayley. She saw it and opened her mouth to scream – but her brother clamped his hand over her mouth just in time. He held onto her until she calmed down – but the rat made a noise as it scampered under another bin, knocking something over. In the silent town, the clattering noise felt as louder as a gunshot.

The nearest man heard that. He turned and headed our way, keeping in contact with the others on a radio. We couldn't hide there any longer. I pointed towards the boarded window of a building. Everyone understood. I got out my claw hammer and ripped the nails out as quietly and quickly as possible. Once the board was loose, we crawled through the broken window into a dark room that smelled just as bad as the street outside. I put the board back after getting inside, hoping the man would not notice it wasn't secured.

My eyes adjusted to the darkness. We were in the stock room of a butcher's shop where all of the frozen meat had defrosted. We stayed quiet as the man passed the boarded window and tested the exit door, which was locked, fortunately. He sniffed the air and muttered something. He kicked something. The rat squeaked.

"Jeez. There are huge rats here, guys. No sign of them. I'm coming back."

*

That was a few hours ago.

Now it's dark and we're hiding on the top floor of an old furniture store opposite the pub. The black car is still parked in the middle of the street. There's also another one parked next to the pub that belongs to some other members of their group. It's a white van. There are also five motorbikes. I've seen at least fifteen men out there. All tooled up with guns, knives and baseball bats. The men have stopped looking for us now it is dark – but they might start again in the morning. Earlier they unloaded our van into their van. Then they took some crates of beer that I'd included in our shopping haul into the pub where it looks like they are having a party eating and drinking our supplies. A few men have been left on guard at their cars – but they don't look too vigilant. I've got some ideas about what we could do – but my ideas could make things worse.

We could do nothing and hide until morning, hoping the gang will leave after having an all-night feast on our hard-earned supplies.

Or I could sneak back to the garage and release the zombies. The zombies would then attack anyone on the street, including me – if I didn't get away fast. But they could make the gang panic and flee the town.

Alternatively, we could sneak up on the men guarding the cars. Angela and I could take them out with crossbows and air rifles – but we'd have to be fast and accurate. Then we could steal their van.

None of my options are good.

Does anyone out there know what I should do?

(Ben received no answer to his question.)

ENTRY SIX

It's been a week since my last entry. A lot of really bad things happened in that time – and it's all my fault. Nobody helped me make a decision – so I made no decision at all, which created a worse situation ... Maybe if someone had answered my last blog we'd all be at our camp now, happy and alive, but nobody helped me choose what to do. I feel sick about what happened next – but I can't blame anyone else. Ultimately, it was my indecisiveness that caused the trouble and cost my family so much.

It's hard writing about that – but I will because you need to know everything.

*

Last week we were on the top floor of an old furniture store, watching a gang across the street. There were about fifteen of them – but only four of us. The gang were enjoying themselves in a pub with some of the supplies we had taken from an Asda inside the M25 danger zone. The rest of our stuff was in a van parked on the street guarded by a couple of armed thugs. I'd had various ideas for taking them on – but I couldn't decide what to do. Instead, we all started arguing about it. Jason and Hayley wanted to strike back immediately – but I was reluctant to get them involved.

"It's one thing to kill zombies," I said. "But it's another thing killing living, breathing, thinking humans. It isn't something to be done lightly, guys. Those guys are scum – but they're not zombies. If we start killing other people, we aren't much better than they are. Have either of you killed a living human?"

They shook their heads. Hayley was close to tears. "No – but they stole everything off us, Ben. They deserve to be killed."

"Yeah!" her brother agreed. "They shot at us. They need to die."

Angela was standing in the darkness, peering down at the street, saying nothing.

"What do you think?" I asked her.

"I think we could take out those two at the van with no problems. Then we could steal the van and get out of here."

"That sounds good to me," Jason said. "Let's do it!"

"Hold on," I said. I didn't want to make a hasty decision. "If we kill them, the rest will want revenge. Are you prepared to fight a whole gang?"

"Yes!" Jason said. "We could release the zombies and -"

"No," I said. "I need more time to think. Maybe someone out there on the internet will help."

I wished someone had given me some advice – but I had received no messages on my laptop.

Angela sighed. "The people out there aren't going to help, Ben. There is probably nobody left out there alive, anyway. The decision is down to us. To you. You are our leader. What do you want to do now?"

I didn't know. I walked over to the window where I could see the men down below. I imagined sneaking up on them and shooting them with a crossbow. Could I kill in cold blood? I had never killed a living person that hadn't been trying to kill me. Could I do it? What if I lost my nerve? "Let's wait a little longer. We're going to wait while I think about this, okay? We can't rush the decision. Guys, get some rest."

The kids grumbled – but they settled down on some dusty beds that were so comfortable I heard them snoring within minutes. That was one of the benefits of being in a furniture store – lots of comfy beds. Angela and I moved some soft-cushioned chairs to near the windows so we could watch the street in luxurious comfort. The men outside looked bored. They also looked cold. One was shivering as he smoked a cigarette. He walked up and down the street, muttering to himself. Maybe he would go into the pub, leaving just the one man guarding the van.

For an hour I stared at my laptop – hoping someone would give me advice. But nobody did. Eventually, I turned it off to save the battery charge.

The two men were still guarding the street.

"Ben?" Angela whispered in the dark.

"Yeah?"

"I never thanked you for rescuing me." She paused. "Whatever happens, I want you to know I'll always be grateful that you found me. You saved my life, Ben. Thank you."

"You never talk about what happened. Do you want to tell me?"

Angela was quiet for a minute – but then she answered, keeping her voice low. "I was kidnapped by a gang of men just like the ones out there. They did bad things to me. They kept me locked up with a group of other women they used as ..." She breathed deeply. "It was a living hell. Once we tried to escape – but they caught us. They killed two teenage girls in front of me – but they locked me in that shed as punishment. They thought they could make me more compliant if they left me to starve for a week. I'm glad you found me before they returned, Ben. I'd rather die than be captured by a group of men like them." Her glistening eyes reflected the moonlight. "Those men out there remind me of the others. They're parasites, not people. We could kill them all while the kids are sleeping, Ben. Just you and me. We don't have to involve the kids. We could come back for the kids after it's done – after we've done what needs to be done."

"There are too many of them," I said. "The risk is too great. We can't go up against them all. It'd be suicidal. We're not soldiers. We're just survivors. We have to be smarter than that, Angela."

"Yeah, I guess so. You're right. Forget it. We're better off waiting." She sighed. "If you want to get some sleep, I'll keep watch. There's no need for us both to be watching."

"Sure?"

"Yeah. I'll wake you if things change out there. Take your own advice, Ben. Get some rest."

I was tired. I had not slept much the day before in the lock-up garage. I didn't think there was any harm in napping for a while because I'd be in better shape to think of a plan afterwards. I closed my eyes and rested my head on the deep upholstery. I almost moaned in pleasure. The easy chair was the most comfortable thing I had sat on in months. So comfortable … This building would make a great home if …

I jerked awake upon hearing a noise like a gunshot. No – not a noise like a gunshot. An actual gunshot. From outside. I jumped out of my chair completely alert, reaching for my shotgun. It wasn't there. And the other chair was empty. Angela had gone out alone. All that talk … I should have known what she intended to do. She was taking on the gang by herself.

The kids were sitting up. Hayley looked around for Angela "What happened? Where's Angela?"

"Outside," I answered. A quick look out of the window showed me enough to figure out what was going on outside. There was a dead gang member on the road with a crossbow bolt in his chest. He'd been killed silently as we planned, but the other gang member was crouched behind a car, shooting towards the van. It was his gun that I had heard. From my high position, I could see Angela crouched behind the van, shooting back with her shotgun. She hit the man and he went down – but more members of the gang were already on the street, firing at the van from behind the other vehicles. Angela was trapped in the middle of the street. She kept returning fire – but they outnumbered her. She needed help – fast.

"Jason, the big rocket!" I shouted.

"I'm on it!" he said, understanding what I needed. While he was busy, I lifted my chair and hurled it at the window. The noise it made crashing through alerted the gang to my position - providing a new target for the enemy – hopefully diverting their attention from Angela. Some started shooting towards our building as I took cover behind the brick wall next to the window.

"Jason!"

"I'm coming!"

Jason had opened our bag of weapons and found the biggest firework. It was one normally used for professional displays containing a serious amount of gunpowder. With bullets whizzing over his head, he crawled across the floor to me. I lit the firework when Jason passed it over. I shoved it into a metal wastebasket that would hopefully contain the blast, then pointed the rocket towards the pub. The basket jolted in my hands as the firework ignited. The firework streaked out, screaming, as it whooshed across the street like a glowing missile. The rocket smashed through a bottom-floor window into the pub, where it exploded with a series of bright flashes and loud bangs.

I doubted it hurt anyone inside – but it caused confusion. Smoke spewed out onto the street and burning phosphorus and magnesium shot into the sky.

Angela used the momentary distraction to run for the side street filled with bins – but I saw her stumble as at least one bullet hit her in the back. She dropped the shotgun and staggered on –

barely reaching the corner before more bullets got her.

I prayed she wasn't badly wounded.

Unfortunately, I had no time to worry about her when we were in just as much danger. A crackle of gunfire blasted out the windows around me – sending broken glass into the air. Hayley and Jason dived behind a double bed as the men ripped apart the room with their bullets.

I'd jeopardised the safety of the kids for Angela – so we had to move now before the men figured out a way of killing us. I grabbed the bag of weapons, yelling at Hayley and Jason to run for the stairs. We had to get out of the shop via the back exit. It was a wise decision – the first of the night. Behind me, a Molotov cocktail landed on the floor, shattering, the petrol setting fire to the furniture. I reached the top of the stairs with smoke stinging my eyes. Hayley and Jason were running ahead. I followed them down to the main floor, which was filled with kitchen and dining furniture. Another three or four Molotov cocktails had been tossed into the display room, spreading a fire, which was a pretty dumb move because it prevented the gang from coming into the building from the front entrance. They had stopped themselves from trapping us upstairs. Instead, they were trying to burn us to death. Luckily, the flames didn't stop us from escaping through the rear exit, out into the cold night. I closed the door behind me before dashing towards some houses on a small estate behind the High Street.

We hid around the side of a home just as a couple of men ran around the back of the warehouse. They approached the exit cautiously. One opened the door and tossed a Molotov cocktail inside. He probably thought he had caught us in the building – which meant they did not expect us to be outside, watching them. I heard one on his radio. His words confirmed my theory.

"We're at the back. They're toast. You got the other one yet?"

I didn't hear the reply – but the men ran off down the street. By then the furniture store was fully ablaze, casting a yellow-orange glow over the streets. Thick black smoke rose into the sky as parts of the roof caved in. The fire was spreading to the other buildings nearby. The gang must have decided to torch the whole street. Maybe the whole town.

I could hear the gang shouting and firing their guns – but they were some distance away. It sounded like Angela was still causing them trouble. Good for her!

Hayley and Jason could also hear the fighting. Jason grabbed my arm. "Ben, we have to go back! We need to help Angela!"

We'd all die if we did that. Right then, the bad guys thought we were dead. They would not look for us. But if we went to help Angela we would all die.

"We can't," I heard myself saying. It didn't sound like me saying it. It sounded like a pathetic coward – but I wasn't afraid for myself. I didn't want Hayley and Jason murdered by those men. "We can't rescue her, Jason. They have her surrounded by now. If we try to fight them, we'll all die. We have to save ourselves. We have to let them keep thinking we're in that burning building."

"No," he said. "We have to go back!"

I shook my head. "No, Jason. Not now."

"You coward!"

I grabbed his shoulders. I looked into his eyes. "Would Angela want you to risk your life for her?"

"No," he said. "But that doesn't mean I wouldn't do it. We can creep up on those guys and shoot them with our crossbows. We can –"

Just then I heard a scream.

ENTRY SEVEN

The high-pitched scream startled me – until I realised it was one of our enemies. When I heard him screaming for help because he had been hurt, I didn't feel bad. I felt relief because Angela was still alive and eluding capture. Good on her. She had lost her shotgun – but she was fighting with her other weapons. Any thoughts of abandoning her to save myself vanished once I knew she wasn't captured.

I switched on my walkie-talkie to her frequency. "Angela, if you can hear me, get to the alpha site. H and J will come for you while I provide a distraction. You copy?"

Angela answered my question by her turning her walkie-talkie on and off, creating a short burst of static. That was the code for yes. That told me she had heard me – but she was too busy to speak because the gang were hunting her. I silently wished her luck, hoping she could get to the alpha site. Whenever we went somewhere, we always designated some places with codes so we could talk on the walkie-talkies even if someone was listening to it. If Angela could get there, she could hide inside and wait for Hayley and Jason. They both had good enough emergency medical training to treat her bullet wound (at least temporarily) until we could get back to the camp.

Hayley and Jason were staring at me. Waiting for commands.

"Okay – I'm going to do something seriously dangerous," I told them. "You guys find Angela at the school. Stay there until I give you the all-clear on the walkie-talkies. If my plan works, those guys will be leaving this town really really fast."

Jason's eyes widened. "You're going up against the gang on your own?"

"Not exactly on my own," I said. "I'm going back to the garage to let out the zombies. Now go! Save Angela!"

They dashed off. I grabbed my bag of weapons and headed back to the High Street through some back streets. I avoided crossing the street until I was far from the parked vehicles belonging to the gang. I crossed between some abandoned cars. I was very lucky. I narrowly dodged detection by a two-man patrol of motorbikes scouting the area. I could see several men on the street outside the pub. The leader was giving orders on a radio. He was not dressed like the others. He was wearing a black suit. He looked like a businessman – except for the rifle in his other hand. That made him look like Tim Roth in *Reservoir Dogs*.

"Find her and kill her!" I heard him shouting. I was tempted to take a shot at him with my crossbow – but the range was too great. And shooting him would not get rid of the rest. I had to stick with my insane plan.

I sneaked around the rear of the pub and some other buildings until I was back at the garage where I'd left our van. The noise on the street had excited the zombies trapped inside the garage. They were banging on the doors and moaning. I checked nobody was looking my way before creeping up with my bolt cutters. What I was about to do was incredibly risky, but I didn't hesitate. I snapped off the lock. The zombies moaned louder, sensing they were close to a living tasty human. I returned my bolt cutters into my bag, strapped the bag over my shoulder, and then grabbed the bottom of the garage doors. I pushed them upwards until the doors continued opening under their momentum, releasing the hungry zombies lurking in the dark.

I'd expected a dozen – possible twenty – but the garage had been completed filled with them. There were over a hundred of them. I wondered how they had been lured inside – probably with a fresh corpse as bait – just as they started to move forward, lurching towards me. They had been trapped in the garage for months – but they had conserved their strength by going into a hibernation state, waiting for an opportunity to feed again.

They saw me and poured out of the darkness, gnashing teeth, slobbering, groaning.

They wanted to make me their dinner.

No time to dawdle.

I turned and ran, knowing they would follow me like rats following the Pied Piper. I could hear them chasing me – but I didn't have the time to look back. I didn't have time to go around the side of the garage either because so many zombies had already blocked that exit. I had to head into the street where I could not avoid being seen by the gang. The zombies chased me into the High Street. My bag of weapons was weighing and slowing me down – but I didn't want to ditch it because I needed it to fight them and the gang. My shoulder ached as I sprinted towards the pub where the leader and a couple of bikers were standing. They saw me and the horde of zombies at the same time. I tossed a lit firework at them before they could aim their guns. It wouldn't kill them – but it had the desired effect of making them scatter as it exploded. The leader ran into the pub, but the other men were left on the street. Through a cloud of acrid black smoke, I dashed past them and hid behind the corner of the pub, leaving the gang members to fight the zombies.

I dropped my bag to get out my air gun. Around the corner, I could hear the gang members shooting at the zombies.

"There's too many!" one shouted.

I heard a man running my way. He appeared around the corner – and I shot him in the face. At close range my air pellet was fatal. It blasted a small hole in his forehead. He looked surprised when he fell over, his limbs twitching. A second later a green-faced zombie was feasting on him, ripping his throat open. It turned to look at me

– another meaty meal – before returning to its current feast, sinking its yellow teeth into the soft flesh of my man's neck.

I grabbed my bag and hurried away.

A minute later I heard more gunfire as the other gang members encountered the zombies. The zombies were spreading out for fresh food.

I had to make my way to the alpha site now.

The school was behind four rows of houses on the other side of the High Street.

I got there without encountering anyone living or dead.

The school was a modern brick building with flat roofs and a concrete playground behind a chain-link fence. I'd seen it only from some distance when we were hiding from the gang during the day – but now I could see some words sprayed on the main entrance doors in red paint.

ZOMBIES INSIDE!
KEEP OUT!!!

ENTRY EIGHT

I could hear angry moaning on the other side – but something wasn't adding up. The message sprayed on the primary school's doors looked like the one on the garage where I'd found over a hundred zombies – but the paint was fresher and smelled of chemicals. On closer inspection, I noticed it wasn't even dry. I grinned. The message was a fake designed to fool the gang. Someone had tagged it recently. I knew it had to be one of my friends. With the sound of a motorbike heading my way, I quickly approached the door. It was locked from the inside with a chain. The moaning continued.

"Hey! It's me! Let me in!"

The moaning stopped. I heard the chain rattling. The door opened. Hayley appeared, holding her favourite anti-zombie weapon, her nail gun. The nail gun looked comically huge in her small hands. She looked at me and grinned. "You made it!"

"Yeah. Quick. Someone's coming."

I entered the school and shut the doors behind me. We secured it with a padlock and chain. I could hear a bike roaring up the street. It slowed as it went by – but it didn't stop at the school. It accelerated away. Whoever was driving it didn't want to stick around to fight the zombies. They were leaving the town, and I couldn't blame them because it sounded like a hell of a fight was going on back where I'd released the zombies. All the gunshots and screaming sounded like a New Year's Eve firework display. Right now, the gang were too occupied with staying alive to bother hunting for us. Good.

"The warning was a brilliant idea," I said. "Did you think of that?"

She nodded proudly. "I didn't want the bad guys coming in. I thought they'd be scared of zombies. You think it will work?"

"You had me fooled – until I smelled the fresh paint. Where'd you get it?"

She rolled her eyes like I was stupid for asking. "Duh! This is a school, Ben. There's like loads of stuff in the art class."

"I don't suppose you found an Uzi?"

She frowned. "What's an Uzi?"

"A type of machine gun. It was a joke."

"Oh," she said. "No. Nothing like that. Just art stuff. Your jokes aren't very funny, Ben."

"Have you cleared this place for zombies?"

"Of course!" she said, sounding insulted. "There aren't any. The whole place is empty. Jason's in the staff room with Angela. Should I stay here and guard the door?"

"No – the gang won't be looking for us any longer. They've got bigger problems. Let's go to them."

We hurried by several classrooms filled with small desks and child-sized plastic chairs that made me feel like a giant. I could smell crayons and chalk and plasticine. The smells reminded me of my childhood. It was strange being inside a school again. Especially one that was empty of children and teachers. I wondered what had happened to them. I hadn't seen any small zombies coming out of the garage – so maybe the kids had escaped. I liked to think that, anyway.

Jason and Angela were in the windowless staff room, where Jason had set up a few torches so there was some reasonable light. The room smelled of blood and iodine. Angela was lying flat on a cheap-looking leather sofa, stripped down to her bloody T-shirt. Jason was crouched beside her, inspecting the small bullet wound in her back. Blood flowed out with every heartbeat. The blood loss itself wasn't a lot – but that was only what I could see on the outside. Her internal damage could be much worse. The bullet could have perforated an artery or entered an organ. Angela was gasping and breathing shallowly as Jason cleaned the wound with iodine. Her face was pale and damp with cold sweat.

"No ... exit wound," she said when she saw me. "That's bad, right?"

"We'll get it out," I said. "Jason, can you see the bullet?"

He shook his head. "Too much blood."

"Okay – let me look."

I stepped closer and shone a torch on the wound. I'd have to cut wider to have a better look – but Angela was already in pain. She'd go into shock if I started butchering her. I spoke to Jason quietly so she would not hear our conversation.

"We'll have to look inside for the bullet – but it will hurt her. You've given her painkillers?"

"Yeah, I've given her some of the morphine," he said. "Ben, I don't know what to do now. *This isn't a cut on her finger.*"

Since the beginning of the zombie apocalypse, I'd had to learn some survival skills, like basic medical treatments, but I'd never done major surgery. There were two types of injury, according to some medical books I'd read: hollow organ damage and solid organ damage. Hollow organ damage was caused when a tube carrying a fluid was nicked. For that kind of injury, you needed to clean the area and sew it up and pray gangrene didn't kill the patient. The other kind of injury could stop an organ from working. Her liver, kidneys, spleen and bowels were all kind of close to the entry wound. If any of them had been damaged, there was nothing I could do.

"Okay, we'll have to cut her open," I said. "Angela, I'm going to give you a local anaesthetic."

I took some things out of our emergency medical kit. They

included a scalpel that I sterilised with alcohol. An injection of lidocaine into the area around Angela's wound made her skin go numb before I started cutting. Making the first cut was the hardest thing I had ever done. I hated hurting her. She grimaced when the scalpel sliced her flesh. Hayley held her hand.

"Ben knows what he's doing," she said. "He'll get it out."

I loved her confidence in me – but I was nervous. Doctors swear upon the Hippocratic Oath. *Do no harm*. I wasn't a doctor. What if I made things worse?

Very carefully, I widened the hole so I could feel inside for the bullet. That increased the amount of blood coming out. Angela gasped as my fingers probed. I swore to myself. I couldn't feel the bullet. It had gone too deep. There was no way of finding it without an x-ray. And even then I wouldn't know what I was looking at. All I could do was sterilise the damaged tissue and stitch her back up, hoping she'd stop bleeding when her blood clotted. I covered her wound with a gauze pad and left her to rest. She didn't look well, though. I'd seen zombies in better health. It was possible the bullet had missed her organs and done only minor damage that could heal itself. Possible? Yeah. Likely? No.

We'd just have to wait and see.

ENTRY NINE

We hid in the school all night, while outside the zombies attacked the gang. I could hear rapid gunfire at first – but it lessened as more of the gang died, ran out of ammo, or fled the town. For hours I feared someone would try to break into the school, bringing the horde of zombies with them, but the message Hayley had sprayed on the doors seemed to do the trick. Of course, that message would only deter humans. Zombies would not read it. If anyone of them got inside, we would be in serious trouble, so I patrolled the classrooms with my crossbow and machetes until it was dawn.

By then it was disturbingly quiet outside. Peering through the windows, I could see nothing moving. The town looked deserted, though I knew the zombies had to be somewhere.

I returned to the staff room, where Hayley and Jason were guarding the unconscious Angela. Angela was not looking better. She was feverish and talking to someone in her sleep called Ryan. It was weird – but I felt jealous of Ryan. Had he been her boyfriend before Day One? He was probably dead now. I sighed. I was really worried about Angela's condition. I'd given her some antibiotics – but they wouldn't fix her bullet wound. He really needed to see a proper doctor – not an ex-banker with a basic knowledge of first aid.

I'd gone online to see if I could find someone able to treat her – but my messages had been unanswered. There were not many people with electricity and internet connectivity in England. The Pure Bloods had grabbed most of the doctors, forcing them to work for them. Angela's condition was getting worse – but I had no skills to help her.

The only person I knew with the medical skills to save her was

Sadie, who was back at our camp with Neal. Sadie had been a nurse before Day One. She could help – but only if we could get out of this godforsaken town.

I spoke to Hayley and Jason. "Okay – I'm going to sneak up on the roof to do a recon." I loved saying things like that. It made me feel like I'd been in the Army. "I'll keep in contact on the walkie-talkie."

I left Hayley looking after Angela. Her older brother Jason took over the patrolling in the long corridor running the length of the school's main building.

"Ben, do you think Angela's going to die?"

"Not if I can help it," I said.

"She looks bad."

"I know – but Sadie might be able to do something."

"What if she can't?" he said.

"We'll deal with that after we've got her out of this town."

I climbed the stairs to the flat roof, where I stayed low and scanned the area through my binoculars. The sun was just poking up over the hills, revealing the extent of the damage done to the town during the night.

It wasn't good. There were dozens of zombies on the High Street, which had been razed to the ground by the fire started by the gang. Their van filled with our supplies had gone. So had the other cars. A couple of bikes were still there near the pub – but we'd never get to them without killing fifty flesh-eaters. We couldn't transport Angela on a bike, anyway. We needed a car or van to get her out of there.

Thick smoke covered much of the town as the contents of the furniture store continued to smoulder, producing the kind of black noxious cloud you'd see after an oil rig exploded. Other buildings were still burning because the gang members had been foolishly tossing Molotov cocktails at the zombies. They'd managed to turn a few zombies into burnt meat – but the sheer number of undead had overwhelmed them. Some had been bitten and turned. I could see them shuffling around, moaning, on the hunt for the living, including their former colleagues.

Fresh zombies like them were ten times faster and more dangerous than the older ones that had come out of the garage.

Speaking of which, I could see our van parked where I'd abandoned it. It looked undamaged by the fires – but it wouldn't go anywhere unless I could fix the leak *and* get some petrol. A better option would be to find another vehicle with some petrol in its tank.

I moved across the roof for a better look in the other direction – only to hear a noise like a man grunting. A pair of hands suddenly appeared grasping hold of the roof's gutter. A hairy head appeared. I aimed my crossbow as a young man, aged about nineteen, hauled himself onto the roof, where he collapsed, laughing with relief. He was wearing biker leathers. I'd seen him before with the rest of the gang. He didn't know I was watching him as he leaned over the roof and called down to the zombies chasing him. "Hah! You didn't get me! Can't get me now, can you, you brain-eating freaks? You're too stupid to climb the drainpipe, aren't you? Hah!"

A low moan from below answered him. The man was smiling until he moved his head and saw me with my crossbow trained on him. Then his face fell. "Whoa! Don't shoot! I'm not a zombie."

"I know that. You're worse. You're with that gang. You tried to kill me and my friends." My crossbow was aimed at his chest. I considered shooting him as payback for Angela. It was hard resisting the bloodlust.

"No, no. Not me. I was with those other guys – but I never hurt nobody. I was forced into joining them by my brother. Luke said we had to join them to stay alive. We had no idea they'd make us hurt other people. They were psychos. I'm not like them, sir. I swear! Please don't kill me! Please!"

I could have released a bolt to kill him – but I was reluctant. I saw the fear in his eyes. That fear was genuine. He was afraid of me. That made me feel like I was the bad guy. It made me hesitate. "What's your name?"

"William – but friends call me Billy."

"William, are you armed?"

"No, sir. I – uh – I lost my weapons."

"If I frisk you and find anything on you, I'll throw you off this roof to let the zoms feed on you," I said. "So, I'll ask you again. Do not lie. Are you armed, William?"

"I have a couple of small knives," he admitted. "And a screwdriver."

"Nothing else?"

"No."

"Take them out slowly. Toss them over here."

One of his knives was in his leather jacket. The other was in his belt with a long-handled screwdriver. He threw them across the roof to me. I added them to my arsenal. "That's all, Billy? No more?"

"No more," he said. "I swear it on my life."

"You are swearing it on your life," I said. "Lie down on your belly with your hands on the back of your head."

He did it. I put my knee on his back while I frisked him. I found some powerful painkillers and other pills in his pockets – but no other weapons. I tied his hands behind his back with nylon rope before taking my knee off him. His hands were firmly secured behind his back when I let him sit up.

"How many of your gang are still here?"

"I don't know. I've been hiding in a building most of the time. I think they're all dead. Undead. Whatever."

"Where's your brother?"

"He's with Quinn."

"Who's Quinn?"

"He's the leader."

"The guy in the black suit?"

"Yeah."

"Where are they?"

"I saw them drive off in the van during the night. Leaving me to die. I can't believe my own flesh-and-blood abandoned me." There were tears on Billy's cheeks. "Looks like Luke cares more about being in Quinn's good books than rescuing his own brother. He doesn't care about me. He's Quinn's number two now your friend killed Mitchell. Me, I'm just a loser. They didn't even try to rescue me. Luke betrayed me."

I left him feeling sorry for himself to check out the far side of the school. There were a dozen zombies down there. They snarled when they saw me. They clawed at the wall, trying to climb it with their bare hands, dragging their fingers over the bricks in a vain effort to climb the side of the building like *really* amateur rock climbers. None had the brains to climb up the iron drainpipe. That was good. I didn't want them climbing onto the roof. We were safe up there – for now.

Unfortunately, the noises they were making were attracting more zombies within hearing range. They were forming a small crowd as they headed towards the back of the school. They'd find a way into the building eventually through the rear exit. I was tempted to shoot them with my crossbow – but I'd never retrieve my bolts with so many of them coming. Each bolt was too precious to lose. I might need them in an emergency. I glared at my captive.

"You've attracted the zombies to our hiding place," I said. "I should kill you for that!"

"I'm sorry!" he said. He sobbed pathetically. "Please don't kill me. Look, sir, I can help you."

"How can you help me?"

"You want to get out of here quickly?"

"Of course," I said. "How can you help with that?"

"I found a car. It's got a fully-charged battery and a full tank of petrol. I was going to use it to escape – but the zombies showed up before I could hot-wire it. Me and Luke are good at that. We used to steal cars on the estate when we … Sir, I'll show you where it is if you promise to take me with you. I don't want to get turned into one of them, sir. Just let me come with you until we're out of this place, sir. Please!"

"Where's the car?"

"It's behind the supermarket. In the car park. A sweet red Audi. It'd take me only a minute to get it started. Unfortunately, the place is swarming with the undead. Well – it was. Looks like most of them followed me when I ran away. We could probably get back to it with no problems if we go around those freaks. I'm really sorry about attracting them, sir."

"Stop calling me 'sir', Billy. I'm Ben. Listen, Billy, I'll promise not to kill you if you help us get our friend out of here, okay? You help me, I'll let you live. Deal?"

He nodded eagerly. "Deal."

ENTRY TEN

I didn't trust Billy one bit – but my car-stealing skills were not on his level. I couldn't hot-wire a car like they do in the old movies. *Gone in sixty seconds?* Not if I tried doing it. *Gone in several days, more like.* Modern cars had too many electronics to just cut some wires under the dash to circumvent the ignition switch. I needed Billy for now – but I would not take my eyes off him. He would have said anything to avoid being chucked off the roof. I grabbed Billy and led him down the stairs into the school.

Jason wasn't happy to see I had a prisoner. He aimed his crossbow. "What's going on, Ben?"

"I found him climbing up a drainpipe," I said. "Escaping a whole bunch of zombies. They're now outside, thanks to him."

"Great," the teenager said. "You tied him up, right?"

"Yeah," I said. "But he's going to help us. Right, Billy? You are going to hot-wire the car?"

Billy nodded. "I'm good at stealing cars."

He sounded proud of it. In this new lawless and lethal world, it was a useful skill.

Better than my degree in Economics.

What use was that?

Keeping Billy's hands tied behind his back, I directed him into the staff room where Hayley was looking after Angela. Angela was awake – but very weak. Her face was white. The bandages over her wounded back were dark with dried blood. She glowered at Billy. He looked down at his feet.

"You caught one?" she said.

"He's agreed to get us a car. It's at the supermarket. Do you feel up to walking?"

"I'll try." Angela attempted to sit up – but she slumped back down on the couch, wincing with pain. "Just give me a minute. I'll try again."

"No," I said. "Rest. I don't want you opening that wound, Angela."

We formulated a plan. Three of us would go for the car – me, Billy and one of the kids - while one person stayed to protect Angela. Jason volunteered to go with me – but I didn't like the idea of Hayley on her own, fighting the zombies at the school. It was better if she came with me and her brother remained with Angela. Jason wasn't happy about his sister going with me to get the car – but I needed him to protect Angela and I needed someone to watch my back when I was with Billy, so she would have to be my back-up. Jason and Angela would meet us at the front entrance after we had the car – but they'd stay locked in the building until I contacted them on the walkie-talkie. Since Angela could not walk, I needed to find some way for Jason to move her by himself. I found the answer in a classroom – a steel trolley. Jason and I carefully lifted her onto it. Jason could push it along the corridor when the time came. Unfortunately, the pain of moving made Angela pass out. When she returned to consciousness, I gave her my air gun as protection. She would have to stay there alone for now because our plan required Jason up on the roof assisting our escape from the school.

I spoke to Hayley out of earshot of Billy. "We're going to have to trust Billy for the moment – but we need to be ready for anything. We'll have to watch each other's backs around him. He's unarmed – but he's one of them. This whole thing could be a set-up. He could have been ordered to lure us out. So watch him. And be prepared to shoot him if necessary – but only if necessary. I intend to let him go if he does help us. A deal's a deal. You ready, Hayley?"

"I'm ready," she said. "Let's get out of here."

Jason, Billy and Hayley followed me into the corridor, which had been quiet during the night, but now it was filled with the sound of banging. The zombies were outside the front and rear entrances, having been attracted to the school by our intruder. Jason and I blocked the rear entrance with a dozen tables and chairs to slow them down if they did breach the building – but we couldn't do that for the front one. That would be Jason and Angela's escape route. The door was held shut with a sturdy lock and chain, rattling as the zombies pushed against it. I just had to hope and pray none of them got inside before we got back with the car.

The four of us ascended to the roof. The air smelled of ash and stung my eyes as smoke drifted from the High Street. The supermarket was visible about a quarter of a mile away. We looked for a way down from the roof that didn't involve a battle with the undead – but they were all around the building now. That was why we needed Jason. He made some noise and waved his arms for attention to attract the zombies while we hid and waited. The moment the area below was clear, I lowered Hayley onto a large recycling bin next to the wall. Meanwhile, Jason was making a racket. There were no zombies near us thanks to his distraction.

"You next," I told Billy. "Climb down now."

"No way. The zombies will get me. I'm not doing it with my hands tied. You'll have to untie me first. I can't climb down like this."

I pulled out one of his knives. He flinched like he expected me to cut his throat – but I cut his wrists loose. "Don't waste any more time, Billy. Move it!"

Billy lowered himself onto the bin. He jumped down onto the ground as I followed. Hayley kept her nail gun on Billy the whole time. The hard look on her small face left me in no doubt that she'd shoot him if he did anything remotely suspicious. Billy held up his hands and stayed very still. I aimed my crossbow at him once I was on the ground.

"You lead the way," I said.

"Unarmed? You're kidding, right?"

"We'll protect you," Hayley said. "Just move it or I'll shoot you with a nail. It'll really hurt."

It was almost funny that a little girl was talking like that to a man like Billy, which was probably why he didn't complain again. "Okay – I'll do whatever you want. Just no nails, okay?"

Hayley glared at him – but she nodded.

"Go down that street as we planned," I said. "It's clear at the moment. We can't wait any longer. Move it."

"This is mental," Billy said, but he did what I ordered. I had my crossbow aimed at his back in case he decided to run. I wouldn't hesitate to shoot him in the back like one of his pals had done to Angela. The three of us moved away from the side of the school out into the open, trying to remain undetected by making no noise and moving slowly so we didn't catch the eye of a zombie – they were more likely to notice us if we moved quickly and non-zombie-like - but we didn't get to the street opposite before we were seen by some of the zombies around the rear of the school. One moaned and lurched in our direction. It was too slow to ever catch us – but other zombies among the crowd pushed the slow one aside and sprinted after us. They were fresh ones. Billy's gang. They moved like living humans. A stealthy escape wasn't possible. They were running after us.

"Run, run, run!" I said, though the words were not needed. Hayley and Billy were already running down the street.

From the rooftop, Jason started shouting even louder – desperately trying to keep their attention on him – but the zombies were suddenly more interested in us, the three Happy Meals they could see on the street.

We were food they could get.

Ahead, a one-armed woman ran towards us from an open doorway. Her nearly-fleshless head only had an upper jaw, but her teeth would cut if she got close. Hayley fired a nail into her skull, splattering pink brain tissue onto the road. The road was clear in front – but the fresh zombies were keeping up with us. I fired a crossbow bolt at the fastest zombie behind me – but my aim was off. The bolt slammed into its shoulder and stuck there, harmless. It didn't slow the thing at all. It just made the zombie run faster. There was no time to reload my crossbow – so I gave the useless weapon to Billy, telling him to hold onto it as we continued to sprint towards the supermarket.

"They're too fast," Billy said.

He was right. We could run – but the fastest zombies would catch up when we tired. "You two keep going. I'll slow them down!"

I switched to my favourite weapons, my machetes, before turning to face the zombie gang member. I stopped running. The zombie charged straight at me – but I hacked off his head with one blow. The head rolled away as his body continued to run for a few seconds before stumbling and falling. More zombies were right behind it – so I attacked them to give Hayley and Billy some breathing space. I decapitated two men and a woman. There was now a safe gap between us and the other zombies. They were chasing – but they'd not catch us if we hurried. I chased after Jason and Billy, who were most of the way to the supermarket. They were almost at the street corner when they stopped and waited for me to catch up.

"Want this back?" Billy said, offering me my crossbow.

"Yeah," I said, taking it. I reloaded it. We hurried around the corner of the supermarket. I could see twenty abandoned cars in the parking lot. I could also see well over a hundred zombies between us and the red Audi. I didn't understand it. They couldn't all have come out of the garage. These were a different group.

"What the hell?" I said. "Where did they come from?"

Billy knew. I could see the guilt in his eyes. He had known about them – but he had not told us.

"Billy?" I said.

"Uh. I forgot to tell you I found some more zombies in the supermarket when I was on the run. They were locked in until I opened the doors. I thought they'd all chased me to the school – but it looks like some stayed behind. I'm sorry." He grinned sheepishly. "Guess I should have warned you, huh?"

"Would have been useful," I snapped. "This is a problem."

Hayley was looking back at the zombies following us. They'd soon catch up. " We're going to get surrounded. Ben, what are we going to do?"

ENTRY ELEVEN

The zombies in the supermarket's car park had not noticed us – yet – but they would if we tried to steal the car. I could have picked them off one by one with my crossbow if I'd had an hour and a safe rooftop – but I could hear the undead horde behind us, getting louder as they neared the corner. As the first zombie appeared, looking like a skeleton with one grey eye in a mostly fleshless face, I fired my crossbow - but nothing happened.

The bolt didn't fire.

I knew what had happened and cursed my stupidity. "Billy, you sabotaged my -"

The sneaky traitor was off running down the street. I swore. Hayley turned ready to fire a nail at him – but the one-eyed zombie was more of an immediate threat. My crossbow was useless so I was basically unarmed until I got something else out of my bag. Hayley had to use her nail gun for taking down the zombie before it got near me. She ran forward and aimed at its head – firing a nail straight through its good eye.

As the zombie died, Billy got to the street corner and whistled before ducking out of sight. The purpose of his whistle was to draw the attention of the zombie shoppers and zombie employees in front of us. They couldn't see the source of the noise – but they did see Hayley and me. Billy had just dropped us in it big time. I muttered something furiously under my breath as I realised Billy had tricked me. There probably was no car with petrol and a charged battery. He had just lied to save his life back at the school. And then he had ditched us at the first opportunity – after leading us into the second ambush in two days.

I was a big idiot for untying his hands. I should have never trusted one of them. I wished I had killed him – but I had bigger worries. The zombies were advancing across the car park. They were also at the corner – blocking our route back to the school.

"Ben?" Hayley said. "What do we do? What do we do?"

Standing and fighting were not an option. "Come on. We'll follow that traitor. Let's hope he knows where he's going. To the corner. Now!"

Billy had escaped down the next street. We raced to the corner, which led to a row of old terraced houses on a cobbled road.

Billy was only twenty feet away. His escape had been prevented by more zombies. A pack of forty were spread out across the street, salivating at the prospect of fresh meat. There weren't any gaps to get through. Billy had picked up a brick, which he was bashing into the head of a bald female zombie while trying to avoid getting bit by others. He was kicking and screaming and fighting for this life. I felt like leaving him to fight alone – but there were fewer zombies in that direction. We had no choice but to fight with him.

My machetes were excellent for close combat in tight spaces – but what I needed for street fighting was something extending my reach. I chose a hefty fire axe, then handed the bag of weapons to Hayley because I needed both hands free. She knew to stay behind me as I raised my axe and charged, hacking my way through the undead like a bloodthirsty maniac.

Several hungry zombies snarled and lurched towards me, gnashing their teeth, so I had to fight two or three at once. Not a problem – normally – but I got my axe stuck in one's head. I struggled to pull it loose – but I had to let it go to kick another zombie backwards and elbow a third in the face.

It was bad. We were getting surrounded. Once that happened, we'd get bitten and turned.

I couldn't let that happen to Hayley.

With a yell, I pulled out my trusted machetes and started hacking away at the zombies. I slashed one zombie with my right-hand machete – chopping off an arm - then slammed my left one into the creature's skull. Pushing it back into the others, using it as a temporary shield, I tried to get my axe back from the one dead at my feet. The axe was caught in the bone. When I pulled upwards, the zombie's neck stretched and tore, leaving me with the axe with the head still stuck on it. The axe with the head attached was a blunt instrument – but I swung it around to fend off a zombie sneaking up on me. I bashed its head with the other head until it went down, head-butted into its second death. Then I stood on the attached head and pulled it off the blade with a sickening squelch. About a dozen zombies were coming around behind us by then – angry undead shoppers wanting to feast. They were closing the distance. To help me out, Hayley fired nails into their kneecaps to drop them. It was an effective way of slowing them down – but it didn't kill them. They crawled towards us. Hayley blasted nails into the heads of the fallen, covering my back as I made a path for us through the others. In my peripheral vision, I could see Billy slamming his brick into the face of a former gang member.

I bet he'd wished he had not whistled.

Nearer to me, the ground was covered with corpses – some truly dead and some twitching and snarling. Hayley and I had to step over some zombies to get to the other side – but it was dangerous stepping on the living dead. One I'd thought I'd killed with an axe blow suddenly lurched its jaws towards my leg – salivating in anticipation of chomping through my flesh – but then its head exploded as Billy appeared, slamming his brick down on its skull.

"Need some help?"

"Yeah," I muttered.

He joined me in fighting our way through the last few blocking our escape. Then we ran until we were clear. We got off the street and rested in the back garden of a house where there were no zombies. For a few seconds we all rested, gathering our breath, momentarily on the same side.

Then Billy stepped away from us – but he didn't run away. He lowered his brick. "Look, I'm sorry about what I did back there. I just wanted to get away. I'll team up with you guys for real this time. I can get us out of this town – but I'll need your help."

"You want us to help you?" I said. "After you whistled to those zombies? You tried to kill us!"

"That was a mistake," he said. "I swear I won't do nothing bad again. I wasn't lying about the car. I could've got it working if the zombies hadn't been everywhere. I have another way out – if you'll listen."

"I'm listening," I said, though I had my axe raised.

"I checked out your van. I know I can fix what's wrong with it in two minutes if we can push it into the garage over the pit. I don't think there are zombies inside now. *You* released them all, killing my friends."

Oh – they were his friends now? Earlier he had made it sound like he had been forced to join the gang. He was bitter about them getting killed.

That was a decision I regretted because it had made it worse for me and my family – but I wasn't going to feel bad about it. "Hey, Billy, I wouldn't have done that if you and your gang hadn't pursued us here. I'm not the only one to blame here. Besides, *you* released the ones in the supermarket, Billy. I figure we're even now. I'll call a truce if you help us get out of here. How do you know you can fix our van, anyway?"

"Before Day One I was a trainee mechanic for CarFit UK. I fixed hundreds of cars. I know how to fix your van. I can weld a plate onto the bottom to repair the tank – but I'd never be able to push the van into the garage on my own, so I need you to help me do that."

"You expect me to trust you again?"

"Look, I can *always* get out of here on foot – but you're the one who needs to get a vehicle for your friend. So, you make the choice, Ben. Want to team up for real?"

He had a cheeky grin I wanted to wipe off his face – but his plan did make me interested. Our van was a zombie-proof box on wheels. It would be great to get it working.

"We'll need petrol," I said, thinking aloud.

Billy looked smug. "No problem. We can syphon it from some vehicles around here. I've seen a couple. All we need is a garden hose."

We agreed to help each other. There was a little greenhouse in the back garden. It was filled with tools we could use to syphon petrol – a garden hose and a large green plastic watering can. It also contained some great gardening tools ideal for fighting the undead – hoes, spades, rakes and pitchforks. They were excellent weapons. Billy swapped his brick for a pitchfork. Hayley grabbed a long hoe. I decided to keep using my axe.

Meanwhile, I contacted Jason on the walkie-talkie. "What's the situation?"

"Pretty nasty," he said. "The zombies are inside the school, dude. Couple of minutes ago, I had to come down off the roof because I could see some of the zombies breaking into the school through a classroom's windows. They would have got to Angela if I hadn't stopped them. I killed some and barricaded the rest into the classroom – but they're slamming themselves against the door. They might break through at any time. Some are now on the roof too because they climbed up when I was gone. I locked the roof so they can't follow me. I keep checking the corridors to see if any have got in through the classrooms – but there are too many windows and doors to guard them all, Ben. We need you here, Ben. Have you got the car?"

"No," I said. "Change of plan. We're going to repair our van."

"The van?"

"Yeah."

"How long will that take?"

"Billy says just a few minutes – once we get there. It'll take us about ten minutes to sneak our way to the garage. That's assuming we don't encounter trouble. So, I'm estimating twenty minutes. Can you hold on until we get there, okay?"

"Dude, I don't know."

"Lock yourselves into a room if you have to. We'll come and get you once we've got the van running, okay?"

"Be quick," Jason said. "Angela's looking worse. She's unconscious again. We've got to get her proper medical treatment, Ben. She's dying."

ENTRY TWELVE

We needed to syphon petrol from three abandoned vehicles to get just enough to fill the five-litre watering can. Billy did that unenviable task, sucking the air out of the hose to create a vacuum to draw out the petrol, while Hayley and I protected him from wandering undead. The worst part of syphoning was the need to suck on the hose until the petrol started flowing because if you were not quick you got a mouthful of foul-tasting unleaded petrol. Billy wasn't fast enough one time – so he was spitting out petrol as we circled around to the garage. I tried not to laugh – but it was funny seeing his face twisted in disgust every time he spat out petrol. He looked like Robert De Niro gurning in the mirror in *Taxi Driver*.

We reached the back of the garage after encountering a couple of emaciated zombies – but they were easy to kill with our gardening tools. Billy was right about the garage being empty of zombies, but they were loitering on the High Street, where a group feasted on a biker's corpse like his organs were the first course in a mediaeval banquet. Two were fighting over his entrails. The group were bound to notice us when we started pushing the van into the garage. Before revealing our location, I sneaked around the van's side to check it was empty inside. Luckily, there were no living or undead hiding there. Then I scouted out the garage. Something moaned in the darkness. So – it wasn't completed deserted. That problem would have to wait until we got the van moving, though.

"Hayley, get in and steer the van when we get it rolling."

She jumped into the driver's seat while Billy and I went around the back. We started pushing as soon as Hayley had the brakes off. The van didn't start to move until we both got our backs into it, really straining. We were silent – but the zombies spotted us. Their moans changed tone, signifying their interest in our flesh and blood.

Billy spat again, cursing. "They're coming."

"I see them," I said. "Push harder!"

"I am pushing harder."

"Push even harder."

We pushed and pushed. The van rolled forward. It started to move on its own momentum once the wheels turned, rolling into the darkness of the garage. We kept pushing harder and harder as the zombies advanced. As soon as the whole van passed under the doors, Billy and I scrambled to get the doors shut. They came down painfully slowly as the zombies ran, crawled and shambled in our direction.

The doors were half down when the first arrived. I recognised him. He was the man Angela had shot in the leg during the ambush. He hadn't escaped with their leader. Now he had a large chunk of his face missing, which had gone pale as he died. He dragged his injured leg behind him, his eyes focussed on me with savage hatred. He remembered me. And now whatever remained of his human mind wanted revenge. I pushed him back with Hayley's hoe – catching it under the chin with the blade. The blade sliced into his throat, crushing his larynx. The undead man stumbled backwards, gurgling through the hole in his neck, his blood running down his chest. I jabbed him a second time – pushing him over. Some of the ones behind him started tearing him apart so they could get past him to the warm, tasty meals in the garage. I didn't want to be fast food. I jumped up and used my weight to drag the door down much faster. The doors slammed down a moment later, plunging the garage into total darkness.

Turning around, I could hear moaning from inside. It was getting louder as the invisible zombie approached me in the dark. Where was my torch? My jacket. Got to get it out now. I fumbled for it while hearing the zombie getting closer and closer. I had no idea where the zombie was until Hayley switched on the headlights, flooding the room with light. Then I could see two zombies. One zombie was lurching across the room towards me. It was an elderly woman with no teeth. She smelled like decayed cabbages. The other zombie was younger, but it was writhing on the floor without any legs or arms, no danger to anyone. I dispatched the pensioner with my axe. Billy finished off the immobile one with his pitchfork through its skull.

A quick search didn't find any more. We were safe – for the moment. But I was fully aware of the danger awaiting me outside. The doors rattled behind us as we pushed the van over the pit. I called Jason while Billy looked for the tools required to get the tank fixed.

"Jason, how are you doing?"

"Uh – worse. They've broken through the rear exit – but they've struggling to get past the barricade because I've added more chairs and tables and stuff to block it. I can hear others crashing around in the classrooms. The air gun is empty of pellets. I've got my baseball bat and other weapons – but I can't fight them and protect Angela for long. Please tell me you're coming, Ben."

"We'll be there soon," I promised. "Just keep yourself alive, Jason. We'll get there. Get to the main entrance. We're coming soon."

I fixed my crossbow while Billy climbed down into the pit with the welding tools. I had my weapon reloaded when he had done the job, which did take him only a couple of minutes. I was impressed – but I didn't show it. I handed him the watering can – while Hayley pointed the crossbow at him, making him understand we were in charge. "Fill the tank quickly."

He nodded. "Yeah. You're in charge, boss."

I moved into the driver's seat as Billy ran around the side. He started pouring petrol into the tank.

"I don't trust him," Hayley whispered.

"Neither do I."

As soon as the watering can was empty, I turned on the ignition and tested the engine. Nothing. I tried again. The engine whined – but stopped. I tried a third time, praying that time for a miracle. The engine roared. Yes. The van was alive again and showing a decent amount of petrol on its gauge. I went around the back and opened the back for Billy – but I wasn't going to let him get in without taking some precautions. I had some gaffer tape. "Billy, I'll drive you out of here – but only if you're hands are tied."

"What? You still don't trust me?"

"It's hard to trust you after you whistled at those zombies. I don't want you getting tempted to do something when I'm rescuing my friends. So, you've got a choice. I either tape your hands or I leave you behind. Do you want me to leave you in this garage when I leave?"

"No," he said sullenly, like a small child being chastised by an adult. "But at least tape my hands in front this time, puh-leeeease."

Hayley covered me as I taped his wrists together. Then I made him sit in the passenger seat with his hands on his lap. He started asking a lot of annoying questions about what we were going to do next. I wished I'd taped his mouth. Maybe I would if he didn't shut up.

I needed to re-open the garage doors – so Hayley took over the driving. She could barely reach the pedals – but she slowly backed the car off the pit while I got myself ready to open the garage doors. Ideally, there would have been enough room for turning the van around – but the space was too tight. Hayley would have to drive out backwards as soon as I opened the door. I'd have to get into the van via the side door before the zombies got me. Timing would be crucial.

First, I turned on my walkie-talkie. "Jason?"

"Yeah?" he gasped. I could hear him throwing something. I could also hear angry zombies in the background.

"We're coming, Jason. Get ready at the main entrance, okay?"

"Got … it. Hurry. Zombies are coming. They're dozens coming down the corridor! I'm trapped!"

"Just keep fighting another minute!"

He was too busy to answer me. The walkie-talkie stayed on. The trouble at the school sounded bad.

"Ready?" I called to Hayley.

"Ready!" she said, revving the engine.

I lifted the garage doors. They clanked upwards. Sunlight poured into the garage – along with a dozen zombies. I ran around the side of the van as they poured through the opening. I dived in the back and slammed the door shut with only a second's grace before the zombies slammed their bodies against the van, desperately trying to get to me.

"Okay?" Hayley said.

"Go!" I yelled.

Hayley backed out at maximum acceleration, colliding with the mass of undead on the street. I felt the impact of the zombies slamming into the rear as the van emerged into the daylight. A couple of the undead crushed under the wheels – but other ones clung to the back and front, crawling over the van like insects. I poked my head up through the opening in the roof and unleashed a couple of crossbow bolts before ducking back inside. I shot two in the face – but I lost two bolts doing it. I'd run out really fast if I used my crossbow unnecessarily. It was stupid wasting them.

For the moment we were free of the zombies – but we were

driving backwards towards the school at forty miles per hour. Hayley was having a hard time steering in reverse. She caught a lamp post with a glancing blow. The lamp post teetered over like a chopped tree as I felt the impact in my teeth. Through the front windscreen, I could see dozens of zombies pursuing us down the road. It looked like we were watching a marathon of the dirtiest people in the world.

"We're almost at the school," Hayley said. "Want me to drive backwards into the car park?"

"No – keep going down the road – then stop and let me take over the driving."

We passed the school going fifty and continued for fifty metres before Hayley stopped. In passing the school I had seen ten zombies crowded around the entrance that I'd have to take care of before Jason and Angela could escape. I swapped places with Hayley, handing her the crossbow. Then I did a quick U-turn before the zombies caught up with us. "Jason! We're almost there! Be at the entrance! Get ready to bring Angela out!"

Jason didn't reply, which was a bad sign, but I hoped he'd heard. There were several zombies in my way as I headed back to the school – and I ploughed into every one of them, smashing and crunching their bones on the bumper and under the wheels. I left behind me a wake of mangled corpses. Billy sat next to me cheering as each zombie got hit by the front bumper.

"Yeah – nail them! You got that sucker! Yeah! Squish them!"

"Hold on, Hayley," I said, turning into the school's entrance. I drove straight at the zombies blocking Jason's way out. My speed was sixty – about the max the van could go. It slammed into three head-on, knocking them flying. Then I drove in a circle catching some more before stopping with the rear pointed at the entrance. I backed up, catching some more, running them over, clearing the entrance. I parked with the rear facing the school with a gap half the length of a car. Between us and the entrance. The entrance was clear for now. I scrambled over my seat into the back of the van, opening the doors. A zombie reared out of nowhere. (It must have been under the wheels.) I threw a machete into its forehead and kicked it backwards. I jumped out with my fire axe in both hands. Hayley covered me with the crossbow as I ran up to the doors. I pulled at them – but they were locked with the chain.

"Jason?"

"Ben? You're here!"

"Yeah. Open the doors!"

"Can't! I'm protecting Angela! I need you to do it!"

I swore. There was a chain on the other side, padlocked to keep the zombies from breaking in. Now I had to do exactly that – while fending off the zombies around me that Hayley missed with her crossbow. I hacked away at the door, pausing only to chop the head off a white-haired zombie. The door was solid. The axe wasn't denting it. It'd take me ten minutes to break it open. The zombies wouldn't wait that long to get Jason. Drastic action was needed.

"Jason! Get away from the entrance! I'm going to drive in!"

I climbed back into the van and jumped into the driver's seat. I drove forwards, braked, then reversed. I hit the entrance at sufficient speed to knock the door off its hinges, flattening it on the ground. Hayley opened the rear doors without me having to tell her. I could see Jason in the corridor fighting off six or seven zombies with a chair like he was a lion-tamer while simultaneously protecting Angela, who was lying unconscious on the trolley nearer the entrance.

"About time!" Jason shouted. "Kind of need some help here!"

With the van wedged in the entrance, no zombies could get at us from the outside, though they were climbing on the van, pounding their fists on the windscreen.

I joined Hayley in helping Jason. I took over the fighting while Jason and his sister lifted Angela into the van.

Once they had her in the back, I swung my axe a couple of times to give myself some space – then I retreated in a hurry.

By some miracle, I got into the van just ahead of the zombies.

Then I slammed the doors shut.

I didn't need to tell Jason to get us out of there.

He was already driving the van forwards, pushing our way through a horde of the undead. There were so many bodies slamming on the windscreen it was dark inside the van until Jason shook them off with some sharp braking and accelerating. He wasted no time driving us out of that town into the countryside, where we eventually shook off the last few zombies.

Nobody looked back at the town.

We were just glad to escape alive.

*

Okay – I've just uploaded my last few blog entries now we're on the road again, safe for the time being. We're on our way to the camp. We should be there in about an hour – if nothing goes wrong.
Angela's still unconscious and looking very sick. Unfortunately, there is nothing I can do. I feel helpless, watching her.

Jason's driving with his sister in the passenger seat. Billy's in the back with me. He's still talking. He wants me to let him join our group. He says he will be a valuable member of our group if I give him a chance to prove it. His mechanical skills will be useful to us, he says.

I don't know.

Can I trust him?

What should I do?

ENTRY THIRTEEN

I allowed Billy to stay with us – but I took no chances. I kept him tied up and I blindfolded him before taking over the driving from Jason. Just because I wasn't going to kill Billy for betraying us didn't mean I trusted him. He had only helped us escape the town under duress. Frankly, I expected him to try something the moment his hands were untied. He seemed the type. But I was willing to let Billy have one more chance to prove himself useful. Of course, I didn't want him to know our camp's location, so he had to lie in the back for the last hour of the journey, not knowing which direction we were going. He looked uncomfortable, but it was the safest option.

Our camp was in a large country estate once owned by a member of the Royal family. The estate had been bought by a footballer and his supermodel wife back in the 1990s. The media had loved them – until their tax-dodging schemes had been exposed. Then they'd become hate figures. They'd abandoned England after Day One to live on one of their private islands, leaving behind their luxurious mansion and fleet of Ferraris, which we had come across a few months earlier. The mansion would have been a great place to live – if it had not been razed to the ground by arsonists. The arsonists set fire to the cars for some reason too – just to trash the footballer's property, I suspected. It had been weird coming across the ruins inside the forested estate. We'd considered camping there out on the open ground, miles from anything living or dead – but we had found a better place in the surrounding forest.

When we drove up the gravel road towards the camp, Angela remained unconscious. Her condition was worrying. Our return should have been a happy time – but too many things had gone wrong for celebrations. Instead of unloading our van of food and medicines, I was bringing back a blindfolded prisoner and a mortally wounded companion. Not exactly the best of presents.

We'd made our camp next to a stream of uncontaminated water providing us with fresh salmon for our meals. The camp was about a mile from the blackened ruin of the mansion, which could just be seen through the trees. The camp was protected from wandering undead by a fence of chicken wire wrapped around several trees, making an enclosure roughly a third of the size of a football field. There were two gates in the barricade for coming and going, allowing vehicles to pass through to the enclosure. I stopped and beeped the horn to let our friends know we were at the north gate. We'd been away a week – but it honestly felt like years. A camper van was on the other side of the barricade beneath some trees. Two people emerged from it. They were Sadie and Neal. Seeing them again, alive and well, made me feel like crying with joy. The pessimist within me had expected the camp to be deserted – but they had stayed and waited for us to return. I was really happy to see them – just like Hayley and Jason, who were in the back, looking after Angela.

That morning Sadie was a slim figure dressed in a black polo-neck jumper and jeans. She was my age – but she looked more youthful, like a girl in her twenties. Her short black hair was fanned out behind her ears like a raven's wings. A crossbow bobbed in her hands as she crossed the camp to the gate.

Following her was an older man in his sixties. Looking like a posh landowner in a BBC costume drama, Neal was wearing a brown jacket and tweed trousers. He was a rangy man with silver-grey hair and a wolfish beard. His head was bandaged after a nasty fall a fortnight ago, which was the reason why he had stayed in the camp with Sadie. His injury had left him concussed and unable to walk – but he looked steady on his feet again. Neal had a rifle pointed in our general direction.

For a horrible moment, I thought my friends were going to shoot at us. Didn't they recognise the van? I waved out of the window. Hayley poked her head out of the roof. They lowered their weapons only after they saw it was us. They hurried to the gate and opened it to let us drive in. I parked next to the camper van. Sadie and Neal were smiling – until they realised we were not returning after a successful mission.

"What – who – what?" Sadie said as Jason and Hayley opened the van's doors, revealing Angela and Billy. "Ben, what happened to Angela? And who is that?"

"She's been shot," I said. "The bullet's lodged inside her. The prisoner is called Billy. He helped us escape from a zombie nightmare – but he's part of the gang responsible for Angela's injury."

"Did he shoot her?" Neal said, poking Billy with his rifle.

"No – another guy." I explained very quickly. "Sadie, can you help Angela?"

She stared at Angela, breathing deeply, frowning.

"Get her inside," she said. "I'll have to examine her."

Neal and I carried Angela into the camper van. Angela moaned just like a zombie, her eyes flickering open just long enough to see where she was. She recognised her surroundings and smiled before closing her eyes again. Sadie gave orders to lay Angela on the table in the kitchenette. It was getting crowded in the camper van with everyone coming in behind us. Sadie told Hayley and Jason to stay outside while she examined the wound under the bright light of an angle-poised lamp powered by solar panels on the roof. The kids looked reluctant to leave – but they stepped outside, looking at me.

"What are we supposed to do?" Jason said.

"Keep an eye on Billy," I said, giving them something to do. I closed the door and turned to look at Angela. Sadie was shining a light on Angela's raw-looking wound. "She's been cut?"

"Yeah, I tried to get the bullet out last night," I said. "But it had gone too deep. I didn't know how to get to it. I stitched her up as well as I could. What's your opinion?"

"She really needs a sterile hospital and a team of surgeons," Angela said. "But since we don't have that, I'll have to do something. I assisted on fifty-something abdominal surgeries – but I never had to cut someone open before. We'll need sterilised instruments. Neal – boil some water. Ben – get the alcohol out of my medical bag. My instruments are inside. Bleach them."

We quickly turned the kitchenette into an operating room. Sadie tested Angela's blood pressure, shaking her head. "She'll need more blood once I start cutting. Anyone know her blood type?"

"She never told me," I said.

"Neal?" Sadie said.

"No. I don't know either."

"Okay – we'll need some O for a transfusion because that's the universal donor group. I'm O – but I can't give blood and operate."

Unfortunately, I wasn't compatible. Neither was Neal. The kids didn't know their blood types – so we couldn't risk using theirs.

That left Billy. I went out to the van and removed his blindfold. He blinked in the sunlight.

It turned out he was Type O, which could be used for anyone, unlike the rarer types. It felt like a miracle. I hated to imagine what we would have done if I had not brought him with us.

"Do you have hepatitis?" Sadie asked him.

"No," he said.

"Are you HIV positive?"

"No! I got no diseases."

I untied him and Sadie soon had him hooked up to a drip that fed his blood into Angela while Sadie prepared for the surgery. Neal and I assisted, handing Sadie her instruments and irrigating Angela's open wound. The operation was the most harrowing thing I'd seen since Day One. Mercifully Angela was too weak to wake up screaming when Sadie started cutting deep into her to get to the bullet. Sadie's gloved hands disappeared into Angela like some kind of sick magic trick. The stench of excrement filled the air. I was relieved when Sadie found the bullet and dropped it into a cereal bowl. The dirty, shiny metal thing was tiny. It was amazing how something so small could do so much damage. I hoped the operation would be over soon – but getting the bullet out was only half of the job. The bullet had perforated Angela's bowel. The whole area had to be thoroughly cleaned and stitched up. It took over an hour. It was the bloodiest, worst thing I had witnessed. And I had seen a man's entrails slop out of his body.

Afterwards, Sadie looked exhausted. Billy didn't look so good either. He was pale after giving his blood and watching the operation. He had vomited once during the op, begging me to blindfold him again so he didn't have to watch. Now he rubbed his tattooed arm near the needle. "Are you guys done with my blood now?"

"No," Sadie said. "We need you to stay hooked up. She needs more blood."

"Aw, come on! For how long am I expected to sit here, getting drained?"

Normally Sadie was calm and collected – but she snapped.

"Until I say so!"

"Jeez! I feel light-headed. My head's fuzzy. You're draining me like a vampire. I'm getting hungry, too. I haven't eaten nothing in days. This is against my human rights."

"We'll get you something to eat," I said. "Now shut up, Billy.

Just sit there, being quiet."

"Hey! I'm helping your girlfriend, aren't I? You should be *grateful and appreciate me*. My blood saved her life. I'm like a hero."

"A hero? We wouldn't have needed your blood if you had not ambushed us." My hand tightened into a fist. Sadie noticed. She shook her head. I calmed down. Billy was pushing my buttons.

"I'd just like some gratitude," he said. "I mean, I didn't have to come here. And I haven't complained about the way you've treated me like a prisoner of war."

He had done nothing but complain. I wished I had gagged him.

"We are grateful," Sadie said, returning to her usual temperament. "You are doing a good thing, Billy. We just need some more blood to make her stronger, okay?"

She was talking to him softly like he was a little boy in need of comfort. It worked.

"Yeah, okay," Billy said. "Just remember I helped. I don't want to be tied up no more."

Sadie ripped off her bloody gloves, walking outside for some air. I followed – leaving Neal to guard Billy. Sadie was shaking.

"Is she going to make it?"

"The operation was a success," she said. "But the danger now is post-op infection. She needs powerful antibiotics or she'll probably die."

"Don't you have them here?"

She shook her head. "Nothing strong enough. That's why I asked you to get some on your journey."

"What do you need?"

She named a few antibiotics. I had heard of some of them. Annoyingly, they had been in our van before we were robbed. "I don't believe it! Billy's gang now have our medical supplies. They include half the stuff you mentioned. If I can get them back, will it help Angela?"

"Definitely," Sadie said. "But you'd have to be quick, Ben. Angela needs to be on them as soon as possible. She really should be on them *now*. She had a fever, which is never a good sign. Post-op infection is one of the greatest killers. That bullet ripped through her intestines, spreading god-know-what bacteria into places where it will cause infection. We need those antibiotics to save her fast."

"I'll talk to Billy," I said. "I'll get him to tell me where the rest of his gang will have gone."

I went back into the camper van and explained the situation to Billy.

"You want to steal drugs from Quinn? Oh, man, you are insane!"

"Where will he have gone, Billy? Where can I find him?"

He shook his head. "If I tell you that, he'll know I betrayed him."

"You said you didn't want to be in his gang," I reminded him.

"Yeah – but Luke's still with him. I don't want Quinn to hurt my brother because I help you."

"You already said Luke left you behind to die. If you want to stay with us and be a part of our community, you have to tell me where they are, Billy. I'll owe you big time."

"You'll have to let me stay here with you guys after I tell you because I won't be safe nowhere else."

"You've got my word," I said. "Now, where have they gone?"

"You know the village where they ambushed you?"

I noticed he had distanced himself from the gang by using 'they' instead of 'we'. "What about the village?"

"Quinn set up our base in the church. He'll have gone back there. It's where we keep our weapons and stuff. The other guys were waiting there."

"You mean the ones we encountered were not the whole lot of you?"

"Hell, no. Quinn's the leader of like a hundred men. Most are bikers and hardcore criminals who escaped from prisons. They were staying back at the base when we chased you – guarding the base. I was kind of surprised Quinn didn't come straight back with the whole gang to wipe out the zombies and you guys. They have the firepower to take on the Pure Bloods in a pretty good battle. They'd only lose because the Pure Bloods have got helicopters and more men."

"Draw me a map of the village," I said. "Show me where everything is. Especially where they would have taken the medicines."

He started drawing a map – but he hesitated before passing it to me. "Listen, Ben, you don't want to go there. Seriously. Quinn's bad news. I've seen him kill children. He's a total psycho. Forget about attacking him. Look for the drugs somewhere else, mate. There's got be a hospital or a clinic with some drugs you can steal."

"Maybe," I said, "but I could spend all day looking and wasting time when I know the drugs we need are with your old buddies."

"Fighting Quinn on his home turf is mad," Billy said. "You'd get killed."

"I don't intend to attack him," I said. "All I need is those medicines. That's what I need. I don't care about fighting him. I just want to sneak in, get the drugs, then get out. Hopefully without anyone noticing. No shooting. Just stealth."

"Solid Snake couldn't get into the village undetected," he said.

I looked at him blankly. "What?"

"He's in the Metal Gear Solid games. You must've played them."

"No," I said. "Never had the time."

"My point is Quinn has men guarding the village. You couldn't get near him – but I could. I could go back saying I'd escaped from the zombies. Then I could get the drugs for you and bring them to you. You could wait nearby. You'd just have to trust me."

ENTRY FOURTEEN

I talked to Sadie and Neal to get their opinions before deciding I'd return with Billy to the village. We had some motorbikes in the camp and enough fuel to make it there and back – so I re-blindfolded Billy and rode out of the camp. I drove fast to avoid the Pure Blood patrols. I was soon near the village, stopping just in sight of the old church. I didn't dare go nearer. I stopped and released Billy.

"You want me to walk from *here*?"

"It's not far," I said.

"What do I tell them when I get there?"

"Say you escaped from the zombies on a bike. Tell them it broke down so you walked the rest of the way."

"Then what?"

"Then you get the drugs and bring them back. I'll hide in the woods over there with my bike so nobody will know I'm around. I'll stay hiding until you get back. If you really want to help Angela and be a part of our group, you'll come back here with the medicines as soon as possible. Angela's life is in your hands, Billy."

I offered my hand to shake. He studied it like it was a trick. "You're really letting me go? You're not like going to shoot me when I turn my back?"

"No. I'm trusting you, Billy."

He shook my hand. "Thanks, Ben."

"Good luck."

Billy trudged off towards the village. Could I trust him? My head said no, but my heart was hoping he'd want to save Angela and do the right thing.

*

Nearly two hours later, I heard a bike coming up the road. The rider was Billy. He appeared to be alone. He stopped where I had let him go. He faced the woods, calling out. "Hey! I got the drugs! Let's go!"

Billy looked like he was alone – but he wasn't. I'd seen a whole bunch of bikers sneaking up on my location from all directions.

They had me surrounded.

At least that was what they thought.

I would have been trapped if I had trusted Billy – but I had not hidden in the woods where I'd told him. I was watching from a hill to the west, observing Billy through binoculars. He was expecting me to come out of the woods to get shot to pieces – but I would have been a fool to trust him. I was disappointed, though. I had hoped …

I slipped away to my bike's hiding place, wishing I had killed Billy earlier. The gang were no doubt sneaking up on where they thought I was hiding as I rode away. They would be disappointed – but not as much as I was with Billy.

*

Back at the camp everyone was pleased to see me, but they were dismayed I'd failed to get the antibiotics. Angela was not going to last much longer without them. Hayley and Jason begged me to take them back to steal the medicines from the gang – but that would be suicidal. I checked on Angela's condition. Her fever was worse. Sadie was wiping her brow, looking very worried. "There's got to be something we can do, Ben. There has to be some way of getting the drugs."

"There is," I said. I had been thinking about the problem on my journey back, avoiding the Pure Blood patrols. "But you won't like it. It's a desperate move."

"We're long past desperate," Sadie said. "Tell me what you're thinking."

My next words tasted bitter. "We could hand Angela over to the Pure Bloods."

"That's crazy. The Pure Bloods? They'd inject her with the necrovitalis virus – or just let her die."

"Not if we make a deal with them."

"What kind of deal?"

"The Pure Bloods would love to know the location of the biker gang. I think they'd be willing to treat Angela for that info because the bikers are a greater threat to the Pure Bloods than a small group of survivors. I'll take Angela to them and make the deal. They treat her, then I'll give up the info."

"No," Sadie said. "It'd have to be me."

"Why you?"

"Once they have the info, the Pure Bloods will have no reason to let you live, Ben. But I'm a nurse. I have the skills they need. I'll agree to stay with them once I know Angela's treated and safe. They won't harm me."

"No," I said. "You have to stay with the kids. You have to look after them. You're like a mother to them."

"Yes," she said. "And you're like a father."

Neal was standing at the entrance. He put his hand gently on my shoulder. "Stop arguing. You both have to stay here, looking after Hayley and Jason. I'm a useless old man. Your lives are worth more than mine if things go wrong. I'll do it."

"You're hardly useless," I said. "You've saved my life more times than I can remember. I can't let you sacrifice yours. Angela wouldn't want you dying at the hands of the Pure Bloods. I'll go. It's my decision. I'm going. Nobody else. Me."

"Then I hate to do this," Neal said.

"Do what?"

He sucker-punched me in the solar plexus. It felt like all the air in my lungs had been ripped out. I couldn't breathe. I couldn't move. Stunned, I was unable to stop him from throwing me out of the camper van. "Sorry, Ben. I'm doing this for your own good."

Next, Neal forcefully ejected Sadie before locking himself inside. Sadie banged on the door begging him to open it – but he ignored her. He started the engine as the effect of his sucker punch wore off. I rushed around to the front, where I could see Neal behind the wheel. There was determination in his eyes. I stood in front of the camper van, hoping to block it from leaving. "Don't do this, Neal."

Neal ignored me. He backed the camper van away from me – then switched into first gear and drove forwards, smashing through the gate out of the camp. I looked at our bikes and the zombie-proof van. I would have chased after him – but all of the other vehicles needed refuelling. No. I was powerless to stop him. Sadie ran after him – but the vehicle raced off and soon disappeared behind the trees. Sadie walked back to the camp shaking her head. "I ... couldn't ... stop him."

"I know," I said.

Hayley and Jason had seen the camper van leaving – but they didn't know what was happening. They rushed towards us, asking a lot of questions that I could not answer then, not with my chest aching from the sucker punch. Sadie answered for me. "Neal's taking Angela to the Pure Bloods. He's hoping to make a deal with them – her life for the location of the bikers."

Tears ran down Hayley's face. "No. He can't trust them. They'll kill him and Angela." She turned to me. "Why didn't you stop him, Ben? You're supposed to be our leader. You're supposed to keep us all alive."

ENTRY FIFTEEN

I'd never catch up with Neal – but I had one more chance of stopping him from sacrificing his life. I grabbed my walkie-talkie and called him, hoping he had his switched on. "Neal, listen to me. Turn around and come back. You don't have to take Angela to the Pure Bloods. We'll figure out something else. Please answer me, Neal."

I waited, looking at Sadie, Hayley and Jason, who were fidgeting and pacing. We were standing in the middle of the camp, which looked empty without the camper van. I repeated my message, calculating Neal would still be in the range of the signal.

Hayley had tears on her cheeks. "Why's he not answering?"

I sighed. "I don't -"

The walkie-talkie crackled. Neal's voice came through so we could all hear it. It sounded far away. "Ben, I heard what you're saying. I'm sorry. You know I'm not changing my mind. It's … right thing. You know the Pure Bloods have everything to treat … in Oxford – hospitals, medicines, doctors. They might let us go after I give them the info. It's … risk worth taking – for me."

"Neal – come back. I will go instead. It was my idea."

"Don't be stupid, Ben. Listen to me before … out of range. This … what I'm doing. I'm going to drive right … and … into Oxford, handing myself into their main checkpoint – but I'm not giving them all our stuff in the van. I'll drop off the important things about a mile down the road from you. You can pick them up in the other van. Got it?"

"Yeah."

"One more thing, Ben. I suggest you leave the camp for somewhere new because if things go south the Pure Bloods might torture me to give you up. Get far away from here and don't leave a note behind." He paused for breath and I heard the growl of static. "Keep those kids alive, Ben. And promise me you won't come after me or Angela."

"I won't promise that," I said. "But I will keep the kids safe. Neal, I forgive you for the sucker punch."

He chuckled. "You got to smarten up, Ben. I ... nev ... ha ... fallen f ... tha ... move. Tell the kids ... love them."

"They're listening, Neal. Tell them yourself."

Hayley and Jason spoke into the walkie-talkie, begging Neal to come back. He said goodbye to them. Then he no longer answered us.

He was gone.

In an hour it would be dark. We decided to stay the night at the camp before deciding what to do in the morning – but first I refilled the zombie-proof van with petrol from our reserves – a couple of barrels we'd siphoned off months earlier – and then Jason and I drove down the forested road until we spotted the things Neal had left behind. They included weapons and our limited supply of tinned food and medicines and extra clothes. We packed everything into the van and returned to the camp, where Sadie and Hayley had prepared a cooked meal of venison roasted over a fire. It was delicious. I would have enjoyed it if Angela and Neal had been there to share it – but their absence was a palpable thing ruining the moment. We ate in silence, brooding over the events that had happened. We warmed ourselves around the fire as the cold night crept into the camp.

We were down to just four of us.

ENTRY SIXTEEN

After Hayley and her brother Jason had gone to sleep in their tent, I stayed awake with Sadie, keeping warm near the fire. We talked for a while about Neal and Angela. We both wanted to rescue them from the Pure Bloods – but we could not work out a realistic plan. We fell into a silence, frustrated. For something to distract our depressing thoughts, I showed her the working laptop I'd found. She was amazed it still worked. She watched me writing on it – adding to my journal of our lives after the zombie apocalypse. "Can I read what you've written so far?"

"Uh – okay."

Sadie read through my earlier entries numbered one to five, the ones I had posted online before my disastrous indecision resulted in Angela being shot. That had been after entry five. Sadie stopped reading them after about half an hour. "I didn't know you used to be a banker. You didn't tell me."

"Would you tell anyone that if you didn't have to?"

"No," she said. "I'd definitely keep that a secret. Do you get any replies to this blog of yours?"

"Not many," I said. "There aren't many people left alive with access to computers. Well – at least that's my excuse. Maybe there are millions of people out there – but they just don't want to contact a loser like me. Back in the day, I never was into social networking. Weirdly, I'm so into doing this now when the world is messed up beyond recognition."

"So, why do it, if hardly anyone reads it?"

I shrugged in the darkness. She didn't see me do that and asked the question again.

"I don't know," I admitted. "I suppose I just want someone to know about us. In the future, when people have forgotten about the zombies and the bad times, they might forget if we don't do something now, leaving a record. That's why I'm doing it. It's a journal for the living."

"I like the idea of this journal, Ben – but I hope you won't post what we're going to do *before* we do it. If the Pure Bloods ever read this stuff you've written tonight, for example, about us, they'll figure out where we are. There aren't exactly many country estates around here previously owned by celebrities. You need to leave it at least a week before posting entries in case they are monitoring the internet."

"Sadie, I promise I won't endanger any of us. I won't update my blog tonight anyway. I'll just write down what's happened for my own benefit later."

"Good," Sadie said, yawning. "Tired. I need to shut my eyes. Will you keep watch for a couple of hours?"

"I'll stay awake," I said. "Get some sleep."

"I'll swap you when you're tired," she said. "Don't let me sleep all night. You need rest, too. We both need to be clear-headed in the morning."

"I'll wake you in a few hours."

It was approaching midnight when Sadie slipped into her sleeping bag and dozed off by the fire. She looked so peaceful asleep. I continued typing my journal until my wrists ached and I could write no more. My eyes were blurry from staring at the laptop. I closed it and yawned. I was tired, too – but someone had to keep guard. My legs prickled with pins and needles when I stood. I shook off my weariness with squats and stretches.

During my exercises an owl hooted, scaring the hell out of me. My heart started thudding. The owl hooted again. Where was it? The darkness beyond the orange glow of the dying fire was impenetrable. I could have believed there was nothing there if I had not been able to hear fluttering wings and strange rustles of the tree branches. Was there a zombie out there? I grabbed my crossbow and I walked around the camp's perimeter, peering into the dark until my eyes adjusted to the silhouettes of the trees and bushes. I tensed every time I heard the tiniest sound. What was that? And that? The woods were alive with hidden things. What was creeping around in the dark? Just small animals probably – mice, rabbits, squirrels – scampering in the undergrowth, but I imagined they were starving zombies lumbering through the woods, drawn by the light of the fire and the smell of roasted venison. We had never encountered any zombies in the area – but I felt uneasy. I could taste my fear. It was bitter on my tongue. I'd spent enough time in the camp to know when something was not right. I trusted my instincts. They have saved my life. I hurried over to Sadie. She was snoring in a very unladylike manner. I hated waking her from a deep sleep – but my gut was telling me we didn't have much time.

"Sadie, wake up."

She snored.

"SADIE."

Her eyes jerked open and her hand gripped the handle of a hunting knife in her belt. "Neal …?"

"No – it's me, Ben. Something is wrong."

She was fully awake in a second. "What?"

"I don't know – but I feel it. Wake the kids. I'll put out the fire."

I hurried over to the fire and kicked dirt over it, plunging the camp into virtual darkness only illuminated by the stars overhead. I turned in a circle, looking hard into the night, not seeing anything strange … until there – between the trees – down below us – I saw a pinprick of light. It grew larger and brighter as it moved closer. There were two white lights close together. The headlights of a vehicle.

Sadie had woken Hayley and her brother. Jason looked like a zombie with his eyes half-closed with sleep. He rubbed his eyes and mumbled. "What's … going on, Ben?"

"We've got company."

"Is it Neal and Angela?" Jason's younger sister Hayley said. She was standing on her tip-toes to get a better look at the lights. "Are they coming back, Ben?"

"I don't know," I said. Was Neal driving back to us?

We stared at the lights. More lights appeared behind the first vehicle. I counted at least four separate pairs of lights. Four vehicles. Coming into the estate on the only road in or out. That was no coincidence. Nobody travelled at night voluntarily if they didn't have to. They had a purpose. I knew what that was. They were searching for us. Hunting us.

"That's not Neal," Jason said. "Is it the Pure Bloods or Billy's gang?"

I doubted Neal would have given up our location so quickly. "I'm afraid Billy must have sneaked a look around when he was here. It's the likeliest explanation." I could see more lights – single beams – confirming my fear. At least a dozen bikes were coming up the main road. It had to be the gang hunting us down in revenge for getting them attacked by the zombies. The vehicles were approaching the burnt-down mansion and the circular road that led up to our location. If they all went in one direction, we could take our van in the other direction and hopefully drive around them … but they must have already figured out that because the vehicles split into two groups. They were approaching us from both directions. We couldn't escape in the van.

"Grab what you can from the van," I said. "We need to hide in the woods before they get here. Quickly!"

Hayley and Jason dashed off to their tent. Sadie grabbed and loaded her crossbow and grabbed her backpack while I filled my own backpack with as much as I could reasonably carry. I hated abandoning the camp – but we could never defend it from two directions at once. I estimated we had less than five minutes before the gang showed up. It wasn't enough time. Everyone had to leave valuable things behind.

When we hurried into the woods to the south, I could hear the bikes approaching on the road. They would be at the camp in a minute.

Around me, the woods were pitch black. We would have been helpless in the darkness – but we all had night-vision goggles taken from an Army and Navy store. The darkness turned to sinister green daylight when I switched my pair on. We headed directly away from the camp, moving quickly and stealthily, resisting the temptation just to run as fast as possible. With time on our side, I would have hidden our footprints in the soft earth, but we were in a desperate rush. We were moving too fast to hide our route from tracking. We had gone about 200 metres when the gang arrived at the camp and drove through the barriers. Someone fired a gun into the air. Others shouted. They were angry because we were not there.

"I KNOW YOU'RE HIDING! YOU THINK YOU CAN ESCAPE US? WE'RE COMING FOR YOU!"

It was then I heard the barking.

It sounded like there were a dozen dogs with the gang – barking furiously into the night. They had to be hunting dogs. At that moment the dogs were probably getting our scent off the things we had been forced to leave behind. As soon as the dogs had our scent, they'd give chase and we'd get caught in minutes since there were no hiding places in the woods where the dogs would not find us.

A cold dread filled me. We were in trouble. We had to get off the private estate to our alpha site – but the shortest route was blocked by the hunting parties. We'd have to sneak around them.

I knew the gang would soon find out which direction we had headed and try to get ahead of us on their bikes – so we hiked another quarter of a mile as fast as we could straight north – making no effort to hide our path because I wanted them to think that was our true destination. We crossed a stream to confuse the dogs and made sure we stayed downwind of them when we emerged from the water upstream heading south. Torches lit the trees not far away, beams sweeping left and right through the darkness. The barking was getting louder and I could hear the men shouting to each other because they did not have to keep quiet as they moved through the woods. "They're this way!"

They continued north – just as I'd hoped. But what would happen when they got to the stream? Would the dogs find our scent again?

Sadie knew the woods better than the rest of us because she had spent more time hunting for food there. "We can go up here – but it's a steep climb. We'll save a lot of time climbing up – but it won't be easy in the dark."

The hill was steep and rocky and almost vertical in places, but that meant the dogs would not be able to follow if we climbed straight up the cliff. Sadie went first. Then Hayley. Then Jason. I was last. Our progress was painfully slow – but we reached the top. I could see flickering torches among the woods below. Hah! The gang were searching in the wrong places – so our trick had fooled them.

Through a gap in the trees, I peered down into the clearing where the burnt-out remains of the mansion were lit up by the lights of a parked van. Someone was standing on the roof looking through a sniper rifle. Looking for us. I recognised Billy even from a long distance. So – I knew for sure he had led his mates to us. I ducked down before he saw me.

After twenty minutes, we emerged from the woods and climbed over the perimeter wall. I relaxed knowing the gang would be searching on the other side – but it was no time to stop for rest. The alpha site was not far. We just had to hike another half mile through the public woods bordering the private estate.

We continued to sneak away, but then something happened. Ahead of me, Hayley stumbled and muffled her cry of pain as she fell. She tried to stand up straight away – but she could not put any weight on her left leg. "Ow! Sadie! My ankle! It hurts sooo much!"

Sadie rushed to her. "Don't put any weight on it. Let me see."

"There was a stupid rabbit hole," Hayley said. "And I stepped right into it. Is my ankle broken?"

"No – it's a bad sprain, though. You mustn't walk on it."

"I have to!"

"No," I said. "I'll carry you."

I removed my backpack and handed it to Jason. Hayley climbed on my back, wrapping her arms around my neck and her legs around my chest. She didn't weigh as much as my backpack, but she was harder to keep on my back. Jason added my backpack to his burden without complaining, though he was noticeably slower when we continued. Sadie led the way through the thinning woods. The alpha site was an electricity substation where we'd hidden some emergency supplies. We had gone half of the distance when I could hear dogs barking on the other side of the perimeter wall.

"This way!" someone shouted.

The dogs were now heading straight for us. Stopping briefly, I sprayed some pepper on the trail to discourage them from following our path. I could hear the hunters getting closer and closer as I hurried away. A minute later I heard yelping and almost felt pity for the dogs. The pepper would not harm them – but it would stop them hunting for a few precious minutes.

I could hear bikes approaching. They'd have us surrounded very soon. I had an idea. "Jason – carry your sister. Sadie, get everyone to the alpha site. I'll make some noise and lead them away. I'll catch up with you guys when it's safe. Just hide until they've gone away, okay?"

"What about you?" Jason said.

"Don't worry about me. I'll figure out something. Just go, Jason. Get your sister out of here."

"Okay," he said.

Sadie looked at me. "Don't get yourself killed, Ben."

"It isn't in my plan," I said, though in truth I did not have much of a plan except to stay alive, somehow.

I swapped Hayley for my backpack. Sadie, Jason and Hayley continued in the direction of the electricity substation while I set up an obvious trail for the hunters to follow. I led them away from the alpha site. With the dogs and men getting closer and closer, I abandoned my backpack under a tree after taking out some weapons. I hid in some bushes until I saw the dogs and hunters. There were five men in the group. I hadn't seen any of them before. They were moving quickly, following the dogs. I aimed my crossbow at the nearest man and released a bolt aimed at his heart. I hit him in the chest a little low, knocking him off his feet. He screamed and tugged at the bolt sticking in his abdomen, his cries so loud they could be heard in space. His friends dived for cover behind the trees as I reloaded and fired again. My arrow slammed into a tree just inches from a man's surprised face. He started shooting back. And so did the others. They didn't know my exact location – luckily – so I didn't get shot as I raced away. Yelling like madmen, they chased me through the trees as more of them arrived on bikes, circling the area, trying to fence me in.

Now I had their attention I had to figure out a way of escaping.

I stopped behind a tree – reloaded my crossbow – then waited for a bike to drive by. I didn't have to wait long. One appeared a few seconds later, ridden by a man with a goatee beard. Another man with a spider tattoo was riding pillion armed with a gun.

I aimed at the rider. My arrow took him in the throat. He lost control of his bike as he was dying, crashing hard into a tree. Spider Tattoo was thrown off and landed on the rough ground, losing his grip on his gun. He groaned and looked for his weapon as I ran over to him before he got his wits back. I kicked him in the head, then finished him with a knife.

I couldn't believe I had cold-bloodedly killed so easily – but I didn't feel any guilt. He would have killed me.

His bike was a smouldering wreck – ruining my getaway plan - but I had a gun now, which was an improvement. When I saw a bike's headlight beaming through the darkness, lighting up the woods to my right, I hurried in that direction and encountered another man on a bike. He was armed with a crossbow – but he didn't see me until I'd already shot him. I ran over to the bike, which was on its side with the wheels spinning. I lifted it and jumped on and rode it through the woods parallel to the road, praying I could get a few miles away before the gang figured out what I'd done. But I'd not gone far when another two bikes appeared behind me, catching me in their headlights. The riders shot at me, forcing me to switch directions and accelerate into the deeper woodland, desperately veering right and left to avoid slamming into trees. It was weirdly exhilarating being chased and riding at a dangerous velocity in the woods – like re-enacting the speeder bike scene in *Return of the Jedi* – but then I struck a rock or something that sent me flying over the handlebars. Then it was no longer exciting because I was landing on hard earth covered with fallen twigs and sharp branches. My momentum sent me rolling thirty feet into the base of an oak tree, where I banged my head so hard it felt like a lightning bolt had exploded inside my skull. I lay there stunned, blood in my eyes, staring up at the night sky, where I could see two identical red moons. In my addled state, I wondered if I'd been transported to another planet by the force of my crash. Only slowly did the moons merge into one as my eyes refocussed. I realised I was still on Earth and laughed to myself for being so stupid. I remembered where I was just before a bright light shone in my face, blinding me. "I got him! I got him! Over here!"

No. Where was my gun? It had to be near me. I had to get it – but my head and body were not responding to my call to action. Everything was fuzzy and confusing. Did I have a concussion? Sadie would know. Sadie! Where was Sadie? At the alpha site? I couldn't let the men get Sadie. I had to keep fighting and drawing them away. I had to find my gun before the man was joined by the others. Where was it? I'd had it in my jacket when I'd been riding. That meant it was still on me, right?

I didn't find out the answer.

I passed out first.

ENTRY SEVENTEEN

"Sir, I think he's awake."

"Make sure."

A hard slap jolted me into full consciousness and splashed blood on the stone floor between my bare feet. Stone? Where was I? A dungeon? My head throbbed with pain as I looked up. The walls were made of stone, too. The only light was from a narrow window with stained glass. Was it a church? Wherever I was, I was naked from the waist up with my hands tied over my head. I was hanging from a steel chain connected to a hook high above, facing a teenage skinhead in a grimy black T-shirt with a skull on it. Not exactly the best way of waking up. My blood dripped off his hand as he stepped back, grinning, his foul smoky breath reminding me of dirty bus shelters and public toilets.

"He's awake now, sir."

"Leave us," the other man ordered. He was standing near a doorway in the shadows, smoking a cigarette that lit his face in a red glow. He was wearing a black suit. I knew him. He was the gang leader, the one who looked like Tim Roth in *Reservoir Dogs*. Dragging on the cigarette, he walked over to me. "You and your friends have caused me some serious trouble. I'm going to make you pay for that. Slowly."

To prove it, he put out his cigarette on my chest. I smelled my flesh sizzling as the pain pulsed through me. I was reeling from that when he slapped my face – not too hard, but it stung and knocked my head sideways. He slapped me again, drawing blood. Then he stopped because my blood was on his shirt. He paused to wipe it off with some spit. "This is going to get messy. Billy!"

Billy walked in immediately. He must have been waiting to be called in. He was not the Billy I had encountered in the zombie-infested town, the one I had believed had wanted to leave the biker gang. This was another man – the real one – revealed like the beetle under a rock. Billy swaggered towards me, smirking. He was standing straighter and seemed taller, more confident.

"Hello, Ben. Bet you didn't expect to see me again, huh?"

"Billy, you could have been free. You didn't have to go back to them."

"You know that story I told you about my brother Luke? It was all made up. I don't have a brother. I just have my uncle Quinn. I'd never betray him. He's saved my life more times than I can count."

Quinn patted him on the back. "You did good, Billy. I'm going to let you have some fun with our guest. Don't do anything I wouldn't do."

Quinn left the room. Billy cracked his knuckles and studied me. "Ben, you're *my* prisoner now. How does it feel to have the tables turned?"

"I'd give it only one star on Trip Advisor. The accommodation could do with some improvements."

"Funny. I don't think you'll be laughing when I'm done with you." He gut-punched me – then he glared into my eyes. "Funny Man, you're going to beg me to kill you. But I won't let you die until you tell us everything I want to know."

"What do you want to know?"

"Where are the others?"

"What others?"

He punched me again. "Do you want to be a human punch bag?"

I spat blood. "No. It isn't my dream job, Billy."

"Where are they?"

"Who?"

"You know who! The kids. The old guy. The nurse. And the crazy woman with the shotgun! My uncle wants them all. If you tell me where they are, I promise I'll make your death quick and painless, Ben. You won't have to suffer if you just tell me where they've gone. I'm not a psychopath. I will have mercy. Just tell me where they are hiding."

"I can't do that," I said.

"Why not?"

"They're my family, Billy. I'm not going to let you hurt them."

"I'm going to torture you, Ben. Save yourself from the pain. Give them up. Tell me where they are."

"Never."

"Never is a long time," he said.

And he proved it.

ENTRY EIGHTEEN

Billy tortured me for hours while I hung helplessly from the ceiling like a carcass in a slaughterhouse. I lived in a world of pain, but I didn't tell him where to find my friends. No – that secret was not going to pass my lips. Hayley, Jason and Sadie needed time to get away. Time I could give them if I stayed silent. Defying Billy was something I could do to help them. My last act on Earth. My stubborn refusal to betray them angered Billy. He beat me until I was pouring blood. After slipping on my blood, he lashed out with his fists, pummelling my back and chest until I pass out, ending the pain for a short time.

I was still dangling from the hook above when I regained consciousness. Billy was gone.

Another man was there, treating my cuts and bruises. He was a frail older man aged about sixty, a Sikh wearing a turban and a long white beard. His legs were in irons so he was a prisoner, too. I was puzzled why he was tending to my wounds. "Who are you?"

"Mohinder Singh. I'm a doctor."

I was suspicious of what he was doing to my wounds. He was relieving the pain and stitching me up – but why if he was part of the gang? "You're a doctor?"

"A surgeon, actually. Well, I was before Day One."

"What are you doing with those men, Dr Singh?"

"Those animals captured me and my granddaughter, Leela, a month ago. They'll hurt her if I don't cooperate. They keep her locked up in another building nearby with some other girls they captured alive. They use those girls like … If I ever did anything against them, they'd hurt my Leela instead of just keeping her as a hostage." He looked close to tears. "They told me to keep you alive because the nephew of their leader nearly killed you. Their leader – he's called Quinn if you don't know it - wasn't happy with his nephew Billy. Quinn wants to find out where the others are you were with before killing you. He's gone out of the village – but he'll probably be back soon. Billy wants to continue torturing you as soon as I'm done. I suggest you tell him anything he wants to know. If you don't, he'll make what they've done to you already seem like nothing. I've seen them feed a man to their dogs. His screams haunt my dreams."

"Can you get me free, Mohinder?"

"I'm sorry. They'd kill me *and* my granddaughter if I did that."

"Can you at least tell me where I am?"

"You're in a church in Grickwich village."

That was the village where they had ambushed me. That was good news. I had studied the village. I knew the layout. I also knew that if Neal had told the Pure Blood about the village, help, of a sort, was on its way. The Pure Bloods were the mortal enemy of vigilante groups like Quinn's gang. If they showed up here, the village would turn into a war zone. If that happened, it was very likely the Pure Bloods would destroy the village and end my suffering. I was happy to die like that if it meant saving the others. "How long have I been here, Doctor?"

"Six hours."

"That's all?" It had felt like days. "So I wasn't unconscious for very long?"

"They brought you in at dawn. I had to treat you for a concussion. You were not in any state to question – but they still hung you up to soften you up for interrogating."

"It's working. I'm in agony."

"I'm sorry I can't take away your pain with some painkillers. They don't let me have access to the drugs." He shook his head wearily. "I hate to see anyone suffer. I became a doctor to help people – not to assist torture. This is barbaric."

"Doctor, they'll kill me eventually if you don't help me. We can escape together – you, me and your granddaughter. Just help me get my wrists undone. We can then get out through that window. There must be a key to the padlock. Where is it?"

"Quinn has it. But I'd never get it off him even if he wasn't with his bodyguards. I used to be a strong man capable of dealing with a man like him – but I'm not any more. I'm seventy-two and too cowardly to risk my life for yours. I am sorry. I really am."

It appeared I'd wildly underestimated his age. "Mohinder, do you want to stay here working for Quinn's gang for the rest of your life?"

"No – but I have no choice."

"Do you want your granddaughter to be free?"

"Yes."

"Then help me. I'll rescue Leela. I promise that. Just get the key and undo me. Then we can all get out of here. You won't be a prisoner any longer then – but you have to do it before I'm too weak to fight. I can't stand much more torture."

I could see him thinking about it – but then Billy returned and the hope left the doctor's eyes. Billy swaggered through the doorway. "Okay, Doc, you've patched him up. Now get out of here. We've got unfinished business – me and him." Billy was carrying a car battery with jumper cables. "I'm going to have myself some fun, Ben. I saw this on an episode of *24*."

Mohinder looked horrified. "You're going to electrocute him? That could kill him!"

"Not *where* I'm going to do it," Billy said. "It will just make him scream for mercy, Doc. Beat it, old man, before I test them out of you." Billy brought the cables together – producing a blue-white spark of electricity that filled with air with smoke and ozone. He taunted Mohinder, laughing as the old man cowered. Billy sneered. "Go!"

Terrified, Mohinder shuffled out of the room, only pausing to look back sadly, apologetically.

Billy grinned. "Now, Ben, where were we?"

He reminded me with a jolt.

ENTRY NINETEEN

Some nightmares only get worse when you wake up. That was what happened to me in the church, where I was a prisoner of an evil sadist called Billy.

Eyes gleaming with sadistic pleasure, Billy threw a bucket of icy water over me to 'help' the electricity flow, then he stepped up to my body with his electroshock device. Two crocodile clips were attached by wires to the car battery – which would send a shock through me once they were connected. Billy brought one clip towards my body – trying to clip it to my already sore skin near my heart. I pulled away as far as possible – which was not much given I was hanging from the ceiling. Billy relished my fear and sniggered. The sick freak was eager to electrocute me. But first Billy pretended to have a conversation with the crocodile clips, doing a weird one-man Punch and Judy show with the clips 'talking' in funny voices. At least voices *he* found funny.

I didn't find it at all amusing.

"Do you want me to bite him here, Billy?" one crocodile clip said. A clip worryingly close to my groin. "Snap, snap, snap!"

"No," Billy said.

"Or here?" the other clip said. It snapped near to my nose. "I'll bite off his nose."

"Not yet," Billy said.

"Let's fry his eyelids!" the first crocodile clip said. "Yeah – that'll hurt! They'll crisp like slivers of bacon."

"No!" the other clip said. "His feet first! Then up and up, one little bit at a time."

"Hmm," Billy said in his normal voice. "I don't know, guys. High or low, which way to go? Hey – I'm a poet but I don't know it!"

He chuckled like a madman. No – not *like* a madman. He was a madman. A madman about to hurt me. Before he clamped the clips to sensitive parts of my anatomy, I decided I had to say something. "Wait, wait! Okay, Billy, you win. You win."

Billy frowned. "I win *what?*"

I sucked in a deep breath. "I'll tell you where the others are."

"Go on," he said. "I'm listening."

"They were gone from the camp when you got there."

"What?"

"Neal drove off in the camper van with them all a few hours earlier. I just stayed behind to get some more things before leaving. By now they've got so far away you'll never get them." I allowed myself a smile just to irritate him. "You lost them."

"We'll see about that," Billy said. "Where were they going?"

I would have shrugged if it had been possible in my position. "I don't know, Billy. I didn't want them to tell me."

"Liar. They are like your family. You must have had a plan to join them. So that means you know where they were going."

I swore to myself. I'd tried to be clever with the half-truth – but it was hard to make up a good lie when someone was torturing you. "Okay – I know where they went. But it's somewhere you won't believe."

"Try me."

"Oxford."

"No way. The Pure Bloods have control of Oxford. They'd *never* go there."

"They did, I swear."

"Oh, well, if you swear *that* makes me believe you. You're just lying to stop my crocodile friends taking a bite."

"No – it's the truth, Billy. They've gone to Oxford."

"That's insane. The Pure Bloods inject people with the zombie virus to see if they are immune. You honestly expect me to believe your friends would submit to that voluntarily, Ben?"

"No, Billy – but Angela was *dying*. You know that. You saw her. She needed powerful antibiotics urgently. The Pure Bloods were her only chance of survival. The others hoped they'd treat Angela if they turned themselves in and fully cooperated with them. Everyone went without me because the Pure Bloods would never accept me – not after I robbed them of supplies from a supermarket they were guarding. The supplies you found in my van. The Pure Bloods would just summarily execute me – but Angela and the rest of my friends had a slim chance of survival in Oxford. The others were willing to risk their lives to save Angela – so they left."

"No, no, NO! Why would risk their lives for Angela?"

"That's what good people do, Billy. They sacrifice themselves for others. You wouldn't understand that because you're a psycho."

"Your story makes no sense. You could have told me that straight away before I started hurting you – if it was true."

"No – I couldn't tell you *then*."

"Why not?"

I had to think of another believable lie. "They only left the camp a few hours before you showed up. For all I knew, they were still on their way to Oxford. They needed all the time I could give them to get there. Giving them more time was the only thing I could do for them. Billy, I couldn't let you harm those kids. They did nothing to you. I had to help them get away – but now they will be safe and you can't touch them. They got away from you."

I laughed to make him believe me. He stared into my eyes for any sign of a lie. I stared straight back, laughing.

"Stop laughing!" He slapped me. "You think they're safe now? Ben, the Pure Bloods have probably killed them already. And I can't see them wasting good medicines on a dying woman. Your precious Angela will be dead, too. All of them will be dead – or undead – because you didn't have the guts to stop them going. How does that make you feel, Ben?"

"I'd rather them be dead than here," I said. "You and your friends are evil, Billy. You're parasites. You rob and kill innocent people. We were just trying to survive when you attacked us. You hurt us first, Billy. Don't you forget that. We just defended ourselves."

"Defended? Your friend Angela killed my friends. I wanted to kill her myself – but now that's ruined. It's not right. Not right at all. My uncle will be so mad!" In anger he hurled his torture device into the stone wall where it smashed apart, plastic and metal flying across the room. Billy snarled. "You know what, Ben? Electrocuting you isn't going to be good enough. I've got something much more fun. Payback for letting out the zombies that killed my friends. Hang around. I'll be back in a minute."

His devious smile worried me as he stormed out.

I looked down at the pieces of the broken car battery. There were some sharp fragments of black plastic nearby. I wondered if I could pick up something sharp and pointed with my feet and somehow use it to pick the padlock securing the chains around my wrists. But how could I do that? I wasn't a contortionist, Harry Houdini, Macgyver or Jack Bauer. I could … not quite … reach anything …

Ten minutes later I heard footsteps and squeaking wheels and knew whatever was coming was going to be bad, much worse than electroshocks and the company of a psychotic nutter.

Billy and Skull T-Shirt pushed a wheelchair into the room, stopping at the doorway. The wheelchair had an occupant – a male zombie strapped into it. He smelled like rotten meat and month-old curdled milk. He was a big one with wide-shoulders and thick, muscular arms and tattoos that had started to turn green with fungus. His body ended at his torso, where I could see pink and grey and purple entrails instead of his lower abdomen and legs.

"Meet Ryan," Billy said. "The moron got bitten four weeks ago because he didn't watch his back. We've been keeping him around because he still has his uses. Ryan likes to eat the rats … and anybody we get sick of having around, like you. My uncle chopped off his legs to make him less dangerous – but he can still crawl pretty fast. He's got strong arms for a dead guy. He used to work out every day. Me thinks he's hungry for a proper meal."

Billy undid the straps, then Skull T-shirt tipped Ryan out of the wheelchair. Ryan flopped onto the floor. The zombie fell onto his grey belly, moaning, his head snapping around so he could stare back at the two living men at the door. He moaned and started dragging himself in their direction, leaving a vile trail of gore behind him.

Skull T-shirt looked scared. "Billy, he wants us!"

"Calm down. Just get the door closed behind us."

"What about the wheelchair?"

"Leave it!"

Billy and Skull T-shirt abandoned the wheelchair and backed out of the room – while the zombie moved towards them. It tried climbing over the abandoned wheelchair, which slammed into the door. Billy and his assistant struggled to get the door closed with the zombie pushing the wheelchair against it. But they manage it. Billy waved me goodbye as he shut and locked the door, leaving me trapped with the ravenous zombie. I heard Billy laughing when he walked away, criticising the teenager.

"Boy, you are such a wimp, man. The dude's got no legs. We had ages to get away."

For two or three minutes, the zombie slammed his head against the door, trying to smash a way through it to the men on the other side, but he lost interest in them once they had moved far away.

It went very quiet.

I didn't move.

I didn't want to draw the zombie's attention.

I hoped the zombie would stay at the door and forget about me – but the smell of my blood was too strong. He sniffed at the air and turned to face me, his jaws gnashing together in anticipation of tearing into my flesh. He saw me hanging there in the middle of the room like a piñata stuffed with tasty treats. The zombie moaned, sending a shiver through my bowels because my spilt blood was exciting his interest.

I was fresh meat. Food for him.

Moaning, Ryan dragged his torso across the floor towards me.

ENTRY TWENTY

Ryan – the legless zombie – half-crawled and half-slithered across the room on his way to get me – leaving me with no choice but to get ready to kick out when his head was in range. I didn't want his snapping jaws to bite a chunk out of me, infecting me with the necrovitalis virus in his putrid yellow-green saliva, so I would have to be careful to time it just right, kicking him with my bare feet as he got close to where I was hanging by my chained wrists. Like a slug, Ryan moved relentlessly, leaving a gooey trail behind him. His entrails were coming out and piling up like sausages – but since he felt no pain it did not slow him down. His hands dragged him to just a few feet away. Soon his gnashing teeth would be within biting distance.

I waited. Nearer. Nearer. *Now.*

I kicked out like I was aiming at a football and trying to make it shoot up into the air. My foot struck Ryan's head a good hard blow – caving in his nose and knocking him backwards. The injury would have knocked out a living human – but it only enraged the zombie. Ryan crawled closer and I did it again – striking him in the top of his forehead, whipping back his head, tearing something in his neck, snapping cartilage. A jagged hole appeared through his neck into his dark throat – but even that did nothing. Only damage to his brain or spinal column would stop him for good.

Unfortunately, kicking out had given me unwanted momentum that sent me spinning around on the chain, making it impossible to kick out a third time when Ryan continued moving forward. By the time I had spun around he was under me, snapping at my heels. I spun around and around and desperately tried to control my motion. But it was hard to do that and avoid Ryan. Ryan was using his strong arms to raise his head to bite my swinging legs. Each time I swung near him, I raised my feet when he tried to bite them. Just avoiding him. Desperately, I struggled to keep my momentum going so my feet were constantly ahead of Ryan's teeth – but I knew I'd tire before he did. In a human versus zombie stamina contest the zombie would win every time. My only chance against him depended on striking his head again with a more powerful kick that could expand the wound to his neck – so I started swinging back and forth until I was moving like a human pendulum. I moved faster and faster, gaining height with each swing, waiting for the right moment to kick Ryan's head. With his arms lifting his body, Ryan was nearly biting me with every pass. I raised both feet as I swung back and lashed out when I swung forward, yelling as I kicked his face so hard his head completely ripped off his neck. It rolled away and slammed into a wall, where it stopped rolling. The rest of Ryan's body stopped moving the instant it was no longer linked to his head, which was still alive in the corner, the eyes staring at me.

"Sorry, Ryan. No meal today."

I gingerly lowered my feet onto the stump of Ryan's neck, taking the weight off my arms. Ryan's corpse was a good but sticky stool to stand on while I recovered my breath and rested my aching muscles. I was in no immediate danger – but I had to get free before someone returned. I yanked down on the chain connected to the ceiling – but it was too secure. Some kind of DIY expert had nailed or screwed it up there. My arms would come out of their sockets before I freed myself.

I thought of the doctor. If only he had not been a coward. He could have got me free.

I was praying for a miracle when I heard what sounded like several automatic weapons firing, followed by shouting, screaming and more gunshots. What the hell? A second or two later an explosion rocked the church and cracked the ceiling, dropping dust and plaster. The impact did what I could have never done – it brought the roof down around me. I dropped onto the zombie as the chain dropped. Hard things struck my back and shoulders. Darkness. Dust. The smell of chalk and sulphur. Blood dripped off my nose. I looked around, stunned at the chaos. The floor was covered in rubble that could have cracked my skull – but I was only scratched. I found myself on the floor on top of Ryan's corpse with the chains piled on me. My wrists were still bound with chains and padlocked – but I was in a slightly better situation. At least I was not hanging from the ceiling.

I could hear more explosions and gunfire outside – which made me think being locked in a room with stone walls had probably saved my life. I could hear bullets thudding into the walls. One broke through the window and ripped a chunk out of the wall opposite. The building shook with another explosion.

Few groups had military weapons. It had to be the Pure Bloods attacking. It looked like Neal had told them where to find the gang in exchange for treating Angela. Good for him! I hoped they were both alive. Then I worried about myself. I wouldn't be alive for much longer if I stayed in the church with the Pure Bloods blasting it. There were two exits – the door and the window. The door had been locked from the other side by Billy. I did not have the strength to break it down. That left the window – which was a suicidal exit as long as people were shooting. Hell – I was safer hiding in the church as long as none of Quinn's gang opened the door – but what if Billy came back? He'd kill me.

Weak from the torture, I struggled to stand up with the weight of the chains fastened to my wrists. My entire body was weak from blood loss and the bruising caused by Billy's beating. I ached in every muscle – even when I blinked. Grunting in pain, I shuffled to the upturned wheelchair, got it back on its wheels, then slumped into it with the chains on my lap. Never before had I been so glad to sit down and rest. I figured I could hide close to the door and lash out with the chain if anyone burst in. They'd never expect me to be free and mobile. I sat recovering my strength as a battle raged in the village – listening to gunfire for what felt like days. Twice more the church shook from explosions, with more debris tumbling down from the roof.

A key rattled the door. This was it. Billy was coming back.

I raised the chain and readied myself to swing it.

The door opened.

ENTRY TWENTY-ONE

I was ready to swing the chain when Billy entered the room – but Billy didn't wear a turban and look seventy. It was Doctor Mohinder Singh. He was peering into the dark room, clutching some sort of club as a weapon – a part of a chair leg.

"Ben?" he whispered. "Are you still alive? Ben?"

I showed myself. "Yeah, Doc. I'm okay."

He looked startled to see me alive – but also relieved. "It is good to see you see, my friend. That monster Billy was telling his friends how he'd locked you in with a zombie. How did you get free and where is the infernal zombie?"

"The zombie's head's over there. I managed to kick it off when I was swinging from up there. Then the roof came down when the Pure Bloods started attacking."

"Ah! So that's what's going on! The Pure Bloods? I had no idea. Things exploded and everyone started shooting. It's complete chaos around here. I heard a helicopter and saw some soldiers in the woods. About ten minutes ago Quinn was shot by a sniper. I was forced to treat him – but he died of blood loss. His men were so busy fighting for their lives that I stole his keys and slipped away unnoticed. I came to free you so we can escape before anyone realised Quinn's dead and starts looking for me. We must get moving *now*."

Quinn's death was the first good news I'd heard since my imprisonment. "I can't move with these chains on me, Doc."

"Do not worry. I shall free you." Doctor Singh stepped into the room and closed the door while he unlocked the padlock. I rubbed my wrists and sighed. I tried standing – but my legs wobbled and the pain of my injuries tripled. "Don't suppose you got something for the pain, Doc?"

"I do." Mohinder had brought in a black medical bag. It was filled with medicines. "Take these with this."

Mohinder handed me four codeine pills and an unopened bottle of Highland Spring mineral water, which had been one of the things I'd found before the gang had stolen my supplies. The cool water eased my parched throat. It was hard swallowing the pills – but they went down after almost choking. I drank half a litre of water and gasped with satisfaction. I was feeling better already. Mohinder told me the painkillers would take effect in about twenty minutes.

"Thank you." I looked at the door. "Can we get out through the main exit?"

"No – a few of Quinn's men are inside, shooting out the doors and windows at the attackers. We'll have to get out through *that* window."

"Okay. Better lock the door so nobody can follow us."

The doctor's hands were shaking as he locked the door. "That wheelchair will never fit through the window. Can you walk, Ben?"

"Guess I'll have to." After the beating I'd taken, I was light-headed and unsteady on my feet, but at least I was no longer chained. Speaking of which, I saw Mohinder's legs were unshackled. "You freed yourself?"

"Yes, my friend. Fortunately, Quinn carried the key on him. He was also carrying every key to the village – including the one to get my granddaughter free." He jangled a large bunch of keys, grinning. "We can free Leela!"

Leela. I'd almost forgotten about her. Mohinder's granddaughter. We'd have to save her, too. And the other girls imprisoned by the gang. "Okay – Mohinder – we need a plan. You have to tell me what to expect out there *before* we leave."

"That way leads to the back of the cemetery. There are some trees for cover and tall gravestones."

"That's good. Anything else?"

"Yes. The gang keep the female prisoners locked in the cellar of a pub down the lane. *The Black Bull*. The cellar is always guarded. That is where we must go to free Leela."

"How many guards?"

"At least two. They have guns."

"We'll need a better weapon than a chair leg and this chain then."

"Agreed, my friend. Agreed!"

The painkillers were kicking in with a warm fuzzy feeling as I hobbled to the window and peered out. There were several old graves fairly close shaded by an oak tree near the church's wall. The gravestones were big ones made of thick granite. If we could slip out unnoticed, we could use the gravestones as shields against the bullets flying around. First, we had to get through the window. It had been broken in three places by bullets – but I needed to knock more glass out with the chair leg. I did it as quietly as possible so I didn't attract the attention of the Pure Bloods or the gang, wherever they were. The glass fell onto the grass outside, making little noise. My pain was just a dullness at the back of my skull when I was ready to go. Afraid someone would see me as soon as I climbed outside, I moved quickly, hauling my sore body over the windowsill. It would be game over for me if a sniper spotted me half in and out of the window – but I was still weak and got stuck. It was hellishly bright outside, the sunlight stinging my dark-adapted eyes. Mohinder pushed me out and I flopped onto the grass. I was out in the open – visible to anyone looking. I was amazed nobody shot at me. A good sign. I crawled over to a hiding place behind a lichen-covered gravestone. My body sweated and ached from the effort. I rested a minute and studied the area. The cemetery went down a hill to the lane. The church was not far from the pub – but it looked like a shooting alley between here and there. Quinn's gang were taking cover behind the thatched cottages and old stone walls. Some of them were shooting into the surrounding woods where the Pure Bloods were positioned. A Pure Blood soldier was calling out on a megaphone.

"WE HAVE YOU SURROUNDED! PUT DOWN YOUR WEAPONS AND SURRENDER!"

He repeated the message over and over.

No bikers were listening. They knew they'd get injected with the necrovitalis virus and very likely turn into zombies if the Pure Bloods got them. They were firing back with everything they had. They had guns and a few rifles and Molotov cocktails that landed well short of the enemy. The Pure Bloods had automatic weapons capable of taking out their enemies from a long distance. It was not an even fight because I could see the Pure Bloods had a black helicopter circling over the village, spying on the enemy, with an armour-protected sniper leaning out, shooting down with deadly accuracy. A biker running from building to building had his head explode with one powerful sniper bullet. Horrified, I watched as something streaked from the woods into a cottage where some gang members were hiding. A second later the cottage exploded. Parts of the thatched roof spun into the air on fire. What was that? An RPG? Dark smoke billowed over the village, drifting as far as the river. Some bikers were trying to escape on their vehicles along the road where they had ambushed me – but the helicopter's sniper was coolly picking them off one by one. I nearly felt sorry for the bikers. It wasn't a fair fight. Closer to me, all the shooting seemed concentrated on the other side of the church. I thanked God nobody was wasting ammo shooting at me.

Mohinder was peeking out the church window. "Ben? Can I come out?"

"Doc, it's clear for now. Just be quick and get down as soon as you're out. The Pure Bloods have got that helicopter about a mile away right now – so move quickly before it sweeps back. The guy won't miss you if he spots you."

Mohinder appeared at the window and climbed up onto the windowsill painfully slowly. I was sure he would get shot – but he didn't. He jumped to the ground and rolled towards me. He stayed low and joined me hiding among the gravestones. We were both breathing hard. Mohinder wiped the sweat from his forehead. "We must get to my granddaughter now."

That was not going to be easy.

There was no natural cover between the cemetery and the pub.

Just then another RPG shot out of the woods.

It struck the pub with a direct hit.

And exploded.

ENTRY TWENTY-TWO

The explosion set the pub on fire, spewing black smoke from the broken windows, leaving me in no doubt everyone inside had been killed by the blast. The shock froze me – but it didn't freeze Mohinder. Instead of staying hidden among the gravestones, he jumped up and cried out in grief for his lost granddaughter. He was wailing and calling attention to himself in the most dangerous way. I grabbed him and pulled him down – but he shook me off and staggered away, moaning, his eyes fixated on the burning building where the gang had been keeping Leela locked up. Tears streamed down his cheeks.

"Get down! Someone will shoot you!"

He wasn't listening. He was no longer rational. Something had snapped inside him. The only thing keeping him sane had been the thought of saving his granddaughter. Her death had destroyed him. He stumbled down the hill like a drunk, shouting his granddaughter's name. "Leela! Leela! Leeeee-laaa!"

I chased after him, keeping my head below the level of the gravestones, hoping nobody would bother to shoot an old man. I was prepared to rugby tackle him to the ground and knock him out if necessary – but then I heard gunfire to my right. A biker was shooting into the woods. He wasn't aiming at me – but the biker was between me and the woods. When the Pure Bloods shot back at the biker, stray bullets slammed into the graves around me like bouncing ball bearings. Ricocheting hot metal zinged past my head, nicking my cheek. I had to dive for cover behind an oak tree and hide for ten seconds – by which time Mohinder was too far away. He was in the No Man's Land between the cemetery and the pub. An easy target.

I watched as bullets whizzed by him, but they all missed. It seemed as if the bullets were avoiding him as he stumbled down the lane, calling for his granddaughter. I believed he was going to reach the pub without a scratch – but then the helicopter flew over and a single shot from the sniper struck Mohinder's turban with such force that his head burst apart. His headless body fell over, spraying blood on the road.

I could not believe my eyes.

Mohinder was dead.

I felt like screaming – but that would call attention to my location. Instead, I turned my anger inwards and gritted my teeth. The helicopter zoomed overhead and continued circling the village, shooting at the bikers, while I struggled to deal with my friend's death. I had not known Mohinder very long – but seeing him die like that hurt more than my physical wounds. I hated the sniper in the helicopter. I wanted to rip him apart with my hands.

I forced myself to calm down. I knew I'd die too if I did not hide somewhere better – but I could not leave the graveyard. Could I hide among the graves? Maybe from the men on the ground – but I could be easily spotted from above. I was safer under the tree. There was a mound of dry brown leaves at the base of the trunk – so I got an idea. I dug down with my bare hands into the soft earth to make a shallow grave for myself to lie in. Then I covered myself with dirt and leaves until the only part of me visible was my nose.

I hid there motionless for hours until the fighting ended. Night came. The Pure Bloods were still in the village when I dared to look around – but their helicopter had flown away. They were in squads going house to house. An occasional gunshot told me they were mopping up any of the bikers they found alive. I could hear some men begging for mercy – but they were shot. One squad was going through the graveyard, searching each row. I didn't feel safe where I was. What if someone searched around the tree? They'd probably see the mound where I was hiding. I was tempted to sneak into the woods – but some instinct told me to stay where I was. It turned out to be the right one because I spotted some men with rifles on the edge of the village. They would have picked me off if I had moved.

After a few long hours the Pure Bloods retreated – but I did not move for another hour. I emerged only when I was certain they had *all* gone. It was just after dawn when I stood up and looked around. The dead bodies of over thirty bikers were burning in the centre of the village on a funeral pyre that smelled like roasting pork. I walked down the lane expecting to see my friend's body there – but I could see a trail where he had been dragged off. His body was among the burning corpses. I felt sick.

I wanted to leave the village then – but first I needed to get myself some new clothes. I stripped a leather jacket off a dead guy I found smouldering on the pyre. His Gortex boots were good, too. I found some other clothes on some other dead bikers before they burned. I guessed I looked like Mad Max when I was dressed again. It was time to leave the village after that.

On my way out, I stopped to check out the damage to the pub, figuring I owed Mohinder something for saving me even after he had died. I had to make sure his granddaughter was dead for my own peace of mind. The pub smelled like a bad barbecue inside. There were two smoking charcoal bodies on the floor with guns beside their blackened hands. One gun was completely ruined by the fire – but the other one looked all right. It was an old revolver with four bullets in the chambers. Not bad. My luck was turning. I stepped behind the counter to see if some beers had survived. The heat had burst most of the bottles and cans – but I found a Sprite and a ginger beer intact. The Sprite was warm – but it quenched my thirst. I saved the ginger beer for later. There was a charred door leading to the cellar. I had the key for it – so I unlocked it. A steep stairway went down into darkness. The brick walls didn't look smoke-damaged.

"Hey! Anyone alive down there?"

No answer.

That was expected. Based on the information Mohinder had told me, the gang had imprisoned a group of young women down there. If any of them had not perished in the explosion and the fire, it was the smart thing to do to stay quiet when they heard a male voice because they would assume I was one of the gang. I would have to go down into the cellar to check it out – but it was so dark down there I needed some light. I found a piece of wood and wrapped some cloth around it – then I set it on fire at the pyre and returned to the pub. My torch lit up the stairway with flickering light as I descended. At the bottom I could see a long passage. There were about a dozen half-naked young women chained to the wall. The first one was dead. The second one was too. They had succumbed to the smoke, suffocating to death. I checked the others. They were dead – but at the far end of the passage, I heard breathing. The passage opened into a larger room where there were some more women. They were also chained up – but they were closer to a vent in the wall, which must have provided some fresh air. There were four survivors. One whimpered when she saw me.

"Hey – don't be frightened. I'm not one of the gang. They're all dead. I'm just wearing some of their clothes." I knew that sounded weird like I was some kind of ghoulish thief. Unsurprisingly, my words did not calm any of them down. "Look, I've got the keys to let you free. See?"

I set the torch down and freed the first woman. She was coughing and terrified when she rubbed her wrists. The only thing she was wearing was a ragged dirty T-shirt. Her arms and legs were marked with bruises. She cowered away from me. "I … can … go?"

"Yes," I said. "But -"

I had been going to say she was better off staying there with the others – but she jumped up and dashed for the stairs. I let her go. That left me with the other three survivors. I unlocked the second prisoner, who was a black-haired teenager wearing a sari. Since she was the only girl wearing Indian clothing, I hoped she was Mohinder's granddaughter. "Are you Leela?"

"Yes," she said. There was suspicion in her eyes. "H-how do you know my name? Who are you? I've never seen you before."

"Your grandfather Mohinder helped me escape from the gang. My name's Ben. Ben Smith. I've come to rescue you."

"Rescue me?" I saw a flash of hope. "Where is he? Where's my granddad?"

"I'm sorry to tell you he's dead."

"Dead? No. He can't be dead."

"I'm sorry. He is. He died in the attack. It was quick. He didn't feel any pain."

"We heard explosions. What happened up there?"

"An RPG hit the pub."

"What's an RPG?"

"A rocket-propelled grenade."

The girl nodded. "Did it kill the scum upstairs?"

"Yeah," I said.

After Leela was freed she looked longingly towards the exit – but she didn't leave. She waited for me to unlock the other two prisoners. One was a tall fair-haired young woman in his mid-twenties called Kim from Australia. The other woman was a little older with short blonde hair streaked with blood. She had been beaten recently. Her eyes were haunted by the bad things that had happened to her. She didn't tell me her name. She just ran away as soon as I had released her.

On unsteady feet, Leela and Kim helped each other out of the cellar – with me leading the way. They both looked like they didn't trust me. I didn't think they believed me until they stepped outside and saw the devastated village. The first escaped woman was running across a field away from us. Leela and Kim called to her – but she didn't stop or slow down. There was no sign of the blonde woman. I wondered if she had fled into the woods or was hiding in the ruins.

Leela looked around, coughing. "The bikers are all dead?"

"I think so."

"Good. Did *you* kill them?"

"Me? No. I was being tortured up there in the church when they got attacked by the Pure Bloods."

She frowned. "Who are they?"

"You haven't heard of the Pure Bloods?" I was surprised. I had thought everyone knew about them.

"I wouldn't have *asked* if I knew," Leela said. "Are they the good guys?"

"Not exactly. They are better than the bikers, I suppose. They don't abuse their prisoners. The Pure Bloods are another group a bit more organised and better armed. They have a military base in Oxford. They are all immune to the zombie virus. They do take in survivors – but there's a big catch."

"What's that?"

"They inject newcomers with the virus as a test to see if they have so-called 'pure blood' like them."

"What happens if you don't have 'pure blood'?"

"You turn into a zombie and they kill you."

"They sound mad."

"Yeah," I said. "That's why I hid from them until they had finished killing the bikers. They're just as dangerous. They didn't take any prisoners today. They just shot everyone. And then they tossed them on that pyre to burn."

Leela stared at the burning bodies. "Is that where my granddad is?"

"Unfortunately, yes."

"I have to see him." Leela scrambled over to the pyre, where she fell to her knees and sobbed. "No – that's my granddad. They threw him on the fire like he's a load of rubbish!"

There was nothing I could say. The other girl – Kim – pulled Leela away. "Don't look. He's gone. Nothing you can do."

"All my family is dead now," Leela said. "What am I supposed to do?"

"You can both come with me," I said. "We'll be safer in a group. I've got friends who can help us – if we can get back to them. You're welcome to come with me."

"Go with you *where*?" Leela said. "There's nothing in this stupid country anymore! It's all like this! A living hell!"

"There's a country estate where I left some supplies. It's about a day's walk. It's better there."

Kim narrowed her eyes. "What if we don't want to go with you, mate?"

"I'm not going to force you. You're free now. You can do what you like. I just think it's better to stick together. There are bad people out there. Plus the zombies."

I noticed Kim had picked up a jagged piece of glass as a weapon. "What do you reckon, Leela? Can we trust this bloke?"

Leela coughed before answering. No offence – but I don't want to go with you. I'll just stay with my friend Kim. We'll be all right without you. You can go on your own."

"Your grandfather wanted me to protect you."

"I don't need protection from a man! We don't need you! I'm

sick of men! You're all a bunch of -" Another bout of coughing doubled her up.

Kim went to her side. "You okay?"

"Hard breathing," Leela said. "The smoke. My throat hurts."

I reached into my jacket and pulled out the ginger beer. "Here. Drink this. It will ease it."

"Thank … you." She accepted the can and gulped some of it down – then she passed it to Kim. "It's good. Have some."

Kim sniffed the drink. "Ginger beer? You couldn't find a strong lager, mate?"

"All I could find," I said.

"Guess it will do," she said, swigging it. "Beggars can't be choosers."

Leela straightened up, breathing heavily. "I suppose we could stay with you for a while – but if you try anything creepy, Ben, I'll kill you."

Kim was crushing the empty beer can when she frowned. "Hey – Pipa's coming back!"

Pipa was the woman I'd seen running away. Now she was running in the opposite direction back to the village. Running and screaming. The reason for her panicked flight was obvious. There were some zombies in the field, lumbering after her. I counted ten – no – more. Twenty. At least that number. They were spread out and moving in her direction. They were not the only ones. There were more in the distance.

"We should have expected zombies," I said. "They must've been attracted by the noise of the battle last night. They must've heard the shooting and started walking. It's taken them hours to get here – but I bet more are already coming from other directions."

Pipa ran up to Kim and Leela. "We're all going to die. They're everywhere. We can't escape."

"No, we'll get out," I said. "I've got a gun. Grab anything you can as a weapon and follow me."

We left the village in a hurry.

ENTRY TWENTY-THREE

We encountered a zombie as we fled the village. It lurched out of the woods gnashing its yellowed, broken teeth. It was a big purple-faced man dressed in a green tracksuit with half his guts exposed. He was dragging a twisted foot chewed by rats until his toes were just bones. He wasn't much of a danger. He would never have caught us in a million years – but he did start to moan and come after us. His moans could attract more, livelier zombies. Because I was in bad shape after being tortured, I would have shot him in the head – wasting a valuable bullet from my revolver – but my three new companions attacked him before I could. Leela, Kim and Pipa smashed his head in with bricks, sticks and a long metal spike respectively. Pipa jammed her spike through his eye into his brain – then pulled it out with brain tissue sticking to the end like pink porridge. They continued to attack him even after his brain was splattered on the ground. Kim battered his head with her rock. Pipa kicked him a few times until she burst into tears. She even spat on the dead man before walking on.

"I wished he'd been one of *them*," she said to the others. She meant one of the biker gang that had held them captive. Leela and Kim murmured in agreement. All three of my new female companions flashed me a nasty look as we continued as if blaming me for something. Their experiences with men had been so bad that I was sure none of them wanted to be following me – another man - even though I had rescued them from the cellar. They were all sick of men.

About a mile on we spotted some more zombies on the road and in a field – so we left the road and continued through the woods. Eventually, we reached another road without having another zombie encounter. Earlier I'd told Leela and Kim it was a day's walk to my old camp – but that was a hugely optimistic estimate. I had not taken into account the state of my health – which had been ruined by being tortured. Billy had worked me over so every part of me ached. The painkillers were wearing off and I was exhausted.

"I need a stop to rest, guys."

"What?" Kim said. "We need to keep going. The zombies might get us if we stop now."

"They won't," I said. "We're past them now. They were all on their way to the village."

"Let's just leave him," Pipa said. "We don't need a man to save us. I'm not even sure he wasn't one of the gang. He is wearing a biker jacket."

"I got it off a dead one," I said. "I was not part of the gang."

"That's true," Kim said. "I remember all of their faces, Pipa. He wasn't with them."

Pipa pouted. "Still – he is a man. We can't trust men. Not after what they did to us back there. He could be taking us to somewhere worse. Let's just leave him and go."

"And go where?" Leela said. "Ben knows this area better than we do. We've been prisoners for so long we don't know what is out here. We need him. We all need a brief rest anyway. My feet are dead sore. I need a break, too."

We rested for twenty minutes. I swallowed a couple of painkillers and gave Leela some for her pain. Leela asked me to explain why I'd been held prisoner by the bikers. I started telling her about the ambush and then the chase that ended at the town where Angela attacked the bikers.

At the mention of Angela's name, Kim's eyes widened. "I don't believe it. You have a friend called Angela? I know an Angela! She was here when I was captured. She was always planning to break out.

She caused the gang so much trouble they locked her naked in a shed with just some raw potatoes to eat as punishment. They left her there for two weeks intending to break her – but something must have happened because they never did bring her back. Quinn told us they had killed her – but I never believed them because they didn't show us her body. I knew she had escaped! It's not the *same* Angela, is it?"

"Yeah, it is. I found her locked in a shed. She never told me about her past – but I knew it was bad. No wonder she shot those guys."

"Good on her," Kim said. "What happened after she shot at them?"

I told them about releasing a whole bunch of zombies. That was part of my story my new companions liked because it had resulted in the deaths of several bikers. They were sad to hear Angela had been shot. Then I mentioned encountering Billy. His name made them all angry.

"Didn't Angela recognise him?" Kim said.

"No."

"That's weird."

"She wouldn't have," Pipa said. "Remember he had a beard when Angela was with us? He shaved it off later on. He looked completely different then. We didn't know his name was Billy, either. They were pretty careful to not use their real names around us at the beginning. They wanted to remain anonymous – but after a while, they stopped caring because it wasn't like the law would ever return."

"You're right," Kim said. "Go on, mate."

I went on to finish my story, ending with how Billy had captured and tortured me.

Kim was first to speak. "You were lucky he didn't do worse. We all knew Billy. He was an evil psychopath. Loved inflicting pain. Did you see him die back there?"

"No," I said. "I don't know what happened to him. Quinn's dead, though. Leela's grandfather saw him die of a bullet wound."

"Billy will have escaped somehow," Kim said. "You can bet on that. He probably convinced the Pure Bloods to let him be their leader. It wouldn't surprise me. I met him a few months back when I was with a group of good people. We were living in a caravan when he showed up on his own. He acted all friendly and I trusted him. He tricked us to come back with him to his camp, which he promised was a safe haven. He lied. They murdered my friends."

"I hate him," Pipa said, gripping her spike tighter. "If I ever see him again, I'll stab him with this!"

"And I'm smashed his pretty-boy face in," Leela said.

Our mutual hatred of Billy helped improve our alliance by the time we were ready to continue. Leela started walking on the grass beside the road because the gravel was too rough on her bare feet. She kept wincing.

"You okay?" I said.

"No. I need some shoes," she said. "And some fresh clothes."

Pipa nodded. "I've been wearing this stinky T-shirt for months. The pigs wouldn't give me anything else to wear. I feel so exposed. Ben, I don't suppose you know where we can get some new clothes?"

We were approaching a junction with a sign. "There's a small town that way. I passed through it a couple of weeks ago. There were some fashion shops. They looked looted, though. And I did see a few zombies."

I was hoping they would not want to go. I didn't like going into urban areas without being armed to the teeth.

"I can't go on wearing this," Pipa said. "I think we should go there. I'm not afraid of some zombies. Not after what I've been through. We can't walk around dressed like this. I feel naked."

"We all need new clothes," Kim said. She looked at me. "Especially you, mate. The Fonz wants his jacket back."

"It would be safer to avoid the town," I said. "I wouldn't recommend going that way. We might find a farmhouse on the other road where the people left some things behind."

Leela, Kim and Pipa moved away and discussed it without me for a couple of minutes. Then Leela spoke for the group. "Ben, you don't have any clothes for us where we're heading – so we might as well take a detour. We need food and water, too. And better weapons against the zombies than this stuff. We all want to go that way. We'll say goodbye here if you don't want to come."

I sighed. "Okay. I'll go – but I'm just saying we'd better be cautious. No rushing into the town to get ourselves murdered or turned into zombies."

"You lead the way," Pipa said. "Then if you get killed, we'll know you were right."

ENTRY TWENTY-FOUR

Buxtonbridge was a small town in Oxfordshire just a mile down the road – a destination for tourists and casual shoppers before Day One. Now it was probably a haven for zombies. I thought it was foolhardy going to the town without good weapons and a good plan – but Leela, Kim and Pipa were keen to do some shopping for clothes and other essentials after their ordeal, so we trudged along the road until my legs were hurting.

The town came into sight around noon. We stopped and observed it from the woods. There was a garden centre and a small Waitrose on the road leading into the market square, where the girls could get some clothes in the boutiques. From a safe distance, we studied the area, looking for dangers. The streets appeared deserted except for a few decaying zombies in the square. The presence of the undead probably meant no living humans were in the town – which was good for us.

The garden centre seemed like the best place to go first because it could contain some garden tools for upgrading our weapons. Pipa wanted to check out the Waitrose first because she was hungry – but I was sure the store would have been ransacked of all food. Weapons were more important. Kim and Leela agreed with me. My new group followed me to the garden centre. It was quiet as I approached, with the girls watching my back. The automatic doors had been pried open by looters so I could see into the store as far as the checkout counters. I saw no zombies among the aisles of garden equipment – but it was fairly dark inside. It was possible there were *some* inside. There were two ways of continuing – silently or noisily. Noisily had an advantage if I'd been fit and armed with a good weapon – because it would attract any zombies lurking inside to the entrance, where I could see them and then fight them in the sunlight. The second option – silently – was something I didn't like doing unless I had no choice. In an area where we didn't know how many zombies were nearby, it was the safer of the options, though.

"Okay – I'll go in to look for some tools with Kim and Pipa. Leela, stay here and watch our backs. Tap on the window if you see more zombies. Kim, Pipa, come with me. Keep together when we're inside. No going off alone."

Kim eagerly joined me at the doors – but Pipa stayed back. She was shaking her head. "Just a sec. Why does Leela get to stay outside where it's safe? How the hell is that fair? I don't want to go into that place. It's dark and we don't even have a torch."

"Leela's got an injured foot," I said. "She can't run like you, Pipa. Besides, we need to make sure the exit is clear. That's why one of us needs to stay outside. Leela can be our lookout."

"I could do that job," Pipa said.

"I'll go inside if Pipa wants to swap," Leela said. "I'm not afraid."

"Sounds good to me," Pipa said, a smug look on her face.

"No," I said. "Leela, you need to stay outside. Pipa, you're not swapping. You're going with us."

"Who made you boss?" Pipa said. "You think because you're a man you should be in charge?"

"No – but we need the fittest people inside. You've already demonstrated you can kill zombies with that spike. If you come with me, you can pick a better weapon for yourself. You want a better weapon, don't you?"

Pipa grumbled – but she joined us at the entrance. I stepped into the dark entrance and listened as my eyes adjusted to the gloom. Kim and Pipa followed me into the store. There was a labyrinth of aisles ahead. To my right, there were some racks of gardening books and a deserted teashop for visitors. On my left were bird houses, displays of seed packets and sacks of flower bulbs. Ahead was a section containing lawn furniture and barbecue equipment. Most of the aisles had been looted and trashed. A sign pointed to the gardening tools at the far end – closer to the other side of the store which opened up to an outdoor area for greenhouses and outdoor plants. A mildewy smell got stronger as I left behind the comforting sunlight and entered the twilight world. Kim and Pipa were so close I could hear them breathing in the semi-darkness.

"Is that you breathing loudly?" Kim whispered.

"No," Pipa said.

Oh – hell.

A zombie jumped out from behind a stack of fertiliser, slamming into me, knocking me to the floor. The mildew smell was coming from inside the zombie's mouth as it breathed on me. I saw its fleshless skull and rotten eyes and teeth. It was on top of me, trying to bite, as I struggled to push it away. My hands were trapped under it and I could not escape. Someone yelled. I heard a whoosh of air and heard a crunch. Something cold and wet splattered my face. The zombie stopped moving. I freed myself from under it, gasping, aching, confused.

"Nailed it," Pipa said. "You got brains all over you, Mr Boss-man. So much for *your* survival skills. You'd be dead if I hadn't killed that zombie. It was going to eat you until I spiked it. Now you owe me your life. We're even."

I would have thanked her if she hadn't been so obnoxious. I stood up, wiping my face of whatever gunk had sprayed me. For once, I was glad it was too dark to see.

"You okay, mate?" Kim asked.

"Didn't bite me," I said.

With her confidence boosted, Pipa took the lead, while I

recovered my wits. We got to the tool aisle without another zombie attack. Other people must have been there before us and nabbed the best stuff – but we found some spades and forks at the back of a display. They were better weapons than what we had – so we returned to the entrance carrying our new tools. (Pipa kept her spike as a backup weapon.) I had a second spade in my hands to give to Leela. I expected to see her waiting outside.

But she wasn't there.

ENTRY TWENTY-FIVE

We looked around frantically – but Leela had vanished in the five minutes we had been inside the garden centre. Kim and Pipa checked around the sides of the building while I crossed the street to look into the Waitrose. The supermarket had been completely emptied of everything. I could see no places for anyone to hide – so I knew she wasn't there. I walked back to the middle of the street and looked in every direction. Where was she? Kim returned with Pipa. She was shaking her head.

"We can't find her, mate. She's gone."

I sighed. "Do you think she'd leave voluntarily?"

"No," Kim said. "She wouldn't leave us."

I didn't think that either – but Pipa shrugged. "Listen, I've been thinking. Maybe Leela got scared waiting outside when we were in the garden centre? She could've run away if she heard that zombie attacking us."

"With her foot injury?" I said. "I doubt it."

"You got a better explanation, Columbo?"

"No," I admitted. "But if she did run away, she must be somewhere nearby. We can't leave her here. We have to look for her."

Kim nodded in agreement – but Pipa glared. "That's crazy. If she doesn't want to be found, we won't find her. This town has loads of hiding places. I say we just continue without her. She'll come back if she wants to be with us. She's a grown woman. We don't have to look after her like she's a little kid."

That made me think of Hayley, making me angry. "Leela's a scared seventeen-year-old who's just lost her grandfather. We can't abandon her."

"Abandon *her*? She abandoned us!"

"We don't know that," Kim said. "Something might've happened to her. We don't know this town. We think it's deserted of living humans – but what it if isn't? What if someone took her?"

"Who?" Pipa said.

"Me," said a man.

ENTRY TWENTY-SIX

Just like that scene in every spaghetti western, a stranger stood in the middle of the street with a couple of guns in his belt. He was dressed in combat fatigues like a soldier and appeared to be alone. He was a man in his fifties with short black hair streaked with grey, a deeply tanned face, hard eyes and a patchwork of old scars on his thick neck. He was smiling at me like he found something funny in our Mexican standoff.

The smile was creepy.

I estimated he was a hundred feet away. He was wearing a bulletproof vest so only a headshot would kill him. I'd shot zombies in the head at a greater distance, but my hand was shaky when I pointed my gun at him because I was weakened after being tortured. I doubted I'd hit him if he had been standing ten feet away. "Don't move! Who the hell are you and what have you done with Leela?"

"Easy now," he said. "Don't get yourself killed pointing that little pea-shooter at me. My friend on the roof over there will have to take you down if you don't drop the gun and kick it towards me. She's a very good aim – so just do as I say and nobody gets hurt."

Was he bluffing? I turned my head and looked at the roof of the Waitrose store, where the long barrel of a very nasty rifle pointed at me. The red dot of a laser danced over my face. No – he wasn't bluffing. I wondered if I could move fast enough to take out the sniper and run for cover back in the garden centre before the man pulled his two guns. In my dreams, maybe. Not in reality.

"Put the gun down," Kim muttered under her breath, as though she had read my mind. I'd nearly forgotten she was behind me. "They could shoot us all if you don't, Ben."

Pipa glared at me. She spoke through her teeth like an angry ventriloquist. "Don't get us killed, Ben."

Kim and Pipa were only armed with garden tools. We couldn't shoot our way out of the situation like Clint Eastwood. I listened to their advice and dropped the gun. I kicked it towards the stranger.

"That's better. You made the right decision, Ben."

He knew my name so Leela must have told him it. Had he hurt her to make her talk? The man had us defeated – but he hadn't shot anyone so I hoped that was a good sign. He walked up to my gun and picked it up to examine it. "Got some bullets left, huh? Mine is empty. Haven't had any ammo in weeks – but you don't need ammo if your enemy doesn't know it." Chuckling, he tucked my gun into his belt. "Think I'll keep this for now. You can all keep the garden tools, though. There are still a few zombies in this town that need bashing." He walked over to me, offering his hand to shake. "I'm Dex. I heard you and your friends had a hell of a night?"

"That's right." I was still wary. "What do you want, Dex?"

"Ben, I don't want anything," he said. "It's what *you* want - that is the question. I've been watching you since you showed up here. I grabbed your friend to find out why you were here. Your friend told me you just escaped from the Pure Bloods and a biker gang. I wouldn't have believed her story if I hadn't heard all the shooting last night. Sounded like Bonfire Night." He looked at Kim and Pipa. "You must be Kim and Pipa. Leela told me you were all kept as prisoners. I'm glad those bikers are all dead. They've been a problem for a while. Killed some friends of mine."

"Where's our friend Leela?" Kim asked.

"Leela's having her injuries treated. She's been well looked after - so don't worry about her. I've done nothing to her except ask her some questions."

"Can we see her?" I said.

"Sure," Dex said. "I only took her because I needed to know

why you were here before introducing myself. I had to be sure you weren't a bunch of Pure Bloods hunting for me."

"Hunting for you? Why? What did you do to them?"

"I'll tell you later," he said. "We need to get off the street now. There's a Pure Blood helicopter coming this way in about ten minutes. They'll spot us if we stay outside."

"How do you know that?"

"Hacked their radio frequency," he said. "No time to talk. Come with me and I'll take you to your friend."

Dex turned his back and headed towards the town centre where I knew there was a market square with some zombies. We followed him. Ahead there were a few zombies crawling and lumbering around the square. Most were harmless – but a couple perked up at the sight of us. They snarled and staggered towards us like drunks at a wedding.

"Stay behind me," Dex said, pulling a meat cleaver from somewhere inside his uniform. The blade gleamed in the sunlight. He dashed ahead, decapitating the zombies in our way with swift, expert swings of his cleaver. He reached the far side of the square and beckoned us to follow him through the door of a nail salon with boarded-up windows. Dex was greeted by a younger man armed with a mediaeval double-edged sword probably nicked from a museum. The younger man was slouching his shoulders until he saw Kim and Pipa. He straightened his posture when they entered the nail salon.

"Hi," he said. "I'm Kris. Nice to meet you, ladies. If there's anything I can do for you, just ask. It'd be my pleasure."

After the ordeal, Kim and Pipa had been through as prisoners of the bikers, neither welcomed his unwanted flirting. They returned his greeting with frosty glares, tightening their hands on their weapons. Kris looked confused. He looked the sort of handsome rogue who expected girls to automatically fancy him. He was ogling Pipa because she was hardly wearing anything after her escape. She folded her arms over her chest and glared at him like she wanted to stab out his eyes.

"Keep your eyes on the zombies," Dex said to Kris. "I'm taking our guests to meet the others. Stay alert. A helicopter's in the area."

"Yes, sir."

Dex led the way through the nail salon up some narrow stairs and along a cold, dark passage into an empty flat probably once lived in by the salon owner. We passed through a pink living room to the girlie bedroom where there was a large heart-shaped wardrobe. Dex opened the wardrobe. It was filled with moth-eaten coats and dresses.

"We going to Narnia?" I said.

Dex grinned. He pushed the clothes aside and lifted a wooden panel, revealing a big hole through into the next building, which I'd seen from the outside was the flat above a burnt-out kebab shop. Dex climbed through and waited for us to join him before putting the panel back in place.

We were in a small dirty bathroom.

"This is one of our secret hideouts," Dex said. "We burnt down the stairs in this building so you can only get here via the salon's entrance. Got the idea for a secret entrance from *The Lion, The Witch and the Wardrobe*. It's a useful hiding pace from the Pure Bloods. They sometimes search this town, looking in the buildings for survivors. We don't want them finding us here – so we hide in places like this."

The next room was crowded with two dozen people – men, women and children. Some men and women were in uniforms. More were in civilian clothes. The room smelled of sweaty bodies. The group greeted Dex with nods and smiles – but they looked warily at me and my companions. We were new and not to be trusted. People were sitting on several sofas and others lying on sleeping bags squeezed into the tight space. Leela was lying on a sofa wearing jeans and a shirt instead of her well-worn sari. Her feet were bandaged. Kim went to her and hugged her. "You okay, Lee?"

"Yeah," Leela said. "I was scared when they suddenly kidnapped me – but they've been really nice to me. They're good people, Kim. Not like the bikers."

Dex approached a scrawny man in an army uniform listening to a military radio. They spoke for a minute – then Dex walked over to us. "You all look like you've been in a war. We've got a doc and a nurse – so just get yourselves checked over. Then when you're done the kitchen's down the hall. Sit down at the table and get yourselves something to eat. We've got hot soup and fresh bread for everyone."

"Thanks," I said. I was still wary of their unexpected generosity – but I was too tired, hurt and hungry to say no. I had my injuries treated by a kind-faced elderly woman who reminded me a little of my grandmother. Her name was Edith. She treated my cuts and bruises and gave me some antibiotics for an infection I didn't know I had. When she was done, I thanked her and wandered down a hall into the kitchen, where I was joined by Kim and Pipa. Like Leela, they had been provided new clean clothes. Kim was dressed in a black polo-necked jumper and black skinny jeans. She looked like a French resistance fighter. Pipa was wearing a khaki army uniform and army boots.

"Where's Leela?" I asked.

Kim answered. "She's staying in the living room resting her feet, mate. She's already had some food, she says."

"That's good."

There were another ten people in the kitchen eating, washing dishes and making soup just like a big family. Dex was there. He introduced us to them. A fat Scottish man was cooking a meaty soup on a camping stove using butane to heat a large steaming pot. He was appropriately named Stu. The delicious aroma of meat and vegetables made me want to weep. Stu served us all bowls of hot broth with hot crusty bread that tasted like heaven. I was amazed they had fresh bread. I had no idea how they had made it. All I knew about bread was it was bought from supermarkets. I would not have had a clue how to make it without electricity and a YouTube video showing me what to do with the ingredients. The bread was the finest food I had eaten since Day One.

"Who are you people?" I asked Dex once I had finished eating.

"We just call ourselves *The Family*."

I thought of Charles Manson. "Sounds like a sinister cult."

"Yeah, I know. We thought about calling ourselves *The Rebels* or *The Alliance* or something like that – but we're not fighting a war and we're not in a Star Wars movie. We're just a group of survivors wanting to stay alive. Honestly, we didn't spend a long time picking the name. *The Family* won by a democratic vote. We were almost called *The Jedi* because we've got a lot of nerds with us. They knew how to survive better than most from watching so many zombie movies. *The Family* won by two votes."

"How many of you are there?"

"There's over forty of us here. There are more, smaller groups of us in other places. We don't like to be in too large a group because we'd get noticed by the Pure Bloods."

"I saw one of their radios, right? How'd you get it?"

"It was mine when I was with them," he said. Dex pulled down his sleeve and showed me his bare arm. It was scarred with human teeth marks. Old bites. From zombies. "I was with the Pure Blood for a while. I was a patrol captain. Before that, I was in the real British army. I was a colonel. My men were stationed outside London when the nuke went off. Back then the official government policy was to shoot anyone bitten. I followed my orders – until the day I was bitten. I wanted to wait to see if I would turn before killing myself – but my men were so frightened they tried to kill me before I turned. I didn't let them. I shot one of them and escaped before the rest shot me. When I didn't turn, I couldn't go back to the army because of what I'd done. I survived on my own for a month. By then the whole country was fighting each other. When the Pure Bloods formed their militia, I volunteered to join up because they wanted guys like me, the immune."

"How long were you with them?"

"Longer than I should have been," Dex said. "At the time I thought they had the solution to the problem because they were fearlessly attacking the zombies and protecting innocent civilians. I wanted to do that, to be a soldier again, defending our country. I didn't know the Pure Blood leaders planned to kill everyone who wasn't immune. I only found out that was going on after a few months when I saw a patrol shooting innocent non-infected people. It made me sick being one of them. One day I saw an opportunity to escape with some soldiers loyal to me – so we stole some guns and supplies and fled. They came after us hard – but they didn't get us all. I've been living off their radar since then – trying to build up a network of small groups of survivors, but it's not been easy. They always have people out looking for me. There's even a reward for any Pure Blood who catches or kills me."

"What's the reward?"

"They get taken off dangerous zombie-hunting patrols and assigned a cushy job at their HQ in Oxford. That's a hell of a reward. Just about anyone would want it because patrolling isn't exactly fun. Pure Bloods might be immune to the virus – but it still hurts when a zombie snacks on you."

"Why's finding you so important to the Pure Bloods?"

"Their leadership can't let anyone quit their army. Especially not someone like me – an early member with my own loyal soldiers. That would give others the idea they can quit too. They'd love to catch us to make an example of me. You know what they do to traitors?"

"I've heard rumours," I said. "I imagine it's bad?"

"Bad isn't the right word. It's *pure evil*. They hang traitors over a pit of zombies so the zombies can chew on their feet. Then they lower them down into the pit very slowly. The zombies eat their way up their bodies like hungry piranhas – but the victims don't die quickly. First, they lose their flesh to their bones. Then they die screaming. New recruits are forced to watch the traitors being eaten alive just so everyone is afraid of betraying their orders. It's an effective lesson, believe me. Hitler would have been proud. Oxford is like a death camp."

"You were in Oxford for long?"

"Yeah – for some time. Why?"

"Two of my friends were taken there. Neal and Angela. What do you think will have happened to them?"

"Captured civilians are locked up in steel cages. Most are immediately injected with infected blood. They're kept as prisoners for two weeks. The ones who turn into zombies are put in the pit. The others are sent to a training camp, where they are psychologically broken down and converted into loyal soldiers of the Pure Blood Army."

"What if they refuse to join?"

"They get the pit."

"Wait a sec. You said 'most' are immediately injected, right?"

"Uh-huh."

"Does that mean *some* people aren't?"

"Yeah. A small number of exceptionally useful people don't get injected with the virus."

"Why?"

"Practical reasons. The PBA don't risk infecting people with unique skills, like scientists and doctors. They keep them as slaves. For everyone else, it's welcome to the cages. 95 out of 100 people injected die within one day. Two more usually die within a week. Another within two weeks. That means just two people survive out of every hundred. It's barbaric. You have better odds of survival playing Russian roulette."

"My friends were taken a few days ago. Is it possible they are still alive?"

"Do they have unique skills?"

"Angela's great with a crossbow. Neal's a brave man."

"Those aren't skills the PBA respect. Sorry. I'm afraid your friends will already be dead. If they are lucky. If not, they're zombies in the pit."

It wasn't the news I wanted to hear. "Can you help me find out for certain?"

"Your friends can't be saved, Ben. I'm sorry that I can't help."

I was feeling extremely tired. "You mind if I sleep somewhere for a few hours?"

"No," he said. "Get some rest. You look like you need it."

I left the kitchen and found a mattress in another room. My eyelids were so heavy I wondered if the soup had been drugged – but I'd seen the others eating the same food. It was probably the painkillers kicking in. I laid down and shut my eyes, falling asleep thinking of Angela, Neal and a pit of zombies.

ENTRY TWENTY-SEVEN

I woke up smelling something delicious cooking somewhere nearby. It smelled like frying bacon – something I had not eaten since Day One. I sat up and saw I was in the same room I'd crashed in – but now I had no aches or pains. Sunlight was coming through a gap in the curtains, turning the walls golden. It felt like a dream because I'd been in agony when I went to sleep – but my bruises had started to fade to yellow. I swung my legs off the mattress and put my feet on the floor, noticing Leela was across the room sitting on another bed reading a paperback copy of *Game of Thrones*. She looked engrossed. I'd started to watch the TV series just before Day One and the zombie plague interrupted all our lives. It made me sad to think I'd never see how it was supposed to end. Leela lowered the book and smiled, looking far healthier than the girl I'd found locked in a cellar.

"Hey! You're awake!"

"Yeah." I felt refreshed and energised. "How long have I been sleeping?"

"Two days," she said.

Her answer surprised me. "You let me sleep *two* days?"

"We didn't have much choice. You needed the rest, Ben."

I'd been brutally tortured by a sicko called Billy. Those injuries were no longer hurting. "What have you been doing?"

"I've been getting to know The Family. I've made a load of new friends here, like a girl my age. They're not like the biker gang. These people don't keep slaves. They help and trust each other."

"That's good to know."

"How do you feel now?"

"Much stronger." I stood up and stretched my muscles, not feeling any pain. "How's your foot?"

"It's great!" Leela said. "Totally healed up. Got myself some new boots. I'm ready to kiss zombie ass."

"That's good." I rubbed my itching chin. I needed a shave. There was nobody else in the room and it was quiet. "Where are Kim and Pipa?"

"Kim's down the hall making breakfast with Stu. Pipa's doing a zombie patrol of the town with Kris."

"Kris? Who's that?"

"Remember the handsome guy with the sword guarding the door? That's Kris."

"Oh, right. Pipa's with him voluntarily? I didn't think she liked him."

"She didn't – at first. But they really like each other now. I saw them kissing last night when they thought everyone was asleep. Pipa loves being in The Family. She's told me she wants to stay with them. Kim likes it here, too. So do I. It's good to be with people helping each other instead of … you know."

I knew. The Family were a group of survivors we had encountered just yesterday – no, that was wrong, it was *three* days ago. Their leader was a soldier called Dex – a former member of the Pure Bloods turned rebel leader. The Family had been kind to us – though Dex had taken away my gun, which I wanted back. Now that I was feeling stronger, I wanted to speak to him again about my friends Angela and Neal, who had been captured by the Pure Bloods. "Where's Dex?"

Leela shrugged. "I don't know, Ben. I haven't seen him today. I heard he's looking for supplies in another town. The Family have to keep moving around to avoid the Pure Bloods. They're looking for a new place because we can't stay here forever. Not with those maniacs out there hunting for them."

The Pure Bloods had murdered her grandfather. It was still a raw wound for her. I had seen him die when a sniper in a helicopter shot him in the head. There had been no reason for doing it. He had not even been armed. "It's about time the Pure Bloods went down. Hard."

Leela nodded. "Yeah – but how can they be beaten?"

"The Family has trained soldiers and weapons. They could fight back somehow – using guerilla tactics. Nobody's safe until the Pure Bloods are stopped. I need to persuade Dex to fight them or we will never be free."

"I don't think they want to fight, Ben. They know they'd lose in a straight fight."

"True – but there must be something we can do. I don't want this country taken over by the Pure Bloods."

"Talk to Dex again when he returns," Leela suggested. "Maybe you can get him to change his mind."

I hoped so. Angela and Neal were probably dead – but what if they were not? What would the Pure Bloods do to them?

I could still smell bacon. "I feel like I'm dreaming, Leela. Can I actually smell bacon frying?"

"You can," she said. "I was waiting for you to wake before going to get my breakfast. You ready to eat?"

"You bet. I'm starving."

We went down the hall to the kitchen. A group of ten people were sitting around the table eating bacon and eggs. Stu was frying more bacon on a sizzling gas hob, assisted by Kim. Kim smiled when she saw me. I sniffed the air. Ah! Sizzling bacon! I had never smelled anything as good. Stu saw me standing in the doorway staring at the food, drooling like Homer Simpson.

"Full English?" he said.

"Yes, thanks."

"Sit down, sit down."

Leela and I took empty seats at the table next to a couple of strangers enjoying their breakfasts. I felt like I was still dreaming as Stu served unbelievably tasty bacon rashers, hot buttered toast, black pudding and scrambled eggs, all washed down by a mug of strong coffee served by Kim. Nothing had tasted finer. "Where did you guys get all this fresh stuff?"

"We have a farm," Stu said.

"Near here?"

"Yeah. It's -"

"Don't tell him the location," a woman snapped. I didn't know her. She was wearing an army uniform with the sleeves cut off so her tattooed biceps were visible. She was around twenty-five and looked like she had seen some serious action, judging by the old scars on her face and arms. Her right ear was just a raw nub because it had been chewed off at some point by a zombie, but since she had not turned into a flesh-eater she had to be immune. Her hair was shaved off, revealing the smooth dome of her skull. "He's new, Stu. We can't trust him yet. Do not tell him more about our farm, okay?"

"Okay, Maggie. Sorry." Stu didn't say another word about the farm. He continued to cook breakfast in silence. Maggie's suspicion and hostility had instantly killed the friendly atmosphere. I could feel the tension as I continued to eat. I felt like Judas at the Last Supper.

I thought I'd try to make friends with Maggie. "So … you've got zombie bites. You must be immune like Dex?"

"Well done, Sherlock. Get a prize for stating the obvious. Yeah – I'm immune. So what? Got a problem with that?"

"No – I was just saying. Were you with the Pure Bloods?"

"Yeah," she said. "Not that it's your business. I don't like talking about that. Just hurry up and eat your breakfast, newbie. Then go away so someone else can have a seat. You're not the only hungry person here. We all are."

Okay. Maggie didn't want to make friends. I accepted that. I ate my breakfast listening to the conversations of the others. I discovered the Family worked like a hippy commune with everyone pitching in to do the chores like cooking and cleaning and zombie patrols. After practically licking my plate clean, I washed up my plate and mug in hot water boiled on a gas stove. The kitchen didn't have any electricity for the dishwasher, of course. The National Grid had stopped functioning months ago – but it felt as close to normal domesticity as I could imagine. It was good doing something mundane and ordinary – taking a break from killing zombies and fighting for my life. I helped Kim slice mushrooms and potatoes, taking the opportunity to talk quietly.

"Can we trust them?" I asked her.

"Yeah, I think so," she said. "I love it here. They've got everything organised. I haven't felt in danger since we arrived. It really is like a family."

"Do you want to stay with them?"

"Yes," she admitted. "Why? Do you want to leave, Ben?"

"No – but I have to think about my other friends – Angela and Neal, who could still be alive as prisoners of the Pure Bloods. Not to mention Sadie, Hayley and Jason. I can't abandon them just because I like this place. I need to talk to Dex about Neal and Angela. Any idea when he's coming back?"

"No – but I'll ask Stu. He knows what's going on."

She did that while I continued the washing up. Kim came back with more information. "Stu says he should be back by tonight. Around eight, he reckons."

"Damn it." I didn't want to wait that long. The more time I wasted doing nothing, the smaller the chance of saving Angela and Neal. I had to hope they were still alive in the Pure Blood base in Oxford.

Maggie dumped her dirty plates in the washing-up bowl, glaring at me. "Clean that, newbie."

"Uh – sure."

She gave me a nasty look before exiting the kitchen. I turned to Kim. "What's her problem with me?"

"She's Dex's second-in-command. In charge of security. It's her job to keep The Family safe. I guess it must be hard for her to trust new people. We could be bad guys waiting for an opportunity to steal things or kill them for their supplies."

I could understand Maggie's fear and suspicion. It was a rational response to a world gone wrong. I had wanted to trust Billy – to give him the benefit of the doubt – but he had betrayed me. Maggie had to be cautious for the safety of The Family. A real hippy commune wouldn't last five minutes in this hard world. The civilians needed soldiers like Maggie to keep them alive.

"Kim, can I ask you a personal question?"

"Shoot."

"If I do leave to look for my other friends, do you want to come with me or stay here?"

"I owe you my life," she said. "If you want me to go, I'll go."

"That's not what I asked. Do you want to stay?"

"Yes," she said. "I do. I like it here."

"Okay," I said. "Thanks for the honesty."

Kim lowered her voice. "Ben, are you planning on leaving?"

"Not yet," I said. "I need to talk to Dex again first."

I hated waiting around doing nothing – so I talked to more members of The Family. A few had been with the group for some months, helping Dex build a network of safe houses. The Family was trying to save lives under the noses of the Pure Bloods, which wasn't easy when the enemy had control of army bases and a deadly militia. The Family had to work covertly while the Pure Bloods could operate in the open.

I had some ideas about how to alter the balance of power – but I kept them to myself for the moment. In one room – an attic space – I found the scrawny guy in charge of the communications equipment listening to Pure Blood coms. There was another younger man there working on a computer. He stopped typing when he saw me enter.

"Hey, you're the 'Journal of the Living' blogger! I'm Lynchpin. Maybe you heard of me?"

"Er ... sorry."

"I was a political activist and hacker before the plague. I hacked into the bank you used to work for, man. I donated their money to charity. Heh. Boy, I hated the capitalist system we used to have – but I'm kind of missing it now. Total anarchy isn't as good as advertised." He chuckled. "Good to meet you, buddy. By the way, I've been reading your blogs. Good stuff. What stopped you posting?"

"I lost my laptop."

"Shame. You've got to regularly update your blog, man. Let everyone know what's going down. Tell you what, I'll get you a tablet hooked up to a solar panel. I'm linked up to what's left of the net, checking out what's going on around the world 24-7. We must let the rest of the survivors in other countries know what we're doing here. Today I've been in contact with a group in Australia and another in Africa. They've been dealing with the zombie problem much better than America and Europe because they had more time to prepare for the plague. Looks like they're winning their fight against them. I wish I'd got out of the UK before they stopped flights out. I'd love to be on a beach somewhere, eating coconuts and fresh fish like Robin Crusoe. That'd be so good."

Lynchpin gave me a tablet to work on, which I took into

another room in another safe building, the local library, where Leela had found her copy of *Game of Thrones*. I spent hours writing my journal while watching the clock. It was quite late when Dex returned. Twenty minutes ago, I went to speak to him about my plan to rescue Angela and Neal from the Pure Bloods. He thought my plan was mad because I didn't even know if they were alive – but I persuaded him to help me get into Oxford to find out what happened to them.

*

This journal entry – number 27 – might be my final entry because I could die tomorrow.

Lynchpin will post this on my blog when he considers it safe to do so. (I can't post it live in case it will jeopardise my plan.) If don't make it back, he's told me he will take over my blog.

So … goodbye for now.

ENTRY TWENTY-EIGHT

"I'm going to Oxford to rescue Angela and Neal," I told Kim and Leela after Dex had agreed to help me. They looked worried and started asking questions, telling me it was too dangerous. "I know it's a dangerous mission – which is why I'm going *alone*. I need you both to stay here with The Family. Look after each other, okay?"

My friends reluctantly nodded. Leela hugged me hard, sniffling back tears. "Don't get killed, Ben."

"Don't worry. Dying isn't part of my plan."

"Are you sure you don't want us to come with you?"

"You can't," I said. "I'm sorry. I appreciate you wanting to, though. But you need to stay with The Family. You'll be all right. Kim and Pipa will make sure of that, right, Kim?"

"You bet," Kim said. "I hope you find your friends alive, mate. I'd just like to say thanks for saving our lives. We'd still be prisoners if you hadn't ..." She didn't need to say more. "When … when do you intend to go, Ben?"

"Everything needs organising," I said. "So it will probably be sometime tomorrow morning. I might have to leave tonight without seeing you guys again."

Leela blinked away tears. "Are you coming back here afterwards?"

"I can't make that a promise," I told her. "But I'll try to contact you by leaving messages on my blog. Lynchpin will watch for it. He'll keep you informed. Well … see you."

I hated saying a final goodbye. My last words to them sounded a little weak even as I said them. Kim walked with me out into the hall. She kissed me gently on my cheek, leaving it tingling. "Good luck, Ben. Rescue your friends and don't get turned, okay? I hope we'll see each other again. In better circumstances. Goodbye."

*

The leader of The Family had agreed to help me get into Oxford to look for Angela and Neal – but he wanted me to do him a favour in exchange. The Pure Blood base was a threat as long as it had helicopters giving them a tactical advantage in any battle – so Dex wanted me to destroy them once I was inside. I had agreed to do it – but I didn't know *how* I was going to get inside Oxford when I met Dex to go over his plan.

Dex was alone in a bedroom that had been turned into an informal school classroom for the younger members of The Family. The room had a dusty chalkboard and rows of little blue plastic chairs taken from the local school. Dex was standing behind the teacher's desk drawing on an Ordnance Survey map of Oxford. There was a red circle around the city centre.

"What's the red line mean?"

"It marks a twenty-foot deep trench filled with zombies. It goes all around the centre of Oxford like a moat. No zombies falling in can climb out and nobody would dare cross it – so it is effectively like a moat around a castle. The base is basically impregnable thanks to the zombie trench."

"Good grief. I can't believe they use zombies for defence. They're supposed to hate them."

"It's pragmatic. Zombies are better than guard dogs at keeping out intruders because they'll moan when someone is nearby. Beyond the zombie trench, there is an electrified fence just in case someone does sneak over the 'moat' of zombies. The entire perimeter is guarded night and day by snipers on the roofs of several high buildings inside the city. The only way in or out, except via helicopter, is a bridge over the trench here. That has a heavily defended security checkpoint, which includes a tank and a bunker filled with loyal soldiers. Nobody gets in or out without being checked by the guards at the gates."

"So ... how do I get in?"

"Well, that's a good question. You can see a frontal assault would be useless. You'd need an army – but I don't have one to lend you. Sneaking over the trench and through the fence is also impossible no matter which angle you approach from. The security is too tight. That leaves you with few options."

"Please tell me there's a secret tunnel into the base."

"No – there's not. Fortunately, I do have a plan. It's an old one – but a good one." He grinned. "What do you know about Troy?"

"It starred Brad Pitt and Eric Bana."

"And?"

"The Greeks used a big horse to – oh! You're going to get the Pure Bloods to invite me in?"

Dex nodded.

And then he told me the rest of his plan.

ENTRY TWENTY-NINE

I never believed the story of the Trojan horse. If I'd been fighting a long war against the Greeks and they suddenly admitted defeat, leaving a big wooden horse behind as a gift, I would not have taken it inside my city's walls. No way. I would have set it on fire. The Trojans must have been idiots to fall for that stupid trick.

Dex planned to use a modified form of that trick on the Pure Bloods, sneaking me inside their Oxford base.

"The Pure Bloods send out zombie patrols on a random schedule," he told me, as I studied a map of the city. "They go out, spend up to a week hunting zombies and catching the living to take back as prisoners, then return to the base. A typical patrol consists of a lead vehicle – a Jeep, say – and a few trucks carrying over a dozen soldiers. The soldiers are always a mix of veterans and new recruits – so they probably won't know each other too well. That's good for us. You are going to sneak aboard a truck and pose as one of them. They should be so tired after a week of zombie killing that they won't realise you don't belong with them. They'll drive you straight through the checkpoint into Oxford. Once inside, you'll be free to look for your friends and destroy their helicopter for me. I'm going to send you in with one of my most loyal soldiers, who will help you on your mission as long as you help us. Maggie!"

His second-in-command, Maggie, entered the room immediately, which meant she had been standing outside, probably listening and guarding Dex. "I volunteered to go with you to make sure the job's done right. I know Oxford well. You'd never know how to act like a Pure Blood if you went on your own, getting yourself caught. Just do what I say when I say it, okay?"

"Yeah, okay," I said. "You were with the Pure Bloods. Won't

they recognise you?"

"No. I didn't have any friends."

That didn't come as a surprise. Maggie had been openly hostile to me since my arrival. I wasn't keen to work with her, even if we had a common goal. "Wouldn't it be safer if I went in alone, Dex? They don't know me."

"True – but you don't know their procedures. Maggie will show you how to act like a Pure Blood soldier."

"Great," I said. "Now, how exactly are we going to get into one of their patrol vehicles?"

"I've been monitoring their coms. I already know the location of a patrol. They've been on patrol in a town they've been clearing of zombies just north of here. They're heading back to Oxford tomorrow morning. They'll be tired and eager to get there – so they won't be vigilant about a couple of extra soldiers joining their ranks. While they are distracted, you and Maggie will slip into one of their trucks. Hopefully, they won't notice a couple of extra passengers joining the ride."

"Hopefully?" I said. "What if they *do* notice?"

"It's simple. They'll kill you."

Maggie was grinning. "Come with me, Mr Civilian. You need to change into a Pure Blood uniform."

I was soon dressed in a soldier's uniform that made me feel like a Nazi war criminal. Maggie inspected me, shaking her head. She was also wearing a Pure Blood uniform – but she looked comfortable wearing hers. With her body hidden under a combat jacket, her head shaved, her androgynous features could pass for male or female. She started frowning.

"What's wrong?" I said.

"You don't look right," she said. "Your hair's too long. They keep their hair short or shaved off completely. Less for the zombies to grab onto. You'll have to shave it off."

I touched my hair and imagined it gone. Goodbye, hair. Hello, skinhead. "Okay, let's do it."

"That's not all. You look too civilian."

"What's that mean?"

"Pure Bloods aren't afraid of getting bitten or scratched because they are immune. You need a zombie bite mark somewhere to fit in."

My eyes bugged out. "I'm not getting myself deliberately bitten. I could get infected."

"Idiot. I'm talking about a *fake* bite mark. I'll sort out that. You shave your head. There's a razor in this bag."

Ten minutes later, I was rubbing my hands over my bare scalp when Maggie returned with some sterilising alcohol and a set of false teeth probably from the mouth of a dead old lady. Maggie sterilised my hand and the plastic teeth – then hammered the teeth into the soft flesh on the back of my hand. They left some nasty-looking imprints just like a fresh zombie bite, oozing fresh blood. I was sure she took some pleasure in hurting me.

"That's better," she said as my blood ran from the wound. "I'll cover it with a bandage so it doesn't get infected for real. Then you'll just look like you've been in a proper combat situation. Show them your wound if you need to prove you're one of them."

The last thing we did before leaving involved getting some Pure Blood weapons from the supply hidden in an attic. The Family had plenty of guns. Unfortunately, they didn't have much ammo. They needed what they had to defend themselves against zombies and other bad people. Dex provided me with an empty automatic rifle, saying, "I can't give you any bullets – it's just for show – so if you want to load it you'll have to nick some from them. Here's your own gun for emergencies, which is still loaded. I've fitted a silencer so it can be used if you need it. Don't use it unless you have no choice. Keep it hidden from the Pure Bloods."

As Maggie collected her weapon, I noticed Dex did give her half a clip of ammo, which didn't seem fair.

"How come she gets ammo for her weapon, Dex? You told me you couldn't spare any."

"Spare any for a civilian. Maggie knows how to handle it. She won't waste it."

Maggie grinned. "I'm ready, boss."

"Good luck," Dex said. "Give them hell."

A black Ford Mondeo was parked in the market square with the engine running. The driver drove us to a mile of the town where the Pure Bloods were patrolling – then he left us to make our way into the town on foot.

Maggie and I arrived at the town after dark. It was easy to see the Pure Bloods had taken over because they did not hide their presence. The town was lit up with powerful arc lights turning night into day. Soldiers were on the streets looting anything valuable. Their vehicles were parked in a supermarket's car park, their headlights blazing. I saw three army trucks, a lorry, a Land Rover, and another vehicle that looked like it had belonged to a scrap dealer. That vehicle was a white truck with a high-walled metal cage on the back. Normally it would have been filled with scrap metal – but it was filled with captured civilians. I counted twenty-three captives – ten men, eight women and five kids. They looked terrified. They'd all be going back to Oxford for injection with infected blood. Maybe one or two would survive that process – only to be turned into Pure Bloods. I felt my heart beating in my ears and had to look away.

Snipers were on the roofs of some buildings, keeping a watch. Luckily for me, Maggie knew about them. She sneaked us past the perimeter guards before we let ourselves be seen. Then we acted like the other soldiers – helping with the loading of goods into the back of the lorry. I was sure we'd get noticed – but the Pure Bloods were not looking for people in uniforms. We blended right in.

At dawn, their captain gave the orders to clear out – so Maggie and I joined the soldiers in the back of an army truck. Maggie sat beside me. More soldiers pushed into the back with us so we were shoulder to shoulder with the enemy. Once the truck was full, I didn't say a word, trying to stay invisible in the semi-darkness. I studied the faces of the men and women working for the Pure Blood Army. I expected to see some trace of evil in their eyes – but most looked like regular people who happened to have the right genes or whatever to make them immune. Only a handful of the recruits looked like complete psychos. We waited to leave for what seemed like hours. Eventually, a weary sergeant looked in the back.

"Anyone done a head count?" he said.

"No, sir," a soldier answered.

I had a sinking feeling as I looked at Maggie. She didn't react – except for nerve pulsing in her neck. A head count was bad news. If they counted two extra soldiers among them, I knew we were as good as dead.

I touched the gun hidden under my jacket as the sergeant started counting.

ENTRY THIRTY

The Pure Blood sergeant started counting heads – but his heart wasn't in it. After counting to six he stopped and sighed. "Oh, forget it. There's obviously nobody missing. Hell – looks like you boys and girls are crammed in there like sardines. Let's get back to the base for some well-deserved R&R!"

My hand relaxed on the gun hidden in my jacket as the soldiers cheered. The laziness of their sergeant was a miracle. He closed up the rear door, shutting us in the dark interior lit just by the light coming through under the door. I sighed with relief once we were on the road. The vehicle's engine was so thunderously loud nobody bothered with a conversation, which was good because I didn't want to talk to the Pure Bloods. I settled back for the journey, praying we would have another miracle when we arrived at Oxford. There was still the checkpoint to pass through. What if they had a more vigorous security routine?

Amazingly, Maggie closed her eyes for a nap like the whole situation didn't bother her, but I stayed awake and nervous. I could never relax enough to sleep surrounded by Pure Bloods. If they found out I was not one of them …

For hours I listened to the rumble of the truck, wishing I knew how far we had travelled. There was no way of knowing that until the truck reached its destination. I was feeling my bottom going to sleep when we stopped suddenly. The engine switched off, replaced by the creepy moan of zombies. I feared we'd driven into a herd of them on the road – but judging by the relaxed faces of the soldiers it was the sound of the zombies in the trench around Oxford. Maggie yawned and checked the time on her watch. She nodded. We were at Oxford. The back doors opened and hard sunlight poured in, rudely awakening the sleeping soldiers.

Their sergeant was standing outside showing his ID to a checkpoint guard in black body armour. Another soldier peered into the truck with a weapon raised. He spoke into a radio.

"R4 is back," he said. "Yes, sir. Okay – you can go ahead."

The sergeant banged on the side of the truck.

And then we were on the road again.

ENTRY THIRTY-ONE

The army truck stopped for a second time and the sergeant opened the back again. "Okay – everyone get out. We're home. Get yourselves out of those dirty uniforms and get a good shower, you filthy maggots. Nobody wants to smell you right now."

The Pure Bloods climbed off the truck. I joined them, standing outside a college building in the heart of Oxford. The other vehicle – the one containing the prisoners – drove past me on its way somewhere else. Every face pressed against the bars looked afraid. They had a right to be. I knew their fate.

I hated the soldiers around me laughing and joking about the things they had done on their mission. I overheard some talking about shooting the bikers. So, they had been involved in that massacre? Great. I smiled and pretended I was just like them, while I got my bearings.

I was on Oxford's High Street surrounded by beautiful college buildings. It was weird being in Oxford after Day One. It used to be known as the "City of Spires" for its beautiful Gothic skyline of towers, but it should be renamed the "City of Spikes." The Pure Bloods loved spikes. That was clear the moment I stepped off the truck and saw a pile of mutilated, rotting zombies on spikes set in the middle of a college's grassy quadrangle. There was a banner above the undead flapping in a light breeze, with a message on it: **Know Thy Enemy. Stay Pure.** There were more spikes on movable barricades near several strategically important buildings. Maggie explained to me the barricades could be shifted quickly to block an attack of zombies if the primary defences were breached – which seemed unlikely considering the whole of Oxford had a formidable zombie-blocking trench around it. Looking down one road to my south, I could see rows of iron spikes where the trench ran along the riverbank of the Isis, which was what the Upper Thames was called in Oxford. It looked like the river had teeth.

Maggie and I mixed among the crowd as the soldiers headed for a cloistered building that looked like an ancient monastery of stone towers and dreaming spires. The Pure Bloods hurried through the cloisters into the building – but Maggie and I paused and waited behind a pillar until we were alone.

"Where are we?"

"We're in the south-east area of the base near Christ Church," she said. "It's a barracks now."

"Have they turned all the colleges into barracks?"

"No – just Christ Church, Oriol, Merton and Corpus Christi. The other buildings are used for keeping supplies … or for research."

"What kind of research?"

"I haven't a clue. I know they have a lot of lab equipment in those buildings – but I didn't have the clearance level to go in. You'd have to have a Level 6 pass. I was just a Level 1."

"What do you think goes on?"

"I heard rumours of them doing biological experiments on zombies – but I never mingled with the scientists. They keep to themselves. They live in a different part of the city from the soldiers. I think they're working on a cure. At least I *hope* they are working on a cure. The Pure Bloods could be doing something else, for all I know." She sighed. "We better get moving before someone notices us, Ben. Just follow me and act like a soldier."

My plan to save Angela and Neal depended on finding them alive and well – so I was eager to start my search. But I also had a second part to my mission that I could not ignore either. I had agreed to help The Family destroy the helicopter used by the Pure Bloods. Maggie showed me where the landing zone was – in a field, heavily guarded *inside* a compound *inside* the compound. We went into an unguarded building for a better look from above. We were in an empty library filled with millions of books that would never be read again. We climbed some stairs to the roof. From the rooftop, we spied down on the compound, getting a far clearer view. I could see most of Oxford below me. Everything looked idyllic like in a Turner painting – except for the presence of the Pure Bloods and their love of spikes.

Maggie looked down over the side of the roof, keeping her body flat on the ground. "Damn it. The security's tighter than it was. They don't want someone nicking their precious helo. There are two watchtowers and sixteen guards. It's going to be hard to get close. Maybe …" She shook her head. "No. I can't think of a good idea. I need time to figure something out."

She rubbed her eyes wearily.

"Okay," I said. "Take the time. But what about Angela and Neal?"

"What about them?"

"I need to find them now. Where will they be?"

Maggie faced me. "If Angela's alive and being treated for her injuries, she'll be kept in the hospital over there." She pointed to the north across the roofs of the ancient colleges. "But Neal won't be over there. He'll be in the internment camp for new arrivals. That's to the east beyond the High Street. That's where the other truck was going. All those non-infected people will be held prisoner until they have been processed."

'Processed' was a clinical euphemism for being injected with the necrovitalis virus and kept in a cage to see if you turn into a brain-eating freak.

If Neal had already been processed, he was very likely dead. Or undead.

"What's the security like at the prison camp?"

"I won't know until I go a recon," she said. "But it's always been tight. They don't want civilians escaping – or do-gooders trying to save them. It will probably be worse than the LZ." She shook her head. "I don't know why I agreed to come on this crazy mission with you. I should have let you do it on your own. It's impossible!"

"I don't understand. Why did you come if you don't think it's a good idea?"

"I was hoping -" She turned away. "Forget it!"

"Hoping what?"

"That I'd save my sister, too."

"I didn't know you had a sister."

"Yeah, well, I do. I have a sister."

"What's her name?"

"Why should I tell you?"

"Because normal people have conversations about stuff like that."

"Not on rooftops in enemy territory, they don't." Staying low, Maggie wormed herself towards me. "We'd better move before a sniper spots us. Let's get inside."

Back in the library, I asked her again about her sister. I wanted to know more because it could mess up my mission if Maggie had her own agenda to rescue her sister.

"What's your sister's name?"

"Vicki."

"How old is she?"

"She's nineteen."

"How long is it since you saw her?"

"Five months. I had to leave her behind when I escaped the Pure Bloods. I hated doing that – but they had her completely brainwashed. She's a true believer. I wanted to take her with me – but I couldn't risk it. She would have thought *I* was a traitor."

Maggie glared into the distance like she had seen an interesting book among the dusty stacks. "I hate myself for letting her down. I should have tried to get her away from them, no matter the risk. I have a chance to fix things – so if get the opportunity to rescue her, I'm bringing her home with me. You got a problem with that, Ben?"

"No – but I wish you'd told me earlier. How do you intend to make contact with her?"

"I'm not. Like I said, she's brainwashed. I'm going to abduct her before we execute our plan."

"You mean that plan we haven't formulated yet?"

"Yes, that plan."

"I love it when a plan doesn't come together."

"What's that mean?"

"Nothing if you didn't watch the A-Team as a kid."

"I didn't. I'm too young."

"Rub it in how old I am," I said. "Look, we have to sort out a plan, but I can't hang around right now. I need to get looking for Angela. Will I have a problem getting into the hospital?"

"No – it's not in a secure area. You can just walk in. The staff will treat your hand if you show them your wound. It's the perfect excuse for being there."

"Good. I'll head over there. You do what you've got to do to get a plan. I'll meet you back here later."

"How late?"

"I don't know. I'll just show up when I can."

"That's not very specific. I'd like a time."

"I can't give you one. If I'm not back by midnight, assume things went wrong and get yourself out of here."

"You still have your gun, Ben?"

"Yes," I said. "Under my jacket."

"Use it on yourself if you're going to get captured. You don't

172

want to be put in the pit with the zombies."

"I like your confidence in my abilities."

"Just giving advice."

"Your advice is to shoot myself? Thanks!"

"I'll kill myself rather than be taken for interrogation," she said. "One bullet in my head from this baby will do that." She patted her rifle. "Head to the hospital on the main streets – not the back streets. It won't look suspicious if a soldier is walking around in plain view – but it would if you started sneaking around, acting like you're avoiding being noticed. As far as everyone here knows, you are one of them. They'll not be looking for someone breaking into their base unless you act weird and give yourself away. Don't act weird, Ben. Got it?"

"I'll try not to act weird, Maggie. I was thinking about dancing backwards with a traffic cone on my head – but now I've heard your advice I don't think I do that. Thanks for the obvious advice. I'll see you later."

"Whatever," she said.

I left the building. I felt vulnerable walking up the street where I could be seen – but nobody gave me a second look in my Pure Blood uniform.

On my journey north through the City of Spikes, I saw some Pure Bloods in civilian clothes. They were just doing ordinary things like shopping and walking their dogs. A pretty young woman was looking after some small children in a park. Traders were exchanging things in the market – clothes for food. Some boys and girls were playing football on the road. I was surprised. I had expected the Pure Bloods to be doing evil things all of the time – but when they were off-duty they seemed surprisingly normal. They didn't even look stressed out by the danger of zombies, which was a perpetual state for everyone else. I supposed it was easy to relax when you were guarded 24/7 and knew a zombie bite would not kill you. Their lives in Oxford looked comfortable. I could sort of understand why some people would be glad to be a part of that. The Pure Bloods had turned Oxford into a safe haven for themselves. It was a shame they had done it at the expense of selling their souls.

Ahead, I saw a modern concrete and glass building. The hospital. My hand itched under my bandage as I entered the busy and brightly-lit A&E department. The artificial light came as a shock because I'd become so used to buildings being dark – but the hospital had *electricity*. I felt as awestruck as Thomas Edison inventing the light bulb. I had not seen an electric bulb working for so long that I wanted to stare in wonder. I was standing there a little dazed when a doctor noticed me.

"Can I help you?" he said.

Just like a normal doctor.

He didn't even look evil.

I was wary, though.

"My hand," I said, waving it for him to see the bandage. "My sergeant told me to have it checked out. Got bit by a zom on my mission. Cleaned it myself – but you know ..."

"Yes, you've got to be careful. It would be ironic if you died from a simple bacterial infection. Let me have a look at it over here." He pulled aside a curtain, revealing an examination bed and blinking electrical equipment.

I had not wanted to be noticed in the hospital – but I could not turn down treatment without drawing attention. I followed the doctor into the cubicle. I sat on the examination bed and offered him my hand to examine. He peeled off my bandage and studied the fake bite wound made by the impression of some false teeth. I was afraid he'd know I wasn't a Pure Blood when he saw the fake wound. "Good news. It's pretty shallow and clean. I'll disinfect it thoroughly just to be sure, then I'll put on a fresh bandage and give you a course of antibiotics. Zombie bites can't give you the virus – but their mouths do contain nasty bacteria, too, just like the living. Come back immediately if it gets any worse."

He treated me and told me to collect the antibiotics from the pharmacy. I headed that way – until I was out of his sight. Then I started my search for Angela, looking in rooms, going from floor to floor. There were sick people in many of the rooms – even Pure Bloods need medical treatment – but I didn't find Angela on the ground floor. There were several floors with hundreds of rooms – with hundreds of opportunities for someone to notice me – so I hoped I could save time by having a look at one of the computers behind a reception desk on the second floor. The computer was hooked into the local network and appeared to be working fine, though it needed a password. I found a password on a piece of paper pasted to the back of the monitor. I typed it in. And I got access to the hospital records. I knew which day Angela had arrived – which helped me find twenty-one patients listed in their records. Only one was listed under a file number with no name, as they probably didn't know it.

PATIENT X, FEMALE, AGE 20-25:
DIAGNOSIS: POST-OP BACTERIAL INFECTION AND SEPTICAEMIA
TREATMENT: INTRAVENOUS ANTIBIOTICS
BLOOD VIRAL STATUS UPON TREATMENT: UNINFECTED BY NECROVITALIS VIRUS ALPHA
CURRENT STATUS: COMATOSE, STABLE.
LOCATION: DEPARTMENT E4, ROOM 204

I stared at the screen, hardly able to believe it.
Angela was alive.

ENTRY THIRTY-TWO

Department E4 was a long way from the hospital's entrance, along dark corridors and up four floors via an unlit stairway. (The lifts were working – but they were guarded so I didn't use them.) Most of the lights on that floor were not working. It looked like there had been a big fight to clear the building of zombies because dried blood and splattered brains were smeared on some of the walls. Not exactly hygienic – but it was an old NHS hospital so maybe the gore had been left from before the apocalypse kicked off. There were also the unmistakeable holes left by bullets. I would hate to have been on the cleaning crew. Departments E2 and E3 were no longer being used due to damage. I stopped to have a look out of curiosity. Trolleys and beds were in the rooms, stacked up, covered in blood. I could see a disturbing amount of broken equipment caused by whatever had happened. After Day One nearly every hospital in Britain had been overrun by zombies. The Pure Bloods must have spent weeks destroying them. I moved on to my destination.

Only a few strip lights were working on that floor – but I did see they were working in the corridor outside Department E4. I encountered nobody – but when I arrived at the entrance doors I found the ward locked. I read a notice: RESTRICTED AREA. PRESS BUZZER TO ENTER. ID MUST BE SHOWN AT ALL TIMES.

Hell. I didn't have any ID. I looked through a small window in the door – seeing an armed soldier on the other side. Room 204 was down that corridor, where they were keeping Angela. I looked at the buzzer, tempted to press it. I had a gun. I could shoot the guard when he opened the door – but that would not solve my problems. Angela was in a coma, according to her medical report. I would have to transport her out of the ward and the hospital without anyone catching us. Blustering in now, without a plan, would be foolish.

I walked down the corridor to another door leading into E4. It was also locked – with a guard posted on the other side. I could hear him talking to a bearded doctor, having a conversation about the patient in room 217.

"Well, I can't stick around all day. See you tomorrow."

I heard a buzz as the door was opened. I had nowhere to hide. My hand touched my gun. I dismissed the idea of shooting the doctor in a heartbeat. Not my style. I don't shoot the living unless I have no choice. The doctor stepped out, looking startled to see me there only a few feet away. The door closed behind him, leaving us standing there.

"Can you help me?" I said. Asking for help is always a good way of disarming someone if there are suspicious, which the doctor was. I could see it on his face. "I'm totally lost."

"This is a restricted area," he said. "What are you doing up here?"

"Oh – I'm sorry." I showed my bandage. "This bleeding place is too big. I'm supposed to get some antibiotics for this bite wound – but I've got confused. I've been wandering around for ages. Where's the pharmacy?"

"You're completely on the wrong floor. Go back down to the ground level. The pharmacy is in the reception area. I don't know how you missed it."

I grinned like I was an idiot. "Right. A3. Thanks, Doctor."

I returned the way I had come – with the doctor watching me. He didn't walk in the other direction until I was pressing the button for the lift. Then he walked in the other direction as I stepped into the lift. I'd noticed he was wearing a laminated ID giving him access to E4. I needed one of those ID cards. I thought about following him and stealing his ID – but a hasty move wouldn't help for long. I pressed the button for Floor 3. That floor was dark and deserted. A large section of the hospital was not being used – probably for many reasons, like saving electricity, zombie-related damage and chronic under-staffing due to the lack of doctors and nurses. No changes there.

Before trying to get into Department E4, I needed to change out of my Pure Blood uniform into a doctor's white coat. A visit to the laundry room sorted that out. The coat had a few stains on it – but nobody would notice in a hospital. I left my army uniform in an empty room on the third floor, then I went looking for a security pass.

There is one place in all hospitals where you are guaranteed to find the staff hanging out. The cafeteria. Even the Pure Bloods didn't change that behaviour. I scoped out a doctor with the right ID on his white coat, which was hanging on the back of his chair as he ate lunch. He looked like he had just started his meal of bangers and mash. He was bald – so I looked similar to him with my head shaved. He was engaged in a conversation with some other doctors – too distracted to notice when I brushed by, stealing his ID. I clipped it onto my coat as I left the cafeteria. I estimated I would have thirty minutes before the doctor finished his meal – time enough to check out the ward and return his ID before he missed it. I rode the lift to the fourth floor with a couple of orderlies. My timing could not have been better, for they were also going to E4. All three of us arrived at the doors as a group. I pressed the buzzer and waited for the guard. He opened the door with his hand on his weapon.

"Show me your ID."

We did. The guard barely looked at my ID We were all let in. The orderlies headed down the corridor, but I stopped at the nurse's station, picking up a chart. Room 204 was just ahead on my right – but I didn't want to head straight there because a nurse was behind the desk watching my arrival.

"You're new," she said.

It wasn't an accusation. Just an observation. She probably knew all of the staff working in the ward. I hoped she would not take a close look at my ID.

"Yeah," I said. "They need me to look at 201's stitches." I had just read that the patient in that room had undergone an appendectomy. "Excuse me."

She nodded and lost interest in me as I entered Room 201. The patient was awake – but he was handcuffed to the bed. There was a bandage on his side and a drip attached to his arm.

"Hey!" he said. "What's going on here? Why am I handcuffed? I did nothing wrong. Why are you treating me like I'm a criminal?"

I had no idea what the Pure Bloods had told the man – but it was clear he didn't know what fate they had planned for him. The Pure Bloods didn't like sick people dying before they were healthy enough to be injected with the necrovitalis virus. That made as much sense as not executing Death Row prisoners if they were ill. The man looked scared and bewildered. He had a right to feel that way. "The cuffs are for security, sir. We can't have patients wandering around the hospital. We have to maintain safety for everyone here."

"This is wrong. You people can't do this. Let me out of here!" He rattled the handcuffs, but then slumped back, exhausted. "Not right ... Help me."

"I'll see what I can do," I said. "Now just relax. You've just had a serious operation. You need time to recover."

He listened to me and relaxed. I hated lying to him – but I couldn't save him from the Pure Blood when he was secured to the bed. I slipped out of the room. The nurse was still there at the station. I picked up some more charts. As I moved from room to room, I discovered every patient was in the same situation, secured to their bed with handcuffs. I wondered what they did if the patient needed to be turned over. Did the guard undo them?

The nurse was no longer at the station when I left Room 203. Once I was sure nobody was taking any notice of me, I slipped into her room. The room was dark. The only light was from the machines by the bed. Someone was in that bed. A young woman with red hair. It was Angela. Alive.

I hurried to her side.

She looked like a beautiful sleeping princess, waiting to be woken by a handsome prince.

I would have to do for now.

"Angela?" I said. "Angela, it's me. Ben. Can you hear me?"

ENTRY THIRTY-THREE

"Angela, can you hear me?"

Nothing.

Angela didn't respond to my voice.

"Angela, can you hear me?"

There was a slight fluttering of her eyelids. I wasn't sure if she had reacted to my question or if it was an involuntarily facial tic. I didn't want to get my hopes up – but there was an increase in the speed of her heart on the monitor. Yes. She had heard me.

To prevent her escape, the Pure Bloods had fastened her wrists with handcuffs to a metal rail on the sides of the bed. They looked like strong cuffs. I'd need the key or a good hacksaw. I was trying to see if I could slip her wrists loose when I heard someone coming into the room. I stopped what I was doing just in time. I pretended I was examining her chart as a curly-haired nurse entered carrying a bag of saline. It was an awkward moment for me. A split-second earlier, when I had touched Angela's arm, her eyes had fluttered open and she had seen me. She had recognised me despite my newly shaved head – but she didn't give the game away by saying my name. Not in front of the Pure Blood nurse. Angela understood the situation and let me know by smiling just for me. Then she closed her eyes and acted unconscious again just as the nurse crossed the room to swap an empty bag for the new one. The nurse glanced at the monitors, then at me. "Uh – we need some help in 207. The patient pulled out his stitches trying to free himself. You done in here, Doctor?"

No – I wasn't done. I had to free Angela.

"Yes," I had to say. "Lead the way."

The nurse hurried out and I followed her – but not before

leaning over Angela and whispering in her ear.

"I'll get you out of here," I said.

She nodded. A tear ran down her face as I left the room.

The situation in room 207 was crazy. The patient – a professional bodybuilder by the looks of his massive muscular body – had ripped the stitches over his stomach, spilling blood on his bed and the floor. He was screaming in pain as he bled out. The guard had left his station to follow us into the room, but he stopped at the doorway, disgusted by the blood.

"What an idiot," the guard said. "Will this take long, Doc? I want some coffee."

The guard was talking to me. What did I know? I had to sound authoritative. "Help me stop him thrashing around. Hold him down so I can re-stitch his wound." Yes – I really said that like I knew what I was doing. The guard obeyed me. He struggled to hold down the patient as I asked the nurse to get me the equipment. It felt surreal as I put on gloves and sewed up the wound with the nurse's help. She was frowning at the job I was doing – but I got the blood to stop flowing. The patient's blood pressure was very low when I had finished – but he was stable.

I felt triumphantly like George Clooney saving a life in ER when I tossed my bloodied gloves in the disposal bin.

"Can I get that coffee now?" the guard said.

"Sure," I said. My hands were shaking.

The nurse was staring at me. "Can I have a word, Doctor?"

"Yes," I said. "What is it?"

She waited until the guard was gone before speaking in a low voice. She tapped her fingers on my ID. "You're not Doctor Blake. I know him. Who the hell are you?"

The fact that she had not alerted the guard was something. I had my gun – but I didn't want to start shooting people. "My name's

Ben. I'm a friend of the girl in 204. I just wanted to see if she's all right. I don't want her to get injected with the necrovitalis virus. You know it will probably kill her. I came to rescue her."

The truth shocked her – but she didn't shout for the guard. "What are you doing with Blake's ID? Did you kill him to get it?"

"No, I borrowed it. He'll probably be missing it soon, though."

She looked relieved. "I don't believe this. You are either insane or incredibly brave. What's your rescue plan?"

"First, I need to get my friend out of here. Will you help me?"

She looked around nervously. "I suppose I'll have to. I hate what we do here. I save lives just to have most of my patients die when *they* inject them. Are you 'pure'?" She said 'pure' like it was a dirty word. I liked her for that.

I read her name on her ID. It was Tamsin. I felt I could trust her. "No, I'm not a Pure Blood, Tamsin. My friends were taken by them so I sneaked into Oxford to save them. I don't want them being turned into zombies."

Tamsin nodded in understanding. "Say you do get your friend out of the hospital, how do you intend to escape Oxford?"

"Truthfully? I haven't worked that out yet, but I will."

"I hate being a Pure Blood. I'll help you – but you can't leave me here. They'd kill me. I want to come with you."

I nodded. "Okay. Will you meet me somewhere so we can talk about a plan?"

"I have a break at two. I'll meet you then. The cafeteria okay?"

"Yes."

"Hey - you'd better return Blake's ID before he notices it's missing."

"I will," I said. "Tamsin, I owe you."

"Just get us all out of here," she said.

ENTRY THIRTY-FOUR

I returned to the cafeteria and slipped the ID back onto the real Dr Blake's white coat. Luckily he had not noticed it was missing. I had thirty minutes to wait for Tamsin so I joined the queue for lunch and selected some dishes from the self-service counters. My tray was laden with free food when I chose a discreet table for my rendezvous with Tamsin, the nurse from E4. As I filled my stomach with hot chicken pie and chips, I worried Tamsin would change her mind and betray me to the Pure Bloods. I was hugely relieved when she sat down at my table. She stared at the mountain of desserts on my tray.

"Sweet tooth?"

"Just taking advantage of the situation," I said. "Don't know when I'll have time for another meal like this. Got to fill myself up now. Thanks for showing up."

"Ben, I've been thinking."

Uh-oh. No good conversation started with those words. In my past life as a selfish banker, they had usually been followed by "we need to break up" or "I want a ring on my finger" - words that had equally disturbed me. "Thinking about what?"

"The patients in E4. We have to help them all – not just your friend Angela. Every single one of my patients must be saved. It'd be wrong to leave anyone behind to be turned into a zombie. You agree, don't you?"

I had been so blinded by thoughts of rescuing Angela that I had not given the other patients a second thought. "You're right. We should save them all – but getting a whole ward of ill people out of Oxford is a far bigger challenge. We'd need transportation, lots of it. I haven't planned for that."

"I'm not leaving them behind. It's all of them – or forget it."

"Okay," I said. "We'll get them all out. How many are we talking, anyway?"

"There are twenty-six patients in E4."

"How many would be able to walk?"

"About half, I think."

"And the rest?"

Tamsin shook her head. "The others are too weak from their operations. They would have to be moved in wheelchairs or on gurneys."

"I suppose the ones capable of walking could move the others if they were dressed up as doctors. I'd need clothes for them all. I suppose I can get them from the laundry - but we'd still need to get off their handcuffs. Who keeps the keys?"

"Whoever's in charge of the ward's security on the shift," she said. "It's always a Pure Blood loyalist. One of the guards keeps the keys on him at all times. He would never give them up voluntarily."

"He won't need to," I said. "I have a gun."

"He has one, too."

"I'll shoot first."

"Wait. I don't want you to *kill* him. I … I could drug him. Slip something into his coffee when it's time to escape. I can get something to knock him out for hours."

"Sounds good."

We discussed how we could get the patients out of the hospital without them being caught. There were several unguarded exits through the abandoned wards. We'd have to move everyone quickly, though, because guards would eventually find out about the missing people. Once we started the plan, there would be no turning back. Tamsin drew a map of the hospital and explained the shift patterns. It was best to get everyone out after dark between ten and four – but there was no point in doing that if everyone got caught inside the base. "Okay, we've got a plan for the initial escape from the hospital. We'll need some trucks to transport people."

"I can't help with that," Tamsin said.

"I'll figure it out," I said. "It might take a day or two. I'll contact you with the details after arranging things. Where do you go when you're not on duty?"

"I live in a flat with some of my colleagues." She told me the address and I memorised it. "You can visit me there. I'll just say your my boyfriend if anyone sees us together."

"I need another ID so I can walk around the town. Got any ideas where I can get one nobody will notice is missing?"

Tamsin frowned – but then she grinned. "Yeah. I do! We have some badly injured soldiers on Ward A6. They came in wearing their uniforms. Their IDs will still be in their rooms. I could probably steal an ID from one of them. It won't be missed for a week."

Tamsin was a godsend. She had another ID for me ten minutes later, belonging to a Pure Blood major called Steve Kerrigan.

"This guy isn't going to wake up and notice his ID's gone, is he?"

"Unlikely. He's got a serious head injury. He won't be recovered for at least a week. That ID will get you into any building up to Level 3 security. Ben, use it cautiously. Don't let them catch you. Do you know about the zombie pit?"

"Yeah," I said. "I heard what they do. They lower people into it as a punishment. Nasty."

"Hearing about it is one thing. Seeing someone being fed alive to a hungry horde of zombies is another. Kill yourself before you let them do that to you."

"I'll be careful," I said. "You be careful too."

ENTRY THIRTY-FIVE

I left the hospital as Pure Blood Major Steven Kerrigan, at least according to my stolen ID. I used his pass to scout around Oxford, looking for weak points in their defences, paying particular attention to the prison compound where I hoped to find Neal. The compound consisted of a high barbed-wire fence surrounding a college building and the grounds around it. Over a hundred people were locked up in steel cages on the grounds. They were guarded by Pure Bloods. The prisoners were crowded like chickens inside the cages – at least twenty people in each cage. Everyone looked miserable and frightened. I couldn't see Neal. He could have been taken for 'processing' - which involved the Pure Bloods deliberately infecting prisoners with the necrovitalis virus as a test of purity. A lottery of life and death. None of them deserved that fate. I couldn't leave any of them behind. I had to rescue them all – but how? It would be difficult. There was a gate leading into the compound. You needed to have the right security pass. You also needed to be expected by the guards. They would not let 'Major Steve Kerrigan' enter without asking some tough questions – so I loitered near the perimeter fence and waited for the right time to catch the attention of a prisoner inside the nearest cage.

The man was bearded and dressed like a roadie for Metallica. He stood beside two scrawny kids and a sunken-eyed woman. They were staying close to each other like a family. I beckoned to him, putting my finger to my lips to tell him to stay quiet. The man shuffled over to find out what I wanted. He was about ten feet away from me when I spoke in a whisper.

"Here," I said. "Take this."

I tossed a ham-and-cheese sandwich through the bars. I'd

intended to snack on it later – but the man and his family needed it more. He caught it and broke the sandwich into three pieces, giving the parts to the kids and the woman, taking none for himself.

"Thanks," he said. "Got another, pal?"

I did. I tossed it to him. He shared it again with his family. This time he did eat a quarter of it himself. "Hmm. Good. Haven't eaten anything nice for weeks. Got more?"

"No – sorry."

"You've got to help us. These people are treating us like we're animals. Please tell me you're not with them."

"I'm not," I said. "So keep your voice down. If they hear us talking -"

"Right, right." He lowered his voice, pressing his face between the bars. "This is a nightmare. Last week we were living in the woods and starving because we ran out of canned dog food. We thought we'd die out there. That's why we came here. Looking for help. But they just locked us up and things got worse. They keep telling us they're going to process us in a few days – but they don't tell us what that means. Some people think they intend to *eat* us like they did in that Charlton Heston movie with the green food. Hey – that's not why you've fed us, is it? Fattening us up for eating?"

"No. The good news is the Pure Bloods aren't cannibals."

"I suppose that's good news. Will you please tell me what's going on?"

"Yes – but keep quiet. I don't want *them* noticing us talking." The guards were walking on the other side of the grounds – but they would return. "I want to help you get out of there – but I need some information first. I'm looking for someone. A friend. His name's Neal. He's tall, in his sixties, with silver hair, probably wearing a brown jacket and tweed trousers. Seen him?"

"Yeah, I saw him. He was here in another cage. They took him out with some others yesterday before they refilled the cage with new people. They put your friend in the big old building behind us. I haven't seen him since then. What do they mean by 'processing', anyway? What are they doing to people here?"

He was probably better off remaining ignorant – but I didn't want to lie. "They test you to see if you're immune to the zombie virus by injecting you with infected blood."

"That's mental. What happens if we're not immune?"

"They kill you."

"Jeez! You have to get us out!" He mouthed the next sentence. *"Please don't let them kill my wife and kids."*

"*I won't*," I mouthed back. "What's your name?"

"Terry."

"Terry, I'm Ben. I'm going to get you out – but I can't do it unless you're ready to go when I come back. You'll have to tell everyone here what happens to them if they're processed. Make them understand most of them will die. You'll all have to be ready when I have a plan worked out. I need information about the security. Do they keep you locked in the cages at night?"

"Yes – night and day. Don't even give us blankets if it's cold. I thought the ones getting processed were the lucky ones. You've got to save us before that happens. How many people are with you?"

"You're better off not knowing," I said.

A guard was coming over.

"I've got to go," I said. "But I'll be back. I swear it."

Terry's gripped the bars tightly. "Swear you'll come back. Don't let us die."

I moved away before I was noticed.

Neal was inside the processing area.

I knew what that meant.

He was probably dead already.

Or, worse, a zombie.

I was too late to save him.

But I could try to save Terry and his family and everyone else.

*

Oxford was a dangerous place for me, but I liked one thing about it under the control of the Pure Bloods. Because they were always prepared for fighting, there was no shortage of weapons and tools easily available for my thieving hands. That afternoon I nicked a new-looking crossbow from a barracks and loaded a holdall with breaking-and-entering tools including a bolt cutter.

Luckily, nobody questioned me as I collected everything necessary for the plan formulating in my head. Any guards catching me in places where I should not have been noticed my rank and assumed I was carrying out my duties. I was fortunate nobody realised I wasn't the real Steve Kerrigan.

During my scouting, I noticed the Pure Bloods parked a large number of their vehicles in one supermarket car park to the east of the colleges. The supermarket had its own petrol station, which the Pure Bloods kept operational by filling the storage tanks from petrol tankers loaded with fuel from a depot somewhere else. I counted six huge petrol tankers parked side-by-side, all full of petrol waiting to be emptied. That meant a load of highly flammable fuel was all in one place like a massive unexploded bomb. I was happy to note the security wasn't tight around the tankers. In fact, no guards patrolled the car park. It was a vulnerability waiting to be exploited. If I could move one of those tankers nearer to the helicopter's landing zone and explode the fuel, it would take out the helicopter, solving that little problem. How I would achieve a prison break wasn't crystal clear yet. I would have to discuss ideas with Maggie since she knew the base better than I did.

Another surprising security vulnerability was at the main security checkpoint where you'd think security would be tightest. The soldiers routinely stopped and searched vehicles coming in – but ones *leaving* were lazily waved through the checkpoint without anyone bothering to look inside. They were just assumed to be empty. A stolen lorry filled with rescued people would not be searched on its way out. That was great news. I could get everyone on E4 into the back of just one lorry with room to spare. I'd probably need one or two other vehicles for the prisoners – but a convoy of lorries could drive straight out of the base in a few minutes. If I timed it so we were escaping as the petrol tanker went boom, the Pure Blood would never catch us and they'd suffer a huge setback to their evil plans for world domination or whatever they intended. My escape plan would take some organising with Maggie and Tamsin – but I felt confident it could work with some luck.

I carried my stolen gear back to the library for my pre-arranged rendezvous with Maggie. Maggie was already waiting for me. "Did you find your friends, Ben?"

"I found Angela in the hospital," I said. "And I know where they're keeping Neal. He's in the internment camp. He's being 'processed' right now."

"Then he's as good as dead already," Maggie said. "Forget him."

Maggie was quite a diplomat. I didn't let her attitude bother me.

"There is some good news," I said. "I met a nurse willing to help us break out some patients locked up in the same ward as Angela. They will die if we don't get them out of here – so they have to be rescued. We also have to save all the people in the internment camp. I contacted one and promised to rescue them. We have to move fast. I figure we should break them out tonight, while there's still a chance to save Neal."

"Jeez. He's just one man. We're not here to save individuals. We're fighting the Pure Bloods."

"Maggie, you're here to save your sister Vicki."

"Yes – but not at the expense of the mission, which is to destroy the Pure Blood's helicopter and their general ability to attack The Family. I've done some serious recon. I can't see a way to destroy the helicopter without it becoming a suicide mission. Not just the two of us."

"Don't worry. I've an idea about that. It'll be risky – but if it works out we'll save hundreds of lives and destroy the helicopter and leave the Pure Bloods wishing they'd never been born."

I could see Maggie was sceptical – but I told her my plan to use the petrol tankers as weapons.

Maggie shook her head, laughing. "Using the petrol tankers as bombs … that's genius."

Wow. A compliment from Maggie? I felt like I'd won an Olympic gold medal.

"We should also be able to move a few empty lorries tonight without anyone noticing. I'll take one and park it behind the hospital. You take another to near the prison. I'll have the patients sneak out of the hospital into the back of the lorry. Then we'll break out the prisoners and get them into the other vehicles. Then we'll move a tanker and set it to explode after we've driven the lorries out of here through the main gates, leaving behind total chaos. What do you think?"

Maggie pulled an ugly face typical of a passport photo – but then she nodded. "It's workable. With more *planning*. I think it's best if we move the lorries during the day when it is less suspicious. After dark, I'll get my sister and bring her back to my lorry while you get the people out of the hospital. Then -"

"Just a second. Your sister's loyal to the Pure Bloods. What makes you think she'll come with you willingly?"

"My sister would never turn me into them because she knows they'd kill me. She'll have to come with me."

"You told me to forget about Neal because he's just one man – but you could jeopardise the mission by trusting your sister, *who definitely can't be trusted*. She doesn't know me. I could knock her out and -"

"No. Look, I know what I'm doing. I'm not stupid. I'm not going to trust my sister. I'll bring Vicki back bound and gagged if necessary – but she's leaving with me. Once I have her safe, I'll contact you on the radio for the final stage. We'll break into the prison together, free the prisoners, then escape before the petrol tankers go boom-boom-boom."

We worked out the details of the prison break, then we made our way to the car park for the theft of the lorries. I found an empty lorry with a full tank of petrol and moved it behind the hospital, parking it discreetly where nobody would look at it twice. Maggie contacted me via radio when she had her lorry in position on a street near the prison.

"Stage two," she said. "Good luck, Ben."

"You, too."

I visited Tamsin's flat and informed her we had to do everything that night. Tamsin looked scared – but she was ready. We were leaving her flat together when something happened.

Our luck ran out.

I'd just stepped outside when a dozen soldiers dashed around the corner of Tamsin's building. They were armed and running towards me. What had happened? Had someone spotted me acting suspiciously? Had Tamsin betrayed me? I looked at her. She looked as surprised as I was. We were caught in the street with no chance of escaping. I didn't even have time to take out my gun and shoot myself to avoid capture because they were already too close. It was over. They rushed at me.

And they ran straight around me on their way somewhere else.

What just happened?

I turned around and watched them running down the street, where they were joined by another group of soldiers, also running. They all jogged down the road, joining a larger mob of soldiers.

More soldiers were joining them from other buildings, heading in the same direction. A young soldier, half-dressed and pulling on a jacket, almost collided with me.

"Sorry, sir!" he said.

"What's going on?"

The breathless soldier stopped to answer me – but he looked excited and eager to run on. "Sir, an intruder's in sector four. A woman. We've got her surrounded – but she's got a rifle. I'm supposed to join my squad, sir. The Colonel ordered us to prevent her escape, sir. I must go, sir. My orders -"

"Go," I said.

The soldier ran off.

I swore to myself.

I heard the crack of a gunshot echoing off the walls of the ancient colleges. That made the civilians run indoors.

The banshee wail of a siren started.

"ARMED INTRUDER IN SECTOR 4! CLEAR THE AREA! CIVILIANS RETURN TO YOUR HOMES IMMEDIATELY!"

"I have to save her," I said, but Tamsin grabbed my arm.

"What can you do? There are hundreds of soldiers. You have to get back inside my flat."

"No. Maggie needs my help."

"Ben, it's a curfew. They'll check your ID if they catch you on the street. We have to get inside. Hurry."

I returned to Tamsin's flat, where I looked out at the street as it cleared of non-military members of the Pure Bloods. The siren continued wailing for five minutes as I heard gunfire in the distance. Then the gunfire stopped and the siren was switched off. Another message came over the Tannoy system.

"INTRUDER CAPTURED! All trained medical staff must report to their stations. Wounded soldiers require medical treatment."

"I've got to go," Tamsin said. "Stay here. I'll come back when it's safe. I'll find out what's going on."

I stayed in her flat for an hour. The sun was going down when Tamsin returned. It was strange seeing electricity-powered lights coming on to illuminate the darkness. Oxford was lit by spotlights and streetlights that made the city look beautiful. The presence of soldiers ruined the view. Tamsin locked the door behind her.

"Your friend injured a few soldiers. But they stunned her and caught her. I heard her own sister betrayed her. She's been hailed as a hero for alerting the guards."

"Hell. I warned her," I said. I wished Maggie had listened to me. "Where's Maggie now?"

"You won't want to hear this. They've taken your friend to the zombie pit."

"Is she dead?"

"Not yet," Tamsin said. "At the moment she's suspended over the pit so the zombies can get hungry. They'll slowly lower her into the pit at dawn tomorrow with a big crowd watching."

"That's sick."

"It's what passes for entertainment among the hardcore Pures. They love to watch people being eaten alive. The good news – if you can think of it as good news – is they think she came back alone to save her sister – so they aren't looking for you."

I supposed that was good news – but not for Maggie. The Pure Bloods would feed her to the zombies if I didn't do something to save her – but saving her would make it harder to rescue Angela, Neal and the others, like Terry and his family.

ENTRY THIRTY-SIX

I had to save Maggie from the zombie pit – even if that meant killing her myself to save her the pain and suffering of being eaten alive. I didn't want it to come to that – so I scouted out the area in my Pure Blood disguise. The zombie pit was in the quad of an Oxford college, where Maggie was suspended by her hands over the pit on a rope attached to a crane. Her legs were just above the heads of the zombies, which meant they could reach up and grab hold of her feet if she didn't kick them away. They were hungry for her flesh. She was like a pendulum swinging over the undead. Their moans were an unholy chorus every time Maggie swung over their outstretched arms.

The only way of getting Maggie down required taking control of the crane. There was nobody in the cab – but a dozen soldiers guarded the quad, keeping a group of civilians away from the zombie pit's edge. The civilians had gathered to watch Maggie's punishment like ghouls at a public execution.

Rescuing Maggie required taking care of the guards and civilians long enough to get access to the crane. I got an idea about what would move them – a crazy idea born of desperation that I told Tamsin.

"That's insane," she said in response.

It was a natural reaction to what I had said.

"Do you have a better idea?"

"No – but how will you make it work?"

"I'll need you to get something from the hospital."

"What?"

"Body parts," I said. "Lots of fresh, juicy body parts."

ENTRY THIRTY-SEVEN

Tamsin met me at a side entrance to the hospital, holding a large plastic bag of human body parts meant to be destroyed in the incinerator. "You're really going to use these, Ben?"

"Uh-huh. I'll see you later."

"Good luck," she said, going back inside. It was her job to rescue the patients, including Angela, locked in E4, while I saved the prisoners and rescued Maggie. My plan was insane – but I had little choice under the dire circumstances.

I put the bag into a larger sports bag, which I carried across Oxford hoping no patrols would stop me. I got to my destination without any trouble, probably with the help of my stolen Pure Blood uniform, ranking me as a major. There was an area on the perimeter of the camp where no guards were watching because there was no real need. There was a trench filled with zombies around Oxford, a sort of defensive moat against attack by other living humans. The zombies couldn't get out of it because the walls were high and covered with spikes – but I'd already collected some long planks of wood, taken from the floor of an abandoned building. I lowered them into the trench, making a six-foot-wide ramp for the undead. They were too dumb to use it without a little bit of encouragement, though. That was why I had the bag of fresh human organs. I laid a trail of fresh meat from the ramp down the street leading in the direction of the zombie pit. As soon as the zombies smelled the blood, they swarmed towards the ramp and began crawling their way out of the trench. There would soon be a hundred or more zombies inside the base. I figured it would take them thirty minutes before they were noticed by the guards. By then I intended to be working on the second part of my insane plan – breaking out the prisoners.

ENTRY THIRTY-EIGHT

Aware that every second saved mattered if my escape plan was to work, I sneaked up to the barbed-wire fence around the prison compound. Daylight was waning. Long shadows hid me from view as I cut through the wire and made a flap big enough to crawl through. I waited until one guard passed my position – then moved quickly, slipping under the wire into the compound. I came up behind the guard with a sap consisting of a sock filled with coins, knocking him out with one hard blow. As he fell down, I saw some people in the nearest cage watching me wide-eyed. I dragged him over to the cage, stripping him of his uniform while everyone inside watched. They included Terry and his family.

"You came back," Terry said. "How are you going to get us out?"

"I have a plan. Put these on," I said, passing him the guard's clothes.

The unconscious soldier was out of sight from the armed guards on the roof – but I could not leave him there for long. Other guards were still roaming the compound. I had hoped the first guard would have possessed keys to the cages – but he didn't. It was a good job I had some bolt cutters. I snapped the lock while Terry dressed. I opened the cage. "Terry, you'll have to act as a guard and help me take out the other guards without the ones on the roof noticing. Everyone else will have to stay in the cage for the moment so the guards don't spot anything amiss."

Terry and I ambushed each guard and replaced them with our freed people right under the noses of the other guards. It took about five minutes. We were just in time because then the electric lights were switched on, lighting up the whole area in stark light. Luckily, the guards on the roof had no idea we had taken over the outside of the prison. Everything looked normal to them. I told the prisoners how to escape through the fence when the time was right. Next, I gave Terry the key to the lorry parked down the street. So far, my plan was working perfectly, but before they could leave the prison compound, someone would have to go into the college to deal with the Pure Bloods on the roof. Several people volunteered to go with me, all glad to help out. Terry and other ex-prisoners wearing Pure Blood uniforms would pretend to guard the cages while I led my volunteers into the college. We knew we had to be careful. We had replaced the guards at the entrance – but there were more enemy soldiers inside who would offer resistance.

I'd already learnt the college's layout from reading an old student guide to Oxford – but it didn't tell me what changes the Pure Bloods had made to the interior while turning the building into a processing centre. Somewhere inside Neal and dozens of prisoners were being held against their will. I wanted to find Neal – but taking out the roof guards was my priority. In my major's uniform, I went ahead of the escapees, heading up a staircase to the first floor. I encountered a Pure Blood who wasn't expecting any trouble. I strode up to him and knocked him out before he knew what had happened. He was tied up and gagged while I continued up to the next floor. We had the roof under our control in a couple of minutes. (Two Pure Bloods died in the attack – but there were no other casualties.) Securing control of the rest of the building didn't take long because the Pure Bloods were unprepared for a prison revolt. We had control over the whole compound in twenty minutes. No alarms were triggered – which was a miracle. After the building was secure, I entered a large lecture room turned into a processing centre filled with eighty steel cages. Each cage contained one person deliberately infected with the necrovitalis virus.

It was obvious ten had already turned into zombies and several were very sick and dying – but over two-thirds were currently asymptomatic. Some had not been injected with the virus yet – which was great news. They begged us to free them. One ex-prisoner had found the keys on a guard. His name was Slater. He wasted no time unlocking the cages holding the uninjected – but he left the sick in their cages.

"Hey," I said. "We're not leaving anyone behind."

"They're turning into zombies," he said. "It's too late to save them."

"Maybe, but we're not leaving them here to be experimented on. Let them all out except the ones that have already turned."

"No way. They'll kill us."

"Listen to me. We're surrounded by enemy soldiers. We need every person we can to fight our way out of this place. Would *you* want to be left behind?"

Slater shook his head – but he didn't open the cages. He tossed them at my chest. "You unlock them if you like, but don't complain to me when they turn against us."

I unlocked the cages, freeing over forty prisoners.

My friend Neal was among them. He grinned when he saw me. "Is this a prison break?"

"Yeah. You okay?"

"I've had better days. The Pure Bloods don't exactly run a five-star hotel. Are they all dead?"

"No. We have control over the prison – but the rest of Oxford is still under their control. Neal, tell me something. Did they inject you yet?"

"Yeah. Couple of days ago."

"Damn. Any symptoms?"

"I'm okay for now," he said. "What about Angela? Did they

keep their word and treat her injuries?"

"They did. Sort of. They treated her – but they intend to inject her with the virus when she is recovered. They only wanted her healthy so they could process her."

"They are insane," Neal said. "Where is she now?"

"A friend's rescuing her from their hospital. I've made a plan to get us out of here – but things are going to get messy and bloody. We have to destroy their ability to come after us – which means blowing up a helicopter and a whole load of petrol. There's also a woman called Maggie I have to save from a zombie pit – so I released some zombies to cause a distraction. It will be like in the town when I opened the garage – but about a hundred times worse because we'll be fighting humans too. Are you fit enough to put on a Pure Blood uniform and act like one of them?"

"You bet," Neal said. "Let's do it. Let's rescue Angela and burn this place down."

ENTRY THIRTY-NINE

Zombies love fresh meat from living victims – but they will stop eating once their victims are dead. Nobody knows why that is – but some people think it is because the transforming necrovitalis virus in dead tissue makes the victim's flesh unpalatable. I don't know if that's true – I can't imagine zombies caring about the flavour of their food - but I do know zombies will not eat their own kind. I wish they would. They are picky eaters. Luckily for me, I knew they would enjoy the human leftovers that I'd put out for them to snack on while I was busy freeing everyone from the prison. When I came out of the prison with Neal and a group of escapees – all disguised as Pure Blood soldiers – I was thrilled to see hundreds of zombies had taken the bait, forming a shuffling crowd exactly where I had wanted.

"You did that?" Neal said. "Are you mental?"

"A necessary distraction," I said. "The Pure Bloods are bound to notice them soon once they spread out looking for more fresh meat. I'm surprised they haven't spotted them already, to be honest."

We were heading for the zombie pit when I heard the first gunshot. It was followed by a high-pitched whistle and shouting and more gunshots and a screaming siren. A voice boomed over the Tannoy system across Oxford.

"Zombie incursion in sector three! This is not a drill. Zombie incursion in sector three! Alpha unit engage enemy -"

While the Pure Bloods responded to my distraction, my group raced to the zombie pit. Maggie was hanging over the pit, mercifully alive, struggling to keep her feet from being bitten by the hungry zombies moaning and groaning like rock fans in a mosh pit. Civilian gawkers and Pure Blood soldiers saw us arrive. A captain was in charge. That was good news for me. In my stolen major's uniform, I outranked him. I strode up to the captain and dead-eyed him.

"The Colonel gave out new orders for the woman. I will take her for interrogation. You are required at the incursion point. The barricades need repositioning immediately in sector three."

The captain hesitated. "I haven't received new orders, sir."

"You're getting them from me, *Captain*. You are needed to protect the base from the zombie threat. Do it – before it's too late."

My glare was frosty. The Pure Blood nodded to his soldiers. They raced off, leaving my people with the civilians. I had to move them on too. "Everyone must clear the area! We've got zombies attacking. Return to your homes and barricade yourselves in."

The civilians scattered. I grinned at Neal. "That was easier than expected."

"I'd hate to think what *you* expected," he said. "So … how do we get her down? Know how to operate a crane?"

"No – but I'll figure it out."

I climbed onto the crane and into the cab. I studied the controls and carefully moved a joystick to see what it would do. I accidentally lowered Maggie into the pit. She yelled at me as the zombies tried to bite her. I hastily reversed what I was doing. She moved upwards. After that little error, I got the hang of it quickly. I lifted Maggie higher, rotated the arm, then lowered Maggie to the safe ground where Neal cut her free. The zombies in the pit sounded furious I'd taken away their meal. They piled against the pit's walls, trying to climb out. Maggie muttered thanks and sagged against Neal, who held her.

"It's okay now," he said. "We've got you."

"My own sister betrayed me," she said. She sobbed briefly before getting her emotions under control. She faced me. "The mission?"

"It's still on," I said. "But I still have to rescue some people, like Angela. They're in the hospital."

"I'll come with you," Maggie said, but she could barely stand.

"No – go with these people. They'll get you to the lorry near the prison. They need you to get them to The Family."

The Family were the complete opposite of the Pure Bloods. They welcomed anyone. Not just the immune. Maggie could get everyone to them, even if Neal and I didn't make it. We said our goodbyes and wished each other luck.

Maggie gripped my hand firmly, shaking it. "Don't get killed, idiot. Who's taking care of the helicopter?"

"Me – once I've rescued Angela. I'll blow it up. That will be your cue to drive the lorry out of the main gates as fast as humanly possible."

We split up then. Neal stayed with me, while everyone else headed for the prison camp to meet up with the others. They'd move to the lorry when it was nearer the time to go. I hoped I'd see them again. The plan required my lorry to be ready to go at the same time. To add to the general chaos, distracting the Pure Bloods even more, I drove the crane over the edge of the zombie pit, jumping out of the cab just before it toppled. The crane crushed a dozen zombies – but it also provided a platform for the rest. They crawled over it like beetles. The strongest ones climbed over the others, gnashing their teeth at me. They were ravenous. They always were.

"That's right. Come and get me."

Neal rolled his eyes. "This area will be zombie hell in two minutes."

"I know. Let's go."

"You don't have to tell me twice."

Twenty zombies were crawling out as we fled the scene. More zombies, more chaos. The Pure Bloods were going to be busy that night. Hopefully too busy to notice two men sneaking their way to the hospital in another sector.

Things were going *post*-post-apocalyptic in a matter of minutes as the escaped zombies spread out and broke into buildings in search of food. Oxford's streets were packed with enemy soldiers fighting the dead.

"Incursion in Sector 4!"

"Zombies in Sector 2!"

"Aaaarhhhuhhh!"

Neal was jogging alongside me down a dark street. "Boy, you've really set a cat among the pigeons. Sounds like the zombies are eating a load of Pure Bloods. I hope we don't end up a zombie desserts."

We reached the back of the hospital, where I'd parked a lorry. Tamsin was supposed to bring everyone to it after drugging the staff on E4, but nobody was inside. Some troops appeared, running down the street in the direction of the zombie pit. They saw us so we just remained at the lorry, looking like we were doing something to fix a tyre. The men ignored us. They had serious fire-power – RPGs and assault rifles – which would make short work of the dead. It looked like they would soon have the situation under control. And then they would have the time to work out it was no accident that had released the zombies. As soon as they knew the living had been sabotaging their base, our advantage would be lost.

"Tamsin's late. I'm going in. Keep the lorry ready."

"Ben, I'm old – but I'm not useless. I'll do more good following you."

I'd wanted to keep him out of harm's way – but he was right. I'd need help moving the sick. "Okay. We're going through the back to get to Department E4. It's a pretty long way down some long corridors and staircases. You up for that?"

"Lead the way."

As we entered the hospital, a loud battle raged outside that slowly diminished in volume as we went deeper and deeper into the building. Neal was puffing and wheezing when we reached the final floor.

"You all right?"

"Didn't ... get much ... exercise in that cage. I'll be fine in a minute."

He didn't look fine. "Sure?"

"Don't worry about it. We've got to save Angela. Concentrate on that, not me."

We both wanted to see Angela again. And get her out of there.

I peered down the corridor. It was empty. A good sign. It was quiet. Far away, assault rifles fired short bursts, sounding like the crackle-pops of bubble wrap. I stepped into the corridor. "Stay here and cover me. Watch the lift and stairs, too."

"How many eyes do you think I have?" he joked. Then he went serious. "You can count on it, Ben. I've got your back. Hurry up. We don't have all night."

I sprinted down the corridor and stopped at the door of E4. It was locked. I had two options. Break it down or press the buzzer for someone to unlock it from the other side. Tamsin should have drugged the Pure Blood guards and medical staff – but what if she had failed? What if the guard was still there? Oh – what the hell! No time to worry. I pressed the buzzer and got my gun ready. If a guard opened the door, I'd shoot him in the head. Someone opened the door. It was a man – but it wasn't the guard. He was one of the patients I'd seen earlier.

"Don't shoot. I'm not one of them. Tamsin! He's here!"

I signalled to Neal that it was safe – then I stepped into the ward, where I saw over a dozen patients in the corridor and more emerging – with help – from the rooms. Tamsin was pushing a young girl in a wheelchair.

"Ben! I'm so sorry we're not ready. I drugged the guards – but it took longer than I expected to make them pass out."

There was a guard slumped behind a desk, drooling on a magazine. And another one on the floor in a pool of spilt coffee. There was also a nurse tied up with a bruised eye. She glared at me. A Pure Blood loyalist. I glared back.

"The lorry's outside," I told Tamsin. "We've got to go now."

"Help us get them out of their rooms, please."

Some of the patients were able to walk on their own – but others were in wheelchairs or lying on trolleys needing assistance. Tamsin had persuaded a couple of nurses opposed to the Pure Blood regime to help out – but the immobile outnumbered the mobile. We would have to move them in stages along the corridor and then to the exit. I estimated it would take twenty minutes. Maybe half an hour. A very long time in a hostile zone.

Angela appeared from her room, shuffling forward, grimacing with every step. It felt amazing to see her. We hugged. She grinned. "Hey, you. Sounds like you started a war out there. You didn't release more zombies, did you?"

"Just a few … hundred. These maniacs keep them in a trench like guard dogs. Seemed a waste not to use them against them. The zombies are on our side – sort of. They're biting Pure Bloods right now, giving them something else to fight. The zombies are hopefully taking chunks out of them."

"Good. I heard they taste like chicken."

She looked pale and unsteady.

I was concerned. "You well enough to walk yourself out of here?"

"My legs feel like jelly. I think I'll use a wheelchair – but I can move it myself. Can you see a spare?"

I found her a wheelchair in a supply room. She slumped into it as Neal entered the ward. Angela broke into a wide grin. "Neal! I'm so glad to see you again."

"Great to see you looking better," Neal said. It looked like there were tears in his eyes. "I'll push you down the corridor. We all have to get moving. No time for a proper reunion."

Everyone helped each other leave the ward and along the corridor past the lift. Nearly everybody was in the corridor when the lift started moving upwards. I had a bad feeling it would be filled with soldiers. "Neal! Someone is coming up!"

Neal and I aimed our guns at the doors. Two soldiers and a doctor were inside. We had them caught by surprise – but they stupidly went for their weapons. It gave me no choice. I shot one in the head and Neal killed the other one with two in the heart. The doctor cowered, raising his hands. I pointed my gun at him while Neal stripped the dead men of their weapons and equipment. He gave one gun to Angela and another to Tamsin.

Tamsin shook her head and gave it to someone else. "No thanks. I'm a nurse. I don't kill."

"You might have to," Neal said, visibly annoyed that she had given away his present. "What the hell. You'll learn or you'll die."

I waved to the frightened doctor to make him come out of the lift. Neal blocked the door with the dead bodies so the lift could not close. I feared someone would have heard the shot. We had to hurry.

The patient with the gun aimed it at the doctor. "Should we shoot him, too?"

"Don't!" the doctor said. "They forced me into working for them."

"He's a liar," a woman said. "His name is Frost. He joked with the guards. He knew they intended to inject us with the zombie virus. He's like a Nazi. We should execute him."

"You," I said to the doctor. "Help us or die. No tricks. No second chances. You do what I say and I promise not to kill you. Do you understand?"

"Yes, yes. Absolutely. Who are you people, anyway?"

"We're the good guys," I said. "You're on the wrong side, Doc."

"You killed those men," Dr Frost said. "You're killers."

"Am I going to have a problem with you?"

He stared at my gun and shook his head so hard his brown hair flopped over his eyes. "No. I'm not a soldier. I'll do what you want."

I whispered in Neal's ear. "Keep an eye on him."

"Will do. I'll shoot him if he tries anything."

As a precaution, Tamsin tied the doctor's hands together with bandages. Frost could still push a trolley – but it would stop him from misbehaving. I wasn't in the mood for trusting another man, not after Billy's betrayal and the trouble that caused.

The doctor pushed a girl down the corridor, and then helped another patient in a wheelchair. The group moved bit by bit.

We were soon all in another corridor in the deserted area that looked like a war zone. Behind me, I heard shouts from where we'd been. My heart thumped like I'd been punched in the chest. I knew someone had discovered the missing patients and the soldiers' bodies. Thirty seconds later, I heard voices and rapid footsteps. I'd taken the precaution of blocking the door behind us. Someone banged on it and cursed. A gunshot echoed in the gloom. The door flew open. Torches shone into the darkness. The stragglers in my group were visible to whoever was coming.

"They're escaping," said the master of the obvious down the corridor. "Stop there!"

Nobody listened.

"Shoot them!" someone ordered. It sounded like a woman. Was

it the nurse we'd tied up?

I wish I'd knocked her out.

Soldiers were taking up positions at the far end. They had assault rifles.

I took up a shooting position behind a broken vending machine while Tamsin continued the exodus with Neal leading the way.

The torchlight was obscuring my view of the enemy – but I saw at least four beams shining down the dark corridor as they moved after us from doorway to doorway. I fired several bursts of bullets set on semi-auto. My bullets struck at least one enemy, who went down yelling. They slammed into the walls and floor and ricocheted into the ceiling smashing lights and tiles, raining down plaster and cables. The soldiers scattered and dived into the rooms on their left or right. They returned fire from the doorways. Bullets hit the vending machine and burst cans inside it, spraying fizzy liquid like mini-geysers. My face was struck by flying metal. They were sneaking closer. I shot back a couple of times just to keep them at bay. The last of my group of stragglers got around the next corner while I kept shooting. I'd run out of ammo in no time. (I'd already reloaded twice in the gaps between shooting and hiding.) It was a miracle I was keeping the enemy back at all because they were blasting the hell out of the vending machine. I poked my gun around and fired blindly. That made some scream. For a second or two, the shooting stopped as the survivors dodged my bullets. Not even the Pure Bloods wanted a piece of lead in their bodies. The vending machine protecting me was starting to look like Swiss cheese. It was no longer in a good position – so I raced to the next corner. I was just in time. One soldier had tossed a grenade that bounced and rolled to five feet from my previous position. When it went off, the vending machine turned into scrap metal. One Tango can hit the wall near me so hard it left a fist-sized dent. I shot back on the run. I hit a man in the arm. More enemies – new arrivals - began spraying bullets and another grenade landed at my feet. I kicked it back and made a mad dash. The grenade exploded and I felt a hot ripple in the air like a wall hitting me. It tossed me several feet and I landed on my back. Pain shot up my spine. Luckily, the grenade's detonation brought down a whole section of the roof. Dust and bricks and burning metal blocked the corridor – preventing the enemy's pursuit. A man in a much worse state than me helped me to my feet. Thanking him, I hurried on and caught up with the others, who had reached a stairway leading down to the exit. Neal was checking the street was clear.

"I don't see anyone out there," he said. "I'll bring the lorry nearer."

He dashed out while everyone gathered at the exit.

Tamsin checked on the weakest with the help of the doctor.

Angela said something to me. I didn't hear it. "What?"

"You okay, Ben? Your left ear's bleeding."

I touched it. My finger came away wet and red. The explosion must have injured me. Burst my ear drum. I hadn't felt it in all of the chaos. I couldn't hear out of it – but my other ear seemed fine, though I was hearing a high whine like a train whistle. "I'm okay. Can you hear the lorry?"

"Yeah. It's coming."

I looked out and saw Neal had parked the rear just outside. The patients would not have far to move. Neal opened the doors for them. There was enough room inside for everyone as long as they didn't move around. The healthiest patients helped the sickest in the back first without anyone giving them instructions. Neal and I kept watch. For five minutes I expected the enemy to appear – but they didn't. It was a long way around the hospital if you couldn't take a shortcut. I was pleased to see the doctor helping out, speeding up the process. Angela climbed into the back and helped the last few up.

The doctor looked at me as the last person boarded.

"You know I'm dead if I stay here," he said. "They'll think I'm a traitor and put me in the zombie pit. Please let me come. I can treat people on the way to wherever you're going."

Neal had heard what he'd said and looked furious. "No. We can't trust you. You turn innocent people into zombies. You're a monster like the colonel in charge. You're all 'just obeying orders' - but that's not an excuse for injecting people with something that kills."

"I've never harmed anyone. I swear it. Before Day One, I was a neurosurgeon, saving lives and doing good. I swear on my life I will help these people if you let me come."

"Neal," I said. "It's your decision."

"Get in," Neal growled. "Before I change my mind."

"Thank you! You won't regret it, I promise!" The doctor hopped up into the lorry. I closed the doors behind him, taking one last look at Angela, who was already tending to someone sicker. She waved at me as the doors closed.

Neal and I hurried into the driver's cab. I took the wheel and started the engine. "We'd better move this thing before we get a parking ticket. I heard they give you a big penalty around here."

I drove away, catching sight of some soldiers in my mirrors just as I turned down the next street. Great. They were looking for us. They had not seen the lorry, though. I hoped they would think we were still in the hospital somewhere. I stopped two streets away. "Neal, I've got to blow up their helicopter if anyone is to get away. You'll have to drive this out of the gates without me."

"That's a suicide mission, Ben."

"It's a suicide mission for us all if I don't. You won't get a mile away if they send the helicopter after you."

"It doesn't have to be you, Ben. Let me do it."

"No. I didn't rescue you to let you die. And don't think you can sucker-punch me a second time. I'm doing it."

"Ben, I was injected with the zombie virus. I'm sicker than I told you. I can feel it inside me, turning me. I'm already dying. At least let me go out in style, saving you and Angela and all of the others. I want this. Let me blow the helicopter to kingdom come."

"There's a chance you're wrong, Neal. You don't know for sure you will die. I can't let you volunteer. It's my job."

Neal lifted his shirt and showed me his bare chest. The skin was a pale blue with streaks of green and grey like a mouldy cheese. "This look like I've got a chance? It's spreading. I'll be a zombie by the morning. There's nothing that can stop it. But I can do something now. Something to save lives."

There was nothing I could do for him — except give him what he wanted. "I'm so sorry, Neal. I wish I had got here faster."

"You got here in time to save Angela. I was a dead man when I made the deal with them. I knew that. My fate was sealed then. If you let me blow up the helicopter, I won't be wasting my final hours turning into a zombie. I'll be helping you."

"Okay." I told him where to find the petrol tankers as I drove on. "I'll drop you off a few streets away."

There were soldiers on the streets, but they were too busy setting up barricades to care about a lorry passing them. Since we were dressed like them, anyone seeing us assumed we had also been given orders to take the lorry somewhere. In the heat of a battle, nobody knew what was going on, as orders and counter-orders caused confusion, which was the perfect cover for escaping. I stopped again. Neal jumped out. There were no zombies or troops nearby. Neal slammed the door and stepped back. "Well, I won't be seeing you again, Neal. So, I guess this is my final goodbye."

"Good luck," I said.

"Get everyone out of this zombie hell," he said. "Go!"

I put my foot down on the accelerator and got the lorry moving. Neal was gone when I looked in my mirror. I wished him luck again. He needed it.

Turning a corner, I smashed into a naked male zombie eating a soldier's face off. They crunched under the wheels, blood and brains spattering my windscreen. More zombies slammed into my vehicle as I flicked on the wipers and clear a window to see through. Looking through the blood smears, I saw a group of the dead chasing a soldier with a jammed weapon. The soldier was backed against the wall of a building, desperately trying to shoot. The zombies lumbered towards him. He had nowhere to escape. He saw me coming and shouted for me to help him. I could drive into the zombies and save him.

But I didn't.

I drove *around* them, leaving the Pure Blood to fend for himself. His eyes widened in disbelief as I drove by. The zombies attacked. Even with only one good ear, I heard his high screams as they bit him and tore him apart, pulling his steaming entrails from his body, chewing and biting, eating him alive.

I didn't let the grisly sight distract me. I had a new problem. I wanted to get my lorry across Oxford avoiding more zombies and soldiers – but it proved impossible. A spiked barricade was ahead, blocking my way. I was on the side with five soldiers on it, with the spikes pointing the other way. Fifty or more zombies were pushing into the barricade, some getting impaled, some pushing others into the spikes. The impaled zombies thrashed and moaned. The zombies behind them tried climbing over the speared ones. Some succeeded and launched themselves at the soldiers. The soldiers didn't panic, though. They were shooting the zombies in their heads. The soldiers were doing a good job of destroying them one by one.

Until I came along and drove straight at the barricade.

The soldiers didn't see me until I was almost upon them.

Driving at sixty.

They scattered, firing wildly. Bullets zinged past me. A few struck the lorry and I heard banging from inside, reminding me that I was not alone, that I had passengers. I had to be more careful with the safety of everyone aboard. I broke through the barricade, smashing it into pieces. A severed hand hit the windscreen, its fingers still moving. I ploughed through the zombie mob and left a trail of destruction in my wake.

I was nearing the point where I had let the dead into the city. The breach had expanded as more zombies climbed free of the trench. They had amassed into a formidable army, well beyond the number I had expected to see. It seemed as though they had swarmed to the smell of fresh meat in their thousands. I bet the Pure Bloods were regretting their zombie-filled trench now. They had completely filled the streets ahead. The Pure Bloods had erected a few barricades to stop them from getting further. Their soldiers were cutting them down in waves – but they kept coming. I turned away from the battle down another road. Something flew over my vehicle shining a spotlight down. The helicopter. It was up in the air, flying over my position. I felt sure the sniper would shoot at me – but then the helicopter raced off towards the breach. I was dismayed to see the sniper aboard shooting the zombies with ruthless efficiency – but I was pleased he had not targeted me. The helicopter was turning the tide of the battle.

I drove past the prison and spotted the other lorry. I pulled up alongside it. Maggie and Terry were in the front. I leaned out my window.

"Maggie, we've got to go now."

"I've just seen the helicopter! You said you were going to destroy it! That was the whole point of this mission!"

"It's busy fighting the zombies. We might make it if we go now. Is everyone in the lorry?"

"Yes – but the helicopter!"

"There's no more time, Maggie. The Pure Bloods are winning the battle. It's now or never. Follow me."

I drove towards the main gates. Maggie drove the second lorry behind mine. There was a barrier crossing the road. There were also some guards. They must have been told to stop anyone exiting because they raised their guns. I poked my rifle out my side window and sprayed them with bullets. They ran for cover. I crashed through the barrier and drove onto the road beyond. Maggie's lorry was right behind. Terry was firing at the enemy all the way out.

The road in front was dark – but behind me, everything suddenly lit up as a truly massive orange fireball erupted into the sky, followed by an ear-splitting boom that rocked my vehicle and almost made me crash.

Looking back, I saw Oxford on fire in several areas as multiple explosions sent roiling white, yellow and orange flames high over the city. The sky was burning with flying debris, including burning bodies of the living and the dead. The helicopter disappeared into a cloud of black smoke and burning petrol rising into the night sky. It appeared again with its tail burning and someone jumping out on fire, falling to a quick death. Another explosion shot something burning bright yellow at the helicopter. It looked like a barrel of oil. The burning object clipped the blades and knocked the helicopter sideways. Out of the pilot's control, the helicopter spiralled down into the thick smoke and exploded into the side of a college building, pieces of spinning broken blades flying over the river. All of the electricity suddenly went off, leaving just the fires lighting the burning streets.

Oxford was no longer the city of spires.

It was the city of fires.

Neal had done it.

He had saved everyone.

He had destroyed the Pure Blood base, turning it into a zombie-infested inferno.

We were free.

ENTRY FORTY

Any pleasure I might have taken at the destruction of Oxford's Pure Blood base was muted by the loss of Neal. I didn't know how I would break the news to Angela, who was unaware of what had happened because she was inside the back of the lorry I was driving, along with many other survivors. I had several miles to go before we got to our destination and I was keen to get there as fast as possible – before dawn if I could do it. Unfortunately, I had not travelled more than five miles on the dark road when the other lorry behind me flashed its lights and stopped. Wondering what was wrong, I pulled over too. I got out and yelled to Maggie, who had already gone to the back of her lorry with Terry. They had their guns out. I looked around nervously, wondering if they had been shot at by someone.

"Maggie, what's going on?"

"Just heard a gunshot inside my lorry!" she shouted back. "Terry, get around the other side. I'll open the door. You cover me."

Maggie took up a position at the rear opposite Terry. I ran to join them. I aimed my gun at the doors, hearing shouts and more shots from inside. There were infected people in there. Had one turned and started killing? Who was shooting? Maggie opened the door. I saw a man with a gun and a body on the floor. A lot of people were crying and trying to get away from the gunman. They jumped out and ran into the pitch-black field. The man was waving his gun in the air, terrifying everyone.

"Drop the gun!" Maggie ordered.

"I had to shoot her," the man said, looking dazed. It was Slater. I remembered he had wanted to leave the sick behind. "She was turning. I saved lives!"

Maggie spoke in a low, commanding voice. "I said *put it down*."

"Put what down?" Slater said, and then looked at the gun as though he had not realised it was in his hand. "Oh." He dropped it and started weeping. "I want to go home," he said, sounding like a little boy lost. "I'm so tired of this. We're always in danger from them. They kill us and kill us and kill us. When will it ever end?"

I looked at the dead body of a young woman with red hair like Angela. The victim's face was grey and mottled. She would have died soon and become one of the zombies. Slater had probably done the right thing – but he had panicked everyone doing it. At least ten people had fled into the darkness. Slater could have waited until the girl had died – by which time we might have made it to The Family's rendezvous point. Now we had lost people in the dark. I cursed Slater for creating a panic.

"COME BACK! IT'S ALL RIGHT! HE'S DISARMED!"

Three people returned. Six or seven did not.

An elderly woman was the relative of one of the missing people. She begged us to look for her eleven-year-old niece Julia.

Maggie sighed. "I'm sorry. We can't wait for them. We have to get going. We're not safe on this road, even with Oxford destroyed. Some Pure Bloods will have made it out. They'll be looking for revenge. Ben, what do you think?"

Reluctantly, I agreed. We couldn't chase the missing down in the dark. "We'd better get that body out of there and leave. But I'll have a quick look for them while your people do that."

I turned on my torch and set off into the field, calling out for anyone in hearing distance to come back. I found one scared teenage boy and persuaded him to go back to the lorry. I also saw another person – a man with black hair – but he ran away from me like I was going to shoot him. I didn't find Julia. I made my way back to the road. I told the elderly woman the bad news. "I'm sure The Family can send someone to look for her tomorrow when it's light. But we can't stay here now. We have to get everyone else to safety, including you."

"No. I'll stay here. Julia might come back. I want to be here if she returns."

"It's dark and dangerous."

"That's exactly why I must stay."

I saw the determination on her face. "Do you have a weapon?"

"No."

"Here. Take this gun." I handed her the weapon belonging to Slater. I figured she would put it to greater use if she needed to protect herself. "Find shelter if you can. Mark an X on the ground outside. I'll tell whoever comes to look for it."

"An X marks the spot," she said. The elderly woman thanked me for the gun. I hated leaving her – but we had to go.

I never did find out her name.

By then Terry had removed the dead body and dragged it to the roadside. Slater was tied up for everyone else's safety. I went back to my own lorry and opened the rear to tell everyone why we had stopped. There were no infected people in my lorry – but several people did need medical treatment. In our escape, a few had got some new bruises, which were my fault for driving like a maniac. I promised everyone we would soon be at our destination. "Angela, you want to ride up front with me?"

"Yeah, sure," she said, hopping down. We closed the doors and went around to the cab. Angela frowned at the two empty seats. "Where's Neal, Ben?"

"Neal's gone," I said.

"Gone?"

"He's dead."

"What?"

"He was turning … so he sacrificed himself. He blew up the helicopter and wiped out the Pure Bloods. For us. He saved our lives."

Angela was silent. We climbed into the cab. I drove on. Angela stared at the road, tears running down her cheeks.

"Neal was a great guy," I said.

Angela nodded. "Ben, I didn't even get time to thank him properly for saving me."

"You didn't *have* to thank him. He loved you. He loved us all. We were his family."

"Yeah," she said. "Oh, God, are Hayley and Jason and Sadie dead, too?"

"As far as I know they are still alive," I said. I told Angela about what had happened after Neal had taken her from the camp – the attack, our escape through the woods, my capture and the Pure Blood massacre, meeting Dex and Maggie, the mission to Oxford. It seemed like such a long time ago when I had last seen Hayley, Jason and Sadie. "Billy's gang captured me – but they didn't get them, which is a good sign they made it to the alpha site unharmed. They should be waiting there."

"Ben, we have to get back to them."

"I know," I said. "But first we have to get these people safe."

Two miles on, a sign flashed by, lit by my headlights.

I sighed with relief.

We were almost there.

ENTRY FORTY-ONE

I stopped the lorry at a caravan site in a farmer's field, near an old farmhouse taken over by The Family. I was welcomed by armed men and women pointing guns and crossbows. They could see me wearing a Pure Blood uniform, which would have required some serious explaining if their leader had not been expecting me. Fortunately, Dex was there. He ordered them to lower their weapons and let me park in the field. My vehicle was followed by Maggie's. The two lorries were emptied of their passengers with the help of The Family. Everyone injected with the necrovitalis virus went to a large tent for a medical examination. They would have to be quarantined. I knew most would die in days – but they would die free, not in a cage. It was the most anyone could do for them when nobody had a cure for the zombie virus. As for the others, they were also isolated for the time being because The Family needed to be cautious. The Family could not welcome a bunch of strangers without taking precautions. Some people – like Slater and Dr Frost – needed to prove themselves trustworthy.

Dex greeted me with a hearty handshake. "Well done. You did a lot better than I hoped. I heard Oxford blowing up from here. Sounded like thunder. I would have enjoyed seeing that. You deserve a good rest before I debrief you. There's a caravan for you and your friend. It has solar panels on the top providing electricity for a hot shower and cooked food. I suggest you get yourself cleaned up and eat breakfast before coming to the farmhouse." He grinned. "I imagine you'll eager to get that PBA uniform off?"

"Yeah," I said. "I feel like a bad guy wearing it."

"That's how I used to feel too. Well – get some rest for that debrief. We'll do it in an hour."

Angela and I were shown to the caravan and then left alone. The caravan smelled like fresh linen on a summer day. Someone had gone to town spraying an air freshener. I appreciated the effort. The caravan looked brand-new. Clean and shiny.

"Wow," Angela said. "This is pretty luxurious for a caravan, like something a celebrity would own. Is this a dream, Ben? Am I going to wake up in that horrible hospital still a prisoner?"

"No – this is real. That's over."

"I still can't believe Neal is gone."

"Neither can I."

"We've got to find Hayley and the others."

"I know."

Angela opened a door and looked into a room. "Uh-oh. There's only one bedroom. Do you think Dex thinks we're a … you know?"

I frowned. "A what?"

"A couple."

"Oh. Maybe."

Angela smiled awkwardly. "That would be … weird, right?"

"Yeah - weird," I said, though I thought it wasn't so weird. If we hadn't just gone through hell, I would have told her the truth, that I didn't think it was weird at all. "Look, I'll sleep on the couch in this compartment. It looks comfy. You can take the bedroom. You need to get a good sleep in a real bed, not a hospital one. Do you need to take more painkillers or anything?"

"No, I'm fine. Very tired – but fine. Thanks for asking."

While Angela went for a lie down in her bedroom, I stripped off my hated uniform in the bathroom, which had a clean toilet and a mould-free shower cubicle. Everything smelled of another air freshener – a lavender one that made me sneeze. I stepped into the shower and turned it on. Hot water! It did feel like a dream. An amazing one. I closed my eyes and enjoyed the hot water running down my weary body. Nothing had ever felt so good. I showered off dirt, blood and sweat, lathering my body with all kinds of luxuriant shampoos and shower gels.

"Ben?" Angela said through the bathroom door.

"Uh-huh?"

"Thanks."

"For what?"

"For coming to find me. Thanks."

"Ben?" she said again, softly.

"Yeah?"

"I wouldn't mind it."

"Mind what?"

"Being a couple. I'd like that. It wouldn't be weird. It would be great."

Her words left me breathless.

"Ben, are you okay? Did you hear what I said?"

"Yes," I said. "I heard. I'd like that too."

"Ben?"

"Yeah?"

"Is there room in the shower for two?"

ENTRY FORTY-TWO

Angela made me forty minutes late for my debriefing in the farmhouse – but it did not matter. Dex was too busy for that when I saw him. One room – a dining room – had been turned into a command centre filled with radio operators, a large map table and a projector displaying a live satellite feed. I was surprised and impressed that The Family had a link to a satellite – but I understood how they had managed it when I noticed a load of cables running from the projector over the floor into a corner, where Lynchpin was hunched over a bank of computers, his fingers typing furiously. Lynchpin was their tech wizard and a former political hacktivist. Amazingly, he had hacked into a functional satellite, providing a great view of Oxford from above in the early morning light. Cyrillic letters on the screen gave me a clue to where the pictures were coming from – an old Russian spy sat somewhere in space, looking down on what was left of England long after its Russian masters had died in the zombie plague.

The picture kept breaking up every few seconds – but it was excellent when it was on. I could see details as small as people on the ground. I could even see them fighting the horde of zombies inside the city. Dex was at the table commanding his guerilla army via a radio headset. They had arrived at Oxford in armoured Jeeps and trucks, setting up attack positions, making it impossible for any Pure Bloods left inside the burning city to escape without surrendering or dying. Maggie was standing next to him drinking coffee and telling Dex tactical information. She acknowledge my arrival with a nod, and then resumed her duty.

There wasn't much for me to do except watch the operation on the satellite feed. I didn't need to ask how things were going. Dex's people had a huge tactical advantage over the Pure Bloods. I was handed a cup of coffee.

"Drink that, mate."

The voice belonged to an old friend – Kim. It felt like a month since I had last seen her. The Australian joined me in watching the screen.

I grinned. "It's good to see you."

"Never thought I'd see you again," she said. "I reckoned you'd croak it when you went off on that suicide mission. Looks like you gave the Pure Bloods a bloody nose."

"Yeah. How did Lynchpin get a satellite working?"

Kim shrugged. "No idea. He's been working on cracking the codes for months."

Dex continued giving orders until the feed went down.

SIGNAL LOST flashed on the screen.

Dex swore. "LP, can you get the picture back?"

Lynchpin shook his head. "The satellite's gone out of range, boss."

"Can't you get another one?"

"It's not that easy. There aren't many working – but I'll scan for a signal. Maybe I can find another. There should be some geostationary weather sats. Not as good as spy sat – but they'll have Britain covered if I -"

"Just do it!" Dex shouted. "I need to keep our people informed on the PBA's movements, LP."

"It's not easy hacking into a military satellite," Lynchpin moaned. "It takes time even for a genius like me."

"We don't have time. Seconds matter. I don't want any of them escaping because I can't see them."

Lynchpin's fingers flickered over a keyboard.

Dex removed his headset to wipe the sweat off his brow. "I'm blind here. I need to update the ground forces, LP. We still have active enemy."

"I might have found something," Lynchpin said. "It's French. They never shared the codes with the UK – but I hacked into a DARPA server last month and they had … Got it. I am amazing. Voilà! Live infra-red in high definition, brought to you by Lynchpin TV."

The picture returned in colour – green and orange and white. It showed heat sources as orange and white, revealing the fires burning inside Oxford had destroyed over fifty per cent of the buildings. The helicopter was still ablaze. Living humans showed up as orange blobs around the hospital and other areas not yet taken over by the zombies. Some were civilians forced to join the Pure Bloods. Others were clearly armed and dangerous. Dex relayed more instructions to his soldiers. They were moving in on the perimeter of the zombie trench. It looked like Dex's people were shooting zombies to make an escape route for the enemy, which was something I would not have done after they had done so many bad things. But Dex didn't see them all as the enemy. He had once been one of them. Dex wanted to save the ones he could. That made him a better man than I was. Personally, I would have let the whole lot burn after seeing what they had done to people in the prison. I honestly didn't understand half of what was going on – but I could see survivors running out of the city with their hands up. Maggie looked worried. I didn't understand why – until I remembered her sister was a Pure Blood. Even though Maggie's sister had betrayed her and nearly her fed to zombies as a result, she still cared about her life. Kim and I could not contribute to the battle – but we helped out by making coffee for the radio operators, keeping them alert until, hours later, Dex declared the operation over.

"The Oxford base is completely destroyed," he announced to

the room. "We've managed to save 124 civilians. 28 Pure Bloods have surrendered. The rest – including their colonel – died. Well done, people. Today we won a major victory. The Pure Blood Army has lost control over the south of England!"

Everyone cheered. Kim banged her cup against mine. "Wish we had some champagne to celebrate. Coffee doesn't quite do it. I'm going to find some beers. Want to join me?"

I really wanted to go back to my caravan, where I had left Angela sleeping. "Maybe later, Kim. I'm dead on my feet. I need some rest."

Most people looked overjoyed by Dex's announcement – but I noticed Maggie was quietly crying in a corner. I went over to her. "Maggie, what's wrong?"

"They found my sister."

"Oh. I'm sorry."

"I'm not crying because she's dead, idiot. She's *alive*. They're bringing her here. I'm crying because I'm actually happy, even though she did let them hang me over a zombie pit. Am I messed up or what?"

"Hey – she's your sister. You love her no matter what she did. The Pure Bloods brainwashed her."

Dex nodded to me. I joined him. "Do you want to debrief me now?"

"Oh – forget that. It's not important now. I just wanted to thank you. I didn't have the guts to attack Oxford until you went in and destroyed their helicopter. I owe you, Ben."

"What happens next?"

"Well, the Pure Bloods still have their other bases – so it's not like we're won the war. I'm not going to be complacent. They will not let us enjoy our victory for long. But it is a start. If there's anything I can do for you, say the word and it's done."

"I appreciate that," I said. "You mind if I talk to Lynchpin?"

"No. Go ahead."

Lynchpin was sitting at his computers, watching four screens at once showing scrolling data I could barely read, never mind understand.

"That was impressive," I said. "How on earth did you get control over a Russian satellite?"

The hacktervist shrugged. "It wasn't too hard. It was an old one sent up during the Cold War. It only had 32-bit encryption. That's like child's play."

"So ... can you get images from anywhere on your computer?"

"As long as a hackable satellite is over it, yeah. Why?"

"I have to go somewhere. I'd like to see it from above. Can you do that?"

"Uh – sure. What are the GPS coordinates?"

"I have no idea – but I do know the location on a map. Will that do?"

"I suppose old-school will work."

I told him about the alpha site, not far from the burnt-out ruin of the mansion where Billy and his biker gang had captured me. Lynchpin pulled up the recorded images, his fingers working magic on his keyboard. "This is the general location. Can't get a live image at the moment – there are no active satellites over the area right now - but I saved all the data from the Russian sat on a hard drive. It will have captured images this morning. Here. Is this what you want?"

An aerial shot of a forest appeared on the large screen. I didn't understand what I was seeing until I saw the mansion and orientated the image in my mind. "Can you get that area bigger?"

"Sure." Lynchpin frowned. "You mind me asking what are you looking for?"

"An electricity substation. My friends were supposed to go

there. I want to see if they are still around. This is confusing. All I can see are trees. It's too distant to make out anything on the ground. Can you zoom in like you did over Oxford?"

"Hold on. I'll look for buildings. Is that it?"

I could see something square surrounded by a perimeter fence. "Yeah. That's the substation. We picked it because of the metal fence."

"Looks like someone is camped there." Lynchpin zoomed in on a tent inside the perimeter. "Looks like your friends are waiting there for you."

"That's great. Thanks for the help."

"Uh-oh – don't thank me yet, dude."

"Why not?"

"I think I've just seen something. Just a sec. Look at this down here."

Lynchpin panned out and pointed at a road. He zoomed in and I saw people, lots of people. People with no heat signature in the IR because they were long dead, but still walking along the road in a vast group, like a herd of cattle. Lynchpin's eyes widened. "Dude, there's a whole horde of zombies heading that direction. Thousands of them. I'm afraid you're friends are camped in the wrong place, Ben. They will soon be in major trouble. Hell – this image was recorded four hours ago. The zombies could already have reached your friends' camp. I'm really sorry, Ben. Looks like they'll be dead by now."

ENTRY FORTY-THREE

"They're not dead unless I see their bodies," I said, glaring at the zombie horde heading for the electricity substation. "That picture is hours old. The zombies might still be some distance off. Can you get a live picture?"

Lynchpin groaned in reply, typing commands into his computer that produced the same response several times: CONNECTION LOST.

"Sorry. I'm not receiving anything. The link's down."

"I need to see what's happening now."

"I know. I'll keep trying."

I left him to talk to Dex, quickly explaining the dire situation. "Zombies are heading for the camp and they don't have a clue. You said you owe me – so help me save them."

"I don't have anyone near that location – but I'll give you anything you need to get there."

"A fast car. A really fast car. Got one of them?"

Dex nodded. "We've got a few sports cars hidden in the barn taken from a dealership. They're brand-new with full tanks of petrol. I kept them in case we ever needed an urgent escape. You can pick what you want."

"That's good. I'll take whatever's the fastest."

"Okay. Consider it done. What else do you want?"

There were plenty of things I wanted. I wrote a list. Dex promised he'd get everything in five minutes. I returned to the caravan to pick up some personal things. Angela was sleeping in the bedroom. I looked in on her. She deserved to know I was leaving, but she was sound asleep. I knew if I woke her she would insist on coming with me – but she was not fit enough to risk her life. And I was unwilling to risk it too. She was safe in the caravan, where she could rest and recover. So, reluctantly, I left a note explaining why I was going without her, which I left for her to find when she woke up. It wasn't a farewell letter – but it felt like it because I was going into a zombie-infested hell zone. I kissed her and sneaked out, wishing I would see her again.

Dex had got everything ready for me. A black-and-white chequered rally car was parked at the gates, the engine revving with awesome power. Lynchpin was standing next to it holding a sat nav. "I couldn't get another live sat feed – but I've programmed in an optimised driving route. It avoids the major zombie zones and worst roads. I hope it helps."

"Thanks," I said.

"I've also had another look at the sat photos. You need to see this enlarged pic. It reveals more detail."

I looked at it and nodded. "Thanks. That'll be useful, too."

Dex strode over to me. He handed me the car's key. "The boot's loaded with weapons. And it has a nitrous tank. Just open the valve and you'll get a speed boost like a mule kick. I also have something else. Here – take these."

He gave me a large combat knife in a sheath and a gun. The gun was a revolver loaded with six bullets. I slipped the knife into my boot and the gun into my jacket. We shook hands.

Dex looked sadly into my eyes. "You understand why I can't go with you?"

"Yeah. You're needed here. Look after Angela."

"You got it. Good luck, Ben."

I jumped into the car, which had been emptied of rear seats so the nitrous tank could fit there. Seconds later, I was racing along a country road at twice the speed limit. There were no police to stop me – or Pure Blood patrols – or vigilantes – or any other vehicles –

so I increased my speed even more. My body was pinned back by the acceleration. Everything flashed past. The last time I had been in a car driving so fast I had been on a German autobahn – a smooth, straight line – but I was on a curvy, potholed, bumpy road. Over one bump, I took off and flew for a second. Landing hard, I lost control, nearly crashing into a stone wall. I braked just in time. Realising I wasn't a Top Gear presenter with a death wish, I had to slow down as I raced through a village and up a blind hill. I pushed up the speed again once I saw the road ahead was clear and straight. I release the nitrous and felt the car bolt forward. I hit a hundred and forty going downhill. The sat nav on the dashboard was barely keeping up with my actual position as I made a sharp turn at the bottom, where the road forked. In a couple of minutes, I encountered the tail end of the zombie horde crossing the road ahead. There were about fifty of them in my path. Slowing down and going around them was not an option. I speeded up and drove straight through them, knocking bodies aside like rag dolls. Blood and gore hit my windscreen. And I glimpsed a disembodied head bounce off the roof and roll like a football. But I made it through, though the rally car made a weird screeching noise as it caught pieces of the living dead in its wheels. The front was splattered with twitching limbs and a rotting brown torso attached to a fleshless skull. The zombie's one eye swivelled in its socket and seemed to stare at me. I jerked the wheel to shake the zombie off. Then I turned on the windscreen wipers and wiped a sludge of decaying body parts out of my vision, not even slowing down.

 I was coming up to another junction. To my right, the road was filled with zombies, thousands of them, all heading towards the substation. It was impassable – but the other road had fewer zombies. It added miles to my journey – but it meant I'd get to the substation from the other side and approach it from the opposite direction, hopefully beating the horde.

The road wasn't clear of dangers, though. More zombies veered into my path, forcing me to steer around them or into them, depending on how decayed they looked. I avoided hitting the fresh-looking ones because they would not break apart on impact with my bumper. I hit the decaying ones dead on. After a mile of hit-and-run splatter-fests, during which my rally car started to resemble Lady Gaga's infamous meat dress, I broke through the horde onto the empty road ahead. I raced to the next junction, then turned down a narrower road, dodging around a smashed bread lorry that had dropped its cargo of wooden crates across both lanes. I smashed through them, turning the crates into kindling.

After that, I avoided another smashed car and got onto the road leading to the substation. I was in an area rich in forest land. A line of pylons appeared over the tops of the trees. They linked to the substation as part of the defunct national grid.

"Nearly there," I said.

I braked. Then I studied the road through binoculars. There was no sign of any zombies down the road as far as I could see. That was a huge relief – but I didn't relax. I restarted the car and drove the remaining distance at a crawl, looking left and right, checking for zombies in the forest. The substation was on my left behind a steel fence. I parked next to a gate marked with grim warning signs.

DANGER OF DEATH!
HIGH VOLTAGE ELECTRICITY!
NO ENTRY!

No electrical power made the warnings an empty threat – but the barbed wire on the fence itself should have kept intruders out anyway. There was a dark-green tent on the other side in front of a small square concrete building under a huge pylon. My arrival must have been heard by anyone nearby, but nobody appeared. If Sadie, Hayley and Jason were waiting there, they would be naturally cautious when a gore-soaked sports car drove up to their hiding place. I didn't want to frighten anyone by going in unannounced. I climbed out and left my door open.

"Hey!" I called out. "Sadie? Hayley? Jason? It's me – Ben!"

When nobody answered me, I walked up to the gate. There was a chain and a padlock. The padlock was locked. I shook the gate. The chain rattled. The silence made me uneasy.

"Hey!" I shouted louder. "Come out! I'm alone! It's safe!"

I heard a noise from the substation building. A door creaked open an inch. Someone looked out through the crack.

I smiled and showed my hands were empty. "See? It's me!"

The door swung open and Jason stepped into the sunlight. His face was bruised. He did not look happy to see me. I drew my gun. Someone was pushing Jason forward, hiding in the shadow, using him as a human shield. There was a gun pointed at Jason's head. Jason's hands were tied up and the other person was shifting from side to side, making a difficult moving target. I felt my heart punch my ribs. Jason shuffled forward. The man behind him was grinning.

"We meet again," he said.

"Billy. You're still breathing? I hoped you'd died."

"I'm not easy to kill, Ben."

"How'd you survive?"

"I had a stolen Pure Blood uniform I slipped on when they started attacking us. I sneaked away dressed like one of them. Had to shoot some of my own people to make myself look like one of them – but I did what was necessary to live. Looks like you did too. Where are the others – Angela and Neal? Are they dead?"

"None of your business, Billy."

Billy sneered. "I knew you'd come back here when I didn't find your body at the church. I've been waiting for you. Your friends have been keeping me company. Drop the gun, Ben."

"Shoot him!" Jason yelled.

Through the fence, it was a tough shot. Clint Eastwood could have done it. Jack Bauer, too. But I was not a deadshot.

"Okay!" I said.

I dropped my gun.

"Kick it away," Billy said.

I kicked it into the dirt.

Billy emerged then into the sunlight, knocking Jason to his knees with the butt of his gun. Billy aimed his gun at me as he came closer. He had the key to the padlock in his other hand. He opened the gate and stepped back, gesturing grandly like a Victorian dandy. "Why do come in and join us, Ben! You are the final guest at my party. Guys, he's here!"

Some more men emerged from the building. Four swarthy-looking men armed with knives and swords. It looked like Billy had the only gun. His new gang looked like they had never seen soap and water. One was as big and ugly as a bear with mange. Two wore biker leathers. The fourth reeked from ten feet away of sweat.

I stepped through the gate. Billy let one of his men frisk me, the big one. "Be careful, Vince. Don't miss anything."

Vince took away my gun. Billy grabbed it off him so he had two guns, one in his hand and one in his belt. Vince emptied my pockets, tossing my things on the ground. I was hoping Vince would miss the knife in my boot – but he found it.

"Billy, can I keep this?"

"Sure," Billy said. "Tie his hands behind his back. Say, Ben, you remember that time you tied me up as your prisoner? Good times, huh?"

Once my hands were tied, Billy punched me in the stomach so I fell down gasping. He stood over me, leering. "Fantastic car by the way. I prefer red Ferraris – but rally cars are great too. What on earth did you do to it – drive it into a slaughterhouse?"

"Something like that," I said. "What have you done with Sadie and Hayley?"

"They're in there," he said, indicating the substation. "Alive for now. I didn't want to kill anyone until I had you, Ben. My brother's dead because of what *you* did. My gang's destroyed, too. You have to suffer for that. I'm going to make you watch me torture the woman, then the boy, then the little girl. I'll only give them a merciful death when *you* beg me to kill them. And then, when they're dead, I'm going to do the same to you."

"You're insane, Billy."

"No – I'm a rational man living in an irrational universe. This world is insane. Zombies don't exist in a normal world, Ben. People like me are the new kings. I love it. This world is my world and you are just an ant under my shoe. I'm going to stamp on you, Ben."

One of Billy's men had gone to my car. He was one of the bikers. He was looking in the back. "Billy, he's got a load of empty ammo boxes in here. What do you want me to do with them?"

"Empty boxes are useless," Billy said. "What do you think I'd want with them?"

"Why don't we just kill them and go?" the man said. "I mean, we've been waiting ages for this guy. I want to go north. Now we have a car like this we can leave."

"Be patient," Billy snapped. "We're going to be here sometime – until I've got my vengeance on this guy. Fisk, bring out the woman and the girl. I want to get started."

Fisk was the second biker. He dragged Sadie out of the building, dumping her on the ground by Billy's feet. She was bound and gagged. Then Fisk went back to bring out Hayley. He carried her over to the same place and dropped her hard on the ground. Hayley grunted in pain, but she did not cry. Billy walked over to Sadie, taking a knife out of his coat. "Ben, what I'm going to do to her is all your fault. Remember that when she starts screaming. Anything you'd like to say before I start hurting her?"

"Yeah, Billy, I've got something to say. You're as good as dead already. You just don't know it."

"Oh – is that right?"

"Yeah," I said. "You've disarmed me – but you didn't disarm the people with me."

Billy laughed. "Oh, I'm supposed to believe you've got an invisible army out there?"

"No – not an army. Just a sniper and a girl you had imprisoned. She's pretty keen to get some payback. Her name is Kim."

Fisk looked worried. "Billy, if he's not alone, what are we going to do?"

"Relax," Billy said. "He's lying. He's on his own. We saw the car coming. There was nobody else in it."

"Billy, you're right and you're wrong. I had passengers. I stopped and let them get out before driving up. They've got you surrounded. If you don't surrender to me, I'll order them to start shooting."

"Yeah, right. If there was anyone with you, why haven't they done anything already, huh?"

"It took them some time to get into position," I said. "But they're ready now."

"I love this fantasy. You couldn't possibly have known I would be here – so you didn't bring anyone with you."

"Billy, I saw you on a satellite image. Your bikes are behind the building. Hidden from view – but not from above. I knew my friends had company when I drove up. I came ahead of them as a distraction."

Billy frowned. "You don't have any satellite photos."

"Then what's on that piece of paper?"

Billy bent down and picked it up and unfolded it. "What the – how did you get this? HOW DID YOU GET THIS?"

"I have powerful friends now," I said. "Guess what? I knew you were here – but I had to draw you out into the open. Maggie, have you got a bead on the guy with the two guns?"

Maggie's voice answered in my ear. "*He's moving around too much. But I'm got his biker buddy in my sights right now. You want me to kill him?*"

"Take the shot," I said.

Fisk's head exploded. The sound of the bullet came from the pylon on my right, where Maggie had climbed. Another shot hit a second man as Billy and the others scrambled for cover. It was from a shotgun fired through the fence. Kim had sneaked through the woods and killed the other biker. That left Billy and Mange Face.

"Kill him," Billy ordered, then dashed towards the substation.

Mange Face faced me with a sword. I had my hands tied – but I had my feet free. I charged at Mange Face and kicked him in the groin. Then I bashed into him and knocked the sword out of his hand. He grunted and turned on me with a knife – slashing at my chest - but I dived onto the ground so Maggie could fire again, which she did, blasting a massive hole through his neck. For a moment Mange Face clutched at his neck as blood pumped down his body. Then he collapsed dead. I saw Billy run into the substation, ducking a bullet that would have taken off his head. He slammed closed the door behind him. I heard the screech of a bolt locking in place.

Kim ran through the gate. She untied my hands and released the others while I kept my gun pointed at the building's only exit. The door was solid metal. I wasn't going to waste any shots – but if Billy poked his face out I was ready to kill him. The building had no other doors and no windows. There was only one way in. I swore.

I heard Maggie's voice through the earpiece in my good ear. "*Ben, I can see zombies. You'd better move it. They'll be on your position in two minutes. I'm going to have to get down and meet you back at the drop-off point.*"

"Okay," I said to her. "Kim, get everyone in the car."

"What about Billy?"

"I'll take care of him. Lend me your shotgun. Take my gun."

I ran up to the substation. The door was locked from the inside. A shotgun blast would do nothing. It looked like Billy was going to get away again.

I wasn't going to let that happen.

I raced around to the back of the building where his gang had hidden their bikes. I shot the petrol tanks and tossed a lighter on the spilt petrol. The petrol started to burn as I ran around to the front of the building. Hayley, Jason and Sadie were crammed into the rally car. They yelled at me to join them. Kim was waiting for me, shooting at some zombies getting too close for comfort. There were hundreds of zombies running and shuffling towards us, drawn by the gunshots.

"Did you get him?" Kim said. "Did you kill Billy?"

"No – but they will. Let's get out of here."

I turned back to the gate and shot the hinges so the gate broke. It was hanging loose as I ran to the car. The fastest zombies were thirty feet away. Kim was behind the wheel, revving the engine. I squeezed into the other side and slammed the door closed, hearing an explosion behind the substation as a bike exploded and pieces of metal flew into the trees. Kim reversed the rally car as the zombies reached us. Some zombies chased us and tried to climb onto the car – but the explosion split their attention, attracting more of them in that direction. As we accelerated backwards, I saw them forming a mob around the substation, trying to climb over the fence and get through the bars. Many pushed through the broken gate to fill the whole area around the building where Billy was locked inside. I grinned. Billy would never get out. He was completely surrounded by zombies. He would either starve to death or be eaten when he unlocked the door.

Kim drove backwards for half a mile before making a U-turn.

We waited to pick up Maggie.

Then we drove back to The Family and our new home.

FINAL ENTRY

That happened several weeks ago. I've been with The Family since that day. I'm at a new location free of zombies and far from the Pure Bloods. I won't say where I am on this blog. It's safer that way. It's peaceful and beautiful and protected. That's all I will say. We've all needed a long rest after everything that happened. It's great to see Hayley and Jason smiling again.

I'm pleased to say Angela forgave me for leaving her behind. She was too happy to see the rest of our family alive to be angry for long.

She's writing her own journal now.

A lot of my new friends are doing the same.

They all want to leave a record for future generations.

For any survivors out there reading this, my *journal of the living*, I'd like you to know we're never going to give up fighting to take back our world.

This entry will be my last – but there are many more stories to tell.

Every one of us has a story.

A journal of the living.

Ben Smith, England
354 days after the zombie apocalypse.

ABOUT THE AUTHOR

John Moralee lives in England, where his short fiction has appeared in magazines and anthologies including *The Mammoth Book of Jack the Ripper Stories*, *Clockwork Cairo*, and the British Fantasy Society's magazine. His novels and anthologies are available as Kindle ebooks and paperbacks.

Journal of the Living is his first zombie apocalypse novel.

OTHER BOOKS BY JOHN MORALEE

Acting Dead – crime novel

Journal of the Living – zombie apocalypse novel

Crowning Achievements: Legend of King Arthur – comic fantasy novel

The Bone Yard and Other Stories – horror short stories

Bloodways – horror short stories

Under Dark Skies – crime stories

Edge of Crime – crime fiction omnibus

Strange Blue World – SF stories

Uncertainty Principle – SF stories

The Tomorrow Tower – SF stories

Future Imperfect – SF stories

BIBLIOGRAPHY

Visions III: Beyond the Kuiper Belt

Visions IV: Deep Space

Visions V: Milky Way

Visions VI: Galaxies

The Mammoth Book of Future Cops

The Mammoth Book of Jack the Ripper Stories

Footsteps in the Dark

Crimewave #1-3

Clockwork Cairo

Switchblade: Tech Noir

Tricks, Treats & Zombies

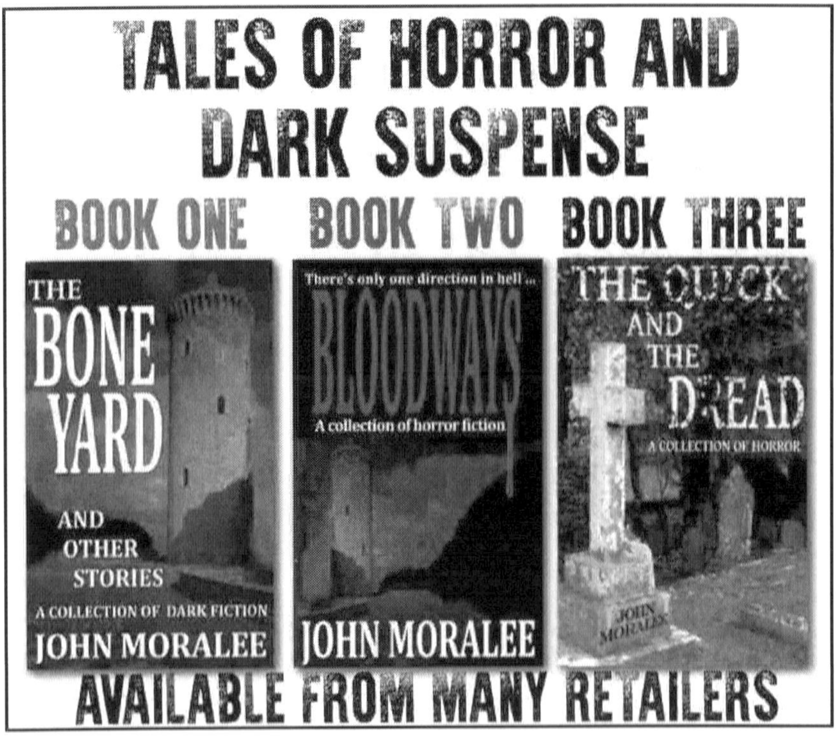
TALES OF HORROR AND
DARK SUSPENSE
BOOK ONE
BOOK TWO
BOOK THREE
THE BONE YARD AND OTHER STORIES
A COLLECTION OF DARK FICTION
JOHN MORALEE
There's only one direction in hell ...
BLOODWAYS
A collection of horror fiction
JOHN MORALEE
THE QUICK AND THE DREAD
A COLLECTION OF HORROR
JOHN MORALEE
AVAILABLE FROM MANY RETAILERS

Thank you for buying this book!

Printed in Great Britain
by Amazon